LB

Sister Cities

Sister Cities

Colette Freedman

This book is dedicated to the original sisters
Jade, Nickella, Susan, Elise and Jill

the movie sisters
Troian, Michelle, Jess, Stana, Amy and Jacki

and the honorary sisters
Sean and Fred

Acknowledgements

I'd like to thank everyone who has been involved with Sister Cities since the beginning. In addition to the original cast, I'd like to thank Leah for being a terrific stage manager, Jack and Jeannine for producing the original production, Kurt and Marc for producing the Edinburgh production and all of the theatres, directors, producers, actors and artists who have been involved in the 20+ productions around the world. I'd also like to thank the innumerable future artists who will hopefully continue to breathe life into this play.

Thank you to B.J. Robbins who believed in this book long before anyone else did.

And thank you to all of the other "sisters" in my life: Brooke, Jen, Jhen, Vanessa, Francesca, Kerry, Bri, Christian, Lynne, Lynn, Sundeep, Rebecca, Julie, Rooney, Diane, Bekah, Stephanie, Devon, Maureen, Myra, Savannah, Mariana, Miata, Emilie, Karen, Sailene, Robyn, Keb, Miriam and Hannah Hope.

My brother David who still takes credit that all of the sisters are based after him.

Zac, Dylan, Max and Scout who prove how loving siblings can be.

And my parents who are, in a word, phenomenal.

PREFACE

Mary prepared to die.

As the weathered brass taps twisted, she watched steaming water flood into the antique claw-foot tub. She glanced down at her tiny wristwatch, which rested on the pink bath towel, now crumpled on the aging linoleum floor. Six o'clock. She'd worn this watch for most of her life. It had been a gift from her second husband, her favorite of the four men she'd married. One of the girls would get it: Austin probably. After all, he was her father. Mary caught her image in the long beveled mirror. She was sixty-three and in spite of, or perhaps because of her lifestyle, she thought she looked good. Her small breasts were still firm, and her dancer's legs, still strong and muscled. She rested her hand on her tight stomach. Who could believe that she'd given birth to four daughters?

Naked, she watched as bubble bath and salts mixed under the taps. Lavender. Her favorite. She loved the odor. It brought her back to a time when everything had been so much simpler. When she had been completely in control. With effort, Mary settled into the tub. She relaxed in the warm water, resting her body against the curve of the porcelain. As she slid down the side of the tub, the bubbles surrounded her head like a watery halo. Thunder grumbled just outside the window. The weather reports said there was a large storm approaching. Mary hoped her daughter would board up the windows. It was a hassle, but it was necessary to prevent water damage. She wondered if she should remind her. No, she'd let it be. Austin was responsible enough to take care of it. Mary raised her daughters to be self-sufficient. To be strong.

And to be able to make the right decision when the time was right.

One

Carolina hated carbohydrates.

"Whole grain or sourdough?" The perky flight attendant stood in front of her with a basket of steaming rolls, waiting for the seemingly inconsequential culinary decision.

Carolina shifted in her seat and wondered if the world was conspiring to make her fat. At 5'9", Carolina was model skinny and she intended to stay that way. She was finally happy with the way she looked. She should be, she'd paid top dollar for it: the caramel highlights in her thick brown hair, the strategically injected Botox, the calorie counted meals delivered to her front door, the morning runs. After all, life was about appearances. Whether she liked it or not, everyone prejudged her value by the way she looked. When Carolina litigated a case in front of twelve strangers, they didn't give a shit that she graduated top of her class at Stanford or had an almost perfect score on her LSAT; instead, they looked at her Bottega Veneta shoes. They didn't care that her husband had left her for a twenty-two-year-old intern who was exactly half her age; instead, they admired her three thousand dollar designer suit. She sighed. No one ever bothered to read the book, they just judged the cover, and she knew that if she could seduce the jury with her words and her looks, she could win the case.

And she usually did. She knew how the game was played and she was one of its best players. When she was with Matthew, she'd relaxed too much, gotten a bit too comfortable and let down her guard. That was the not-so-distant past and she wasn't planning to look back.

Carolina grimaced. Was it only six months ago when she didn't think twice about eating the wheat bread on her daily tuna sandwich? The pimply-faced delivery guy from The Baguette Box routinely brought a cellophane wrapped sandwich and a triple espresso to her desk at twelve thirty on the dot. Every day. Carolina always ate at her desk. She enjoyed the regularity, and her work was too important to blow off for even an hour. She wondered how her colleagues managed the lazy lunches in downtown Seattle: There was simply too much to do and too few billable hours in which to do it. Granted, occasionally she'd play hooky. On one of the rare non-rainy Seattle days when she felt somewhat on top of her workload, she would take a run during lunch. Those were some of her best moments. She'd jog the trail from U-Dub, through the bird sanctuary all the way to the north end of Lake Washington. Sometimes, when it was clear enough, she could even see Mt. Rainier. Carolina loved to run; it was the only time in her life when she could truly let go.

"No bread," she chirped to the flight attendant, who she was sure hated her already, "and another double ... please."

The please was an afterthought, but it was the middle of the night and she knew the flight attendant was really just catering to her. She was probably eager to get back to her *People Magazine* or do whatever flight attendants did on red-eye flights. The rest of the first class passengers, including a B list rock star, were already sound asleep.

Carolina rarely slept. Baltimore told her once that doctors could prescribe pot for insomnia. The marijuana clinics, or 'cannabis collectives' as they liked to call themselves, offered a smorgasbord of options from brownies to buds. Carolina shuddered; she'd opt for insomnia over breaking the law. She would never jeopardize her future judgeship by engaging in anything even potentially felonious. She was a stickler for the rules. As she popped two Ambien, she hoped she would get at least an hour's sleep before she arrived in Hartford and rented a car to her final destination.

⚜ ⚜ ⚜

Dallas loved trains.

Something about the constant whirring of the engine and the rhythmic clacking of the wheels against the steel track calmed her. It reminded her of the metronome she used when she gave private piano lessons Thursday nights and Sunday mornings. She appreciated the precision of the constant tempo: a regulated heart that was never allowed to beat too fast. One of her students had complained that the metronome hindered her creative interpretation of the music; yet, Dallas wasn't interested. Her students needed a limited flexibility: They had to learn the rules before they could break them, and the infallibility of the metronome removed guesswork, so a student could play evenly. Dallas appreciated all aspects of music. She and Peter had season tickets to both the Philadelphia Orchestra and the Opera. She cherished those evenings away from school when she and her husband would sneak into the city and she would allow herself the luxury of losing herself in the music. It was one of the only times that Dallas could truly relax, the way Carolina did when she was running, or Austin did when she was writing or Baltimore did when she was... well, knowing Baltimore it was probably something sexual.

Dallas sighed. She was not in the mood for this impromptu family reunion.

She looked at the reflection of her alabaster skin through the smudged glass and adjusted her Burberry headband. She smoothed down an errant hair, ensuring that her tamed hair was perfectly in place. She would soon arrive in New Haven and take a cab to the ferry dock in Stony Creek. She wouldn't get there until twelve thirty even though Carolina told her to be there by noon. Dallas would be late. She was always late.

She'd had every intention of being early; she wanted to catch the 6:46 Amtrak out of Philly. However, one of the girls on her hall was having an early morning crisis. So she got a late start leaving Ardmore Academy, and had to take the 8:45 train. There always seemed to be some sort of problem at the boarding school, and Dallas was the ultimate problem solver: meticulous, exact and non-judgmental. Peter said it was one of the reasons why he loved her: her ability to stay objective in subjective situations.

He'd offered to come and she'd considered it; yet, the last time she subjected him to her sisters, it had been an unpleasant experience. A few Thanksgivings ago with too much wine and too little forgiveness. Plus her field hockey team was on its way to making Regionals and she needed Peter to step in and coach the matchup against Andover. She was furious that she had to miss the game. But it was out of her control...and the one thing Dallas Baxter-Pierce hated was feeling out of control.

⚜ ⚜ ⚜

Baltimore had a love-hate relationship with motorcycles.

She'd been obsessed with them ever since her first high school boyfriend introduced her to the sleek machines which hugged the road and easily zoomed up inclines which cars struggled to climb. She loved the roar of the pipes in her helmet and the immense power at the tips of her fingers; yet, she hated the fact that her mother was so anti-bike. And Mary's softly spoken voice with her pithy, guilt-infused sentences drove Baltimore crazy.

"It's too dangerous," Mary preached.

"So is life," Baltimore replied, before listening to one of her mother's endless spiels about the risks of riding. Apparently one of her mother's innumerable boyfriends had been in an accident and died. That was decades ago Baltimore thought, and motorcycles had come a long way since then. She grinned; so had boyfriends.

Zooming in and out of cars on the fairly empty I-95, Baltimore calculated she could make the 147 mile route in less than two hours. She'd have to. Her sisters were always giving her shit about not taking things seriously. They were going to be so mad at her when they saw the bike. Still, motorcycles made more sense than cars: They were environmentally friendly and made much less of a carbon footprint. She could easily justify her purchase, which was made possible by a sizable check her father had sent her, courtesy of his band's tour in Germany. Or was it Austria? Baltimore never knew or really cared, but she had no problem cashing her dad's guilt checks: conscience-easing money for missing 99% of her childhood... and adulthood.

Who was she kidding, her sisters were going to be furious. That's why she hadn't told them about buying the bike. The reality was, she hadn't told them a lot of things lately. Baltimore hadn't been home in over a year. Or had it been a year and a half? Why had she stayed away for so long? She loved growing up in the island community. After she left, she never really found roots anywhere else that made her as comfortable. She was always searching, but at twenty-six, people were supposed to still be searching, weren't they? Plus, her mother had always dogmatically insisted that she remain at Harvard and concentrate on her studies.

Baltimore wondered how much there really was to study when getting a Master's degree in Sociology.

She made a right at the sign for Stony Creek and soon spied Carolina getting out of a blue Prius. Baltimore slowed down. She pulled up to the ferry dock as Carolina was walking towards the boat. Perfect timing. Baltimore parked the bike at Stony Market. It would be safe there for the weekend unless Old Man Winters complained. He'd been the store owner since Baltimore was a little girl, and the way he used to flirt with her mother was embarrassing. Baltimore jumped off the bike and grabbed her worn knapsack. Across the street, the ferry driver was carrying her sister's two Louis Vuitton suitcases. She hadn't realized this was a dress-up affair; Baltimore was wearing a tee shirt, jeans, cowboy boots and a leather jacket. She undid her ponytail and shook out her long unruly curls before tucking her shirt into her jeans: a last ditch attempt to look more presentable. Carolina was wearing heels, pantyhose and a business suit as if she'd just come from court rather than flown across the country on the red-eye. Baltimore wondered if she should change.

If necessary, she figured she could borrow clothes from Austin, or even Mom.

April 1963
High Point, North Carolina

Dear Daughters,

Parents are supposed to fuck up their kids; it's part of the evolutionary cycle.

My mother is no exception. I am sixteen years old and I officially hate her. No, hate isn't strong enough of a word. I absolutely loathe my mother. So, I'm going to write letters to my future daughters so that I don't fuck them up the way my mother fucked me up. Genius, right? I mean, what chance did I have? My mother is a nightmare. Selfish, insecure, needy and devoid of any maternal instinct whatsoever. If she lived in the wild, a bear would have stolen her cubs and she would have just walked off. Harsh, but true.

I, Mary Elizabeth Baxter, promise to stop the cyclical pattern and not damage any of my cubs. Not sabotage your dreams. I vow to encourage you and raise you to be the best of the best. To make you feel special and to be there for you. I promise to take you to field hockey practices and piano lessons and pay attention to you.

Future daughters Paula, Johanna, Georgina and Ringo, I vow to love you. For better or worse. In sickness and in health. Til death do us part. What? You don't think a parent can make that vow to her children? I disagree. Marriage vows are the most sacred bond you can make with someone. It is a promise of forever and I promise to love my little Beatles forever. I hope you're okay with your future names. I definitely want to do something thematic and I'm completely obsessed with the Beatles... so I'll probably name you after them. But it's a woman's prerogative to change her mind so, then again, maybe I won't. Where was I? Oh, yes, my horrible mother whom I loathe.

I suppose most stories start at the beginning, but mine started when I was five years old. When my dad died. Until then, I knew nothing but joy. I was immune to disappointment or pain or sadness. My father was my entire world and I spent the first five years of my life being told how special I was, how wonderful I was.

Not by her.

She was far too self-absorbed to even notice me. If you look up the word *narcissism* in Webster's Dictionary, it says JoAnna Baxter next to it. Mama seemed to spend the majority of her time busily looking in the mirror, telling herself how wonderful she was. You think the Queen in Snow White was vain? She never met my mother. I was invisible to her. But Daddy looked at me. He paid attention to me. He gave me tons of confidence and love and set my bar for men impossibly high. I assumed that all men would be as wonderful as my father.

So far, I've been sorely disappointed.

Not depressed, disappointed. There's a big difference. One of my literary idols, Sylvia Plath, just committed suicide by placing her head in the oven. And although it was very Hansel and Gretel-like of her, it was pathetic. Who would ever kill themselves? And she was only thirty, that's so young. Speaking of young, let's get back to me.

My childhood was like a fairytale, I suppose, where an innocent child lives in total happiness until one parent (the good one) dies and the other marries an evil stepparent. Only, Mama never remarried. She just became a tired, bitter alcoholic. And I became an inconvenience. Except when I mixed her martinis. I was useful then. Otherwise, she barely paid attention to me.

Nothing like being abandoned in your own home, over and over again.

Dad was part of the XVIII Airborne Corps. So, my first five years, I grew up in what I thought was the armpit of North Carolina: military housing at Fort Bragg. It was drab, we were poor, but I didn't care. My father was the center of my world and when he was near me, I felt safe. After the Korean War took Dad away from me, I never felt safe again. Mama didn't handle his death well. She didn't handle telling me well either. Rather than straight out telling me my father's brains had been blown out by North Koreans, Mama took me to the movie *Bambi*. And when Bambi's mother gets killed, and his father says, "Your mother can't be with you any more," Mama turned to me and said, "That's what happened to your father."

I spent the rest of the movie completely confused. My father had been shot by a hunter? Every time I pressed Mama for answers, she waved me off, so finally I stopped pressing. She couldn't handle the truth so she started to live in a world of illusion, and she dragged me down the rabbit hole with her. Only inside the hole wasn't the White Rabbit or Peter Rabbit or the Velveteen Rabbit. None of the rabbits from the storybooks and movies were down there, only Mama. Even the Easter Bunny was missing. In one fell swoop my childhood innocence was shattered and I was forced to grow up. I became an oxymoron. An adult child. A five-year-old adult suddenly responsible for her mentally unstable mother who started drinking her first martini of the day at noon.

After Daddy's funeral, Mama packed us up and moved us to a part of North Carolina that made Fort Bragg look like Disneyland: High Point. High Point is literally a one horse town where the horse ran away. It has an almost non-existent population, save two times a year when the furniture market comes to town. The entire community was built to accommodate the big furniture convention, so most of the year it's like a ghost town until the suits who sell upholstery descend on the town like Mardi Gras. For those two weeks, I get to see how the other half lives and I seethe with jealously. The furniture people are like exotic foreigners who come from big cities like New York and Los Angeles and Chicago. The secretaries look like Tippi Hedren with perfect hair and designer shoes, and their bosses smoke cigars that cost more than my entire wardrobe. Nothing makes you feel more inferior than seeing what you don't have and what you can never have.

It also makes you determined to do something about it.

The odds were definitely stacked against me ... I was a scrawny blonde with a dead father and a drunken mother who lived on the wrong side of the tracks. Mama and I lived in a shitty little two bedroom on the outskirts of the city, but we still managed to rent out our house to furniture convention people for one week every April and October. It's like we won the lottery twice a year and then went back to being poor. Mama made enough money during those two weeks to cover both our mortgage and her bar bill for the next 12 months. That shows you how cheap it is to live in High Point. That also shows you how dull, tiny, backwards and hopeless my hillbilly town actually is.

From the minute Dad died and my world fell apart, I wanted to leave, see the world, go to the big cities, live. Because you can't really live in High Point. You can only suffocate. I watch the way Mama keeps getting older, sadder and more bitter. Her body is hunched over and even though she's still a young woman, she looks old. She acts old. She self-medicates with martinis like an old woman and sits in front of the television watching sitcoms like *The Donna Reed Show* and *The Adventures of Ozzie and Harriet.* Ironic that those are the shows she likes. Clearly, she has not picked up any pointers from those perfect television mothers. I am determined not to let that happen to me. Life is for living. I wanted to be like the Tippi Hedren women but every time I approached them and asked them if they'd take me with them, they laughed and treated me like I was a child. I was a child. A determined child. I kept trying to run away, but there was nowhere for me to go because I didn't know anyone and because I had no means to travel and because I was only a child.

So much for the currency of youth.

Still, from the age of five, I meticulously plotted my escape. Oddly enough, my escape didn't come from leaving, but from staying. In sixth grade, Mama deposited me in Miss Tillie's Dance Academy. Mama worked two jobs and when she discovered that dance class was cheaper than babysitting, she enrolled me in class five days a week. In that ramshackle studio next to the Y, my world suddenly began when I was introduced to pirouettes and pas de deux and jetés. I was a fast learner with good lines and natural turnout, and Miss Tillie worked with me personally from the time I was eleven and a half until now. She was a principal dancer with the Alvin Ailey Dance Company who moved back home to, ironically, take care of her mother.

Who says you can never go home again?

I owe Miss Tillie everything. Absolutely everything. She gave me what Mama didn't. What Mama couldn't. She taught me grace and discipline. She gave me the courage to succeed. To survive. She spent hours and days and years teaching me technique and demanding perfection from me. Miss Tillie knew I needed to eclipse our small town and she was determined to help me do it. Last week, she drove me to my audition for her cousin's dance troupe in Chapel Hill.

And... my future daughters... I was accepted! I did it! I got into the CHDT!!!!! The Chapel Hill Dance Troupe. I'm only sixteen, but they think I'm eighteen. I told Mama I got accepted to college early and she's so self-involved and thrilled that she doesn't have to feed me anymore, she didn't even question it.

Next week, my life is officially starting.

Parents are supposed to fuck up their kids; it's part of the evolutionary cycle. But I will try my hardest to color outside the lines and connect the dots into my own pattern.

I will not fuck you up. I will just love you.

Your future mother,
Mary Elizabeth Baxter

Two

"This is the last ferry, Ma'am. We're closing up shop before the storm hits."

"Ma'am?" Carolina rolled her eyes. "Really, Andy? You've known me since we were twelve. Besides, it's not even drizzling."

"Yet." Andy cocked his head at the sky the way sailors did, but Carolina knew very well that Andy Brady wasn't a sailor, but a former Manhattan CPA who was rumored to have had a nervous breakdown. He'd been driving the ferryboat between the mainland and the island for the last five years and led seal watching cruises in the early spring.

"You going to visit your Mom?" Andy asked.

"Um, yes." Carolina wasn't sure how to respond. Technically, she was going to visit her. Everyone on the island knew her mother. Mary was always a favorite, as the Baxters' blue Victorian was often home base for the local kids who spent their summers roaming from house to house. "Can we wait just a few more minutes?" Carolina asked.

"Five minutes, tops. No later than 12:05," Andy said. "I have a wife," he added for effect.

Carolina nodded. Even Andy had someone to share his life with. He and Carolina had played together when they were kids and even dated briefly in eleventh grade. But Carolina ended it abruptly. She wasn't interested in a long-term relationship with a townie. Andy was a good guy, but she wanted to get away and Andy was someone who was tethered to the East Coast. His family summered on the island and lived in nearby Branford. The historical home he grew up in, which had been in his family since the 18th century, was now sandwiched between a strip mall and a fast food restaurant. His older brother Barton, now a local policeman, lived there as well. He'd never leave, unlike Carolina who ran away the second she had a chance.

Carolina let Andy help her onto the small boat. The wind had picked up a little and she was having trouble balancing on her heels. She'd change when she got to the house; she had enough clothes in her suitcases for two weeks even though she planned to only stay for two days. "When's it supposed to start raining?" she asked.

"Weather report says a biggie's due in the next hour or two. Probably close in around fourteen hundred," Andy said as he loaded Carolina's bags onto the boat.

"Fourteen hundred?"

"Military speak," Andy said, winking.

Carolina's father was a military man who had spent most of her life prioritizing the armed forces over her. Consequently, she loathed anything that reminded her of the army, from the hipster fatigue pants Baltimore sometimes wore to civilians who spoke in military timetables to sound important.

"Of course," Carolina smirked. "From all the years you spent in the service."

Andy ignored the dig. "You know how fast storms come in around here."

Carolina nodded. Over the years, she had weathered several flash storms on the island. Her mother expertly made the storms fun for her girls, lighting candles when the power went out, organizing board game tournaments and telling them stories about her gypsy youth. Mary knew how to fill time with fun. Ironic that Carolina only knew how to fill time with work.

"How long's it been since you were last home?" Andy's question interrupted her nostalgia.

"Two years, give or take." Carolina finally spied her baby sister across the street, leaning against a motorcycle and flirting with Old Man Winters. She watched Baltimore throw back her head and expertly feign a flirty laugh. Like mother like daughter. She wondered if being a slut was hereditary. Baltimore was so much like their mother, only Mary would never own a bike. Carolina squinted. The shiny bike looked brand new. Since when did Baltimore own a motorcycle? Not that her baby sister would tell her, they rarely spoke. Their main form of communication was texting.

"Bet your Mom's excited to see you," Andy said.

"Hmm." Carolina's attention was still focused on her sister who didn't look like she was in any hurry to go. "C'mon Balt," Carolina yelled before turning back to Andy. "Have you seen Dallas?"

"Nope, but she'd better get here soon."

"By fourteen hundred?" Carolina couldn't help herself. She watched Andy bristle and realized that she'd yet again managed to offend a member of the weaker gender. It's what her sisters called 'The Carolina Curse.'

"Even the island taxis close down when it gets too bad out," Andy said, no longer trying to make an effort.

Carolina was irritated that Dallas was late. To deal with Austin, she needed someone on her side and Dallas was the most logical choice. Baltimore worshipped Austin, while Dallas was more objective.

"Baltimore, let's go," she screamed again before looking up at the ominous clouds. In Seattle, this would be considered a beautiful day.

⚜ ⚜ ⚜

Austin looked out the window at the approaching ferry. She could make out the small figures of two of her sisters, huddling against the wind. They were Andy's only passengers. He had fewer and fewer passengers these days. Practically everyone had already closed up their summer houses on the island, and the odd tourists wouldn't brave the variable fall weather.

It was quiet on Money Island, eerily quiet. She supposed she should eat something. Her mother chastised her earlier for eating crap. Mary was always giving her a hard time. But Austin liked pizza and macaroni and potato chips. Carbohydrates, especially bread and chips, were comfort foods which ... comforted her.

And bracing for her sisters' arrival, especially for Carolina, she definitely needed some comfort.

1965

Mary stabbed the toothpick into the errant olive submerged in her dirty martini.

She delicately placed the small oval fruit in her mouth, turning her head just slightly so that the soldier in the corner could watch her suck the pimento through the hole before chewing the olive slowly. Very slowly.

Mary knew how to attract a man: She'd lost her virginity three years earlier at fifteen. Sammy Gold was her first love. He was the son of one of the rich furniture bigwigs. He was Jewish, the heir apparent to Gold Flooring, and both her anti-Semitic mother and Sammy's anti-white trash parents were against the relationship from the start. Because of that, or perhaps in spite of it they dated on and off for a year before Mary gave herself fully to him. A week later, Sammy was in a motorcycle accident and was declared brain dead at the scene. His parents kept him on life support for months and Mary remembered how awful it had been visiting him in the hospital: a vegetable with tubes in his mouth. That was not the way to live. That was definitely not the way she wanted to die. Eventually, his parents pulled the plug. No one told Mary; she showed up at the hospital one day and Sammy was just... gone.

Mary shrugged. That felt like a lifetime ago. Her heart had finally healed and she realized that she epitomized the Tennyson quote, 'Tis better to have loved and lost than never to have loved at all." Mary was someone who loved hard and was therefore forced to deal with the consequences when the love didn't turn out the way she planned. She glanced back at the soldier. He was handsome and strong. Mary smiled; she would put *Dr. No* into play. She'd seen Sean Connery in *Dr. No* three times and mastered Honey Ryder's hair flip and confident stride as she emerged out of the sea to capture James Bond's heart. Mary adopted the siren's nuances and had enjoyed several lovers since then.

After all, attracting a man wasn't rocket science.

She'd been observing the soldier since he'd entered the dive bar and had bought the last two rounds for his buddies. Mary liked the way his crisp uniform sat on his toned body. She could see the outline of his muscles through his pressed shirt. Captain Cardoso. She'd seen the name on the small silver name tag attached to his lapel. Mrs. Cardoso. It had a nice ring to it. Mary was all for the free love movement of the sixties; yet, she also wanted to be married. And although she was happy to make love, not war, she also liked the idea of marriage. Everything good about her mother was wrapped up in her marriage to Mary's father, and Mary wanted to experience that goodness as well.

The soldier had been watching her for over an hour. Generally, Mary stayed away from military men; yet, there was something different about this one. His eyes. Mary always had a soft spot for kind eyes. She turned slightly, allowing him to better see her. She had popped into the bar for a drink after rehearsal, merely throwing on a floral peasant skirt over her maroon form-fitting leotard. She took a drink, knowing that the rush of the alcohol had the peculiar effect of making her nipples pop out. Braless, she smiled as she covertly watched the soldier watching her. She flipped her Janis Joplin-like long waves one more time.

And she knew that she had hooked him.

February 1965
Chapel Hill, North Carolina

Dear Daughters,

Better late than never.

I apologize for not writing for two years, but I seriously don't have a spare minute. Whoever invented time was definitely not a dancer. There are not enough hours in the day to accomplish everything I need to do. All I do is dance. Okay, to be honest, all I do is dance all day and have sex all night. Both are equally time consuming. Too much information? Sorry, but I've always been a straight shooter. No point in diluting the truth. Plus, I've never been happier. Mama and High Point feel like a distant memory: characters in someone else's story. And I'm never opening that book again. I am never going back, only forward. I'm creating a new story and you, my future daughters, will each have your own chapters in it. But before you come along, it is just me and my dancing. I dance sixteen hours a day and I couldn't be happier. My feet are always bloody, I have killer shin splints, eight of my toes are completely black and blue and I'm missing half of my toenails, but I'm happy. I'm content. Who would have imagined that little Mary Elizabeth Baxter from High Point would become a professional dancer. And I'm good, I'm really good—it's not considered bragging if it's true. And it's true. Poverty has given me a veneer of authenticity as an artist. I don't have money. I don't have family. I only have my work.

I eat, breathe and sleep dance. It's all I do and all I want to do.

Perhaps Mama taught me an unexpected lesson. There is an upside to self-absorption. Live a life true to yourself, not one others expect from you. Had Daddy lived, maybe I wouldn't have become a dancer. Maybe I would have led a more conventional life, become a teacher or a secretary. Children often make poor decisions in vain attempts to please their parents, to make their parents proud. Maybe my artistic career would have been circumvented if I had a more traditional childhood. But Daddy died and I fell into the artistic world thanks to Mama's selfishness and neglect... and the fact that Miss Tillie's classes were so cheap. It was a happy accident and I wouldn't change it for the world. Nothing makes me happier than dancing. All of the sadness melts away and I am able to truly live in the now. To dance, you have to have the raw guts to conjure the make believe in the moment. To live with complete abandon and trust the music, your director and your partner. You need to release all of your fears and insecurities and, after a childhood where I was forced to hold on to everything so tightly, it feels wonderful to finally let go. Each minute flick of a finger or curl of a toe contributes to the story I am telling through my movement. My entire body is alive. So many people just express themselves from the neck up. They forget to breathe and are trapped in their heads. Can you imagine... being trapped and not being able to fully express yourself? Dance has taught me to use my entire body to articulate my thoughts. Words are important, but actions speak louder than words.

Sometimes, you can tell an entire story without uttering one word.

It didn't take that long before I was promoted to principal dancer. Can you believe it? I'm the youngest one in the company and everyone hates me... but that's because they're all jealous bitches. Especially the twenty-five-year-olds who wish their bodies could do what mine does. I can out *tendu* and *chasse* the best of them. This is a profession for young people and, at eighteen, I am in my absolute prime. I'm going to give it another couple of years and then retire. Not officially from dance...just from dancing. There is nothing more pathetic than seeing someone over the hill who is desperately hanging onto their youth. When it's my time to go, I'll go peacefully. I won't petition the Artistic Director or tearfully plea for a few more seasons. I'll leave gracefully. And I'll be prepared when the moment comes. In my limited spare time, I've been working on some choreography. I think that's where my voice really is, in creating dance. I'm going to work out a routine with some of the other dancers and present it to the Company Manager. You have to step outside of your comfort zone and take chances if you want to succeed. You must face your biggest fear if you want to win. I suppose abandonment is my biggest fear. Both my parents ditched me: Daddy in death and Mama in life. The first piece I'm choreographing is called *Mother Nature.* Only my Mother Nature doesn't nurture...she destroys.

I will nurture you girls. I will build you up. You have my word.

I don't know how old you'll be when you read these letters, but I'm assuming you'll be old enough to know about sex. Or at least have a deep appreciation of it...like your mother. Dance companies are all about the sex. Everyone is fucking everyone. It's the most insular environment I've ever been in. I've already slept with the three straight dancers, but I have my eye on someone special who is outside of the company. Okay I have my eye on two guys, but one of them probably isn't going to work out.

The first guy's name is James. He's a musician who sings and plays the electric guitar. Yum. He's tall, lanky and incredibly sexy. He's amazing in bed, but I'm pretty sure he's destined for stardom and, the fact is, there is only room for one star in a family and that's me. The other guy's name is Roger. Captain Roger Cardoso. Okay, I know what you are going to say, I've already warned myself... stay away from military men, they'll break your heart. Trust me, I know. But I love Roger. He is so sexy. His muscles actually have muscles and his hands... wow, I've never seen hands like that. Most men think the way to a woman's heart is through jewelry. Mine is definitely through foot rubs.

Show me a man who can give a good foot rub, and I'll show you a future spouse.

Roger comes into Chapel Hill from the base every weekend. He's desperately in love with me and has already proposed... but I'm eighteen, a little young to get married. Aren't I? How white trash would that be? Still, he'd offer financial security and it could be my ticket out of here. Roger's family is loaded. Filthy rich loaded. Like Howard Hughes... without the airplanes.... and the issues. They live in Fort Lewis, Washington, and he's a second generation army brat. His great great grandfather was a Brazilian billionaire, whose money came from coal. Roger is not a billionaire, or even a millionaire, but he is comfortable. Very, very comfortable. Shit, what am I thinking? I swore off military men since dad died and proved they'll abandon you one way or another... but Roger is so... strong, virile, exciting. And sexually, he's exceptional. He takes his military persona into the bedroom with him and there is nothing in the world more exciting than being tied up and fucked.

Sometimes, he even wears his cap.

The games we play... well, I probably shouldn't go into too much information as these letters might get slightly pornographic, but let's just say that you all need to date a military man at some point in your lives. Maybe even marry one.

He's possessive in the bedroom and would probably kill me if he knew about James, but I'm excellent at keeping secrets.

Because secrets aren't really lies, they are more like hidden truths.

The frustrating thing is that Roger could be deployed any minute. Troops are heading over to Vietnam every day and Roger could be next. Girls, I am very anti-war. And this is coming from an army brat. I've seen what wars can do from first-hand experience. I want to protest Vietnam. I want to use my voice to make a difference, to affect people. But I also want to support Roger, especially if I end up marrying him. It's all so confusing, but my possibilities are infinite. At least, my youth perpetuates the illusion that my possibilities are infinite.

I'm not sure what I'll do, but I'll think with my heart. Too many people waste their lives thinking with their brains. A dancer's success comes from her natural instinct. And when you have a strong instinct, you must follow your heart because if you don't, you've wasted everyone's time, especially your own.

And time is the most precious commodity we'll ever have.

I love you future daughters and I can't wait to meet you,

Mary Elizabeth Baxter

Three

"Pee, gotta pee. Gotta pee," Baltimore shouted as she flung her knapsack on the couch and bolted up the stairs.

Carolina followed her, lugging her two overpriced suitcases. The house hadn't changed. Come to think of it, she didn't know if it had ever changed. The orange shag carpet was worn from several decades of small feet trouncing all over it. The furniture was mismatched, but not in the quirky shabby chic style: It was simply mismatched. Their mother was the island hoarder. A perpetual collector, whenever she saw a neighbor getting rid of a couch or a chair, Mary Baxter always claimed it before Goodwill could. There were too many books to count and their heaviness made the old bookshelves sag, groaning in silent protest from the excess weight.

As she ran her hand along the shelf, Carolina remembered the classics like old friends. She'd read all of them. Her sisters had as well. Mary was insistent upon it. Carolina remembered her mother's insistence that her daughters become voracious readers. "You can hold a book in your hand and it becomes alive in your mind when you read it. It takes you on an adventure. Yet, if an illiterate man holds the same book, it is simply pulp."

A self-educated high school dropout who had eventually gone back and gotten her GED and college degree, their mother was intent on her four daughters going to good schools. She had insisted that her daughters be properly prepared for the outside world that was filled with men and disappointment; the two often hand in hand.

Despite its lack of upgrading, from the analog television now equipped with the lame bunny ears to the red rotary phone, the house looked good. Welcoming. Carolina remembered first moving into the house full time when she was seventeen. Nothing like being uprooted in the middle of high school. Hell, she had been uprooted for most of her young life. So had Austin. Dallas and Baltimore spent most of their lives in the blue island house. It was the only home Baltimore ever knew. Carolina supposed that her baby sister had had the most normal childhood, at least the most settled one.

She suddenly felt the familiar feeling of envy rearing its aggressive head. She usually kept most of her emotions tightly locked away; yet, being back home...spending the last fifteen minutes in the water taxi with Baltimore, she knew she was in for a long weekend. As she surveyed the cozy living room, she admitted that the blue island house had felt more like her home than any other. It had been in her father's family for many generations and he had given it to Mary. Carolina spent her summers there for as long as she could remember before her mother decided to move the family there permanently. As the oldest, she got to pick her room first and she remembered her delight at choosing the small cupola on the third story of the house with four windows, one facing every direction. She used to plot out her life there, the things she would accomplish. She would work hard in school and become a famous lawyer. She would kiss frogs to meet her prince. She would save the world. She chuckled; one out of three wasn't bad. And she had met her prince charming, she just hadn't counted on the fact that he would turn back into a toad.

Carolina loved her room, which she had painted the perfect shade of Carolina Blue and she made the patchwork curtains herself with her mother's Singer sewing machine. Her basketball trophies were still there. Her scrapbooks. Her memories. Mary kept all of her girls' rooms the same so that they'd feel comfortable coming home. Carolina was glad her smart phone had a great camera. She'd take some pictures of her room. And the view. Perhaps it would inspire her for the next phase of her life. She looked up the stairs and imagined sleeping in the four-poster bed her mom found in town. She remembered her mother's story of how she had charmed... or was it seduced the owner to ferry it over to the house, schlep it up the stairs and assemble it himself. Yes, it would be nice to spend a few nights here, she convinced herself.

As Carolina walked around the living room, she began to clean up... a habit. She turned off the antiquated television, picked up a few empty frozen dinner containers balancing on the closed roll top desk in the corner and tidied a pile of unopened mail on the table. A large pile. Why wouldn't Austin open it, she wondered? Carolina always went through her own mail meticulously, separating bills from correspondence and shredding the rest. One could never be too careful with identity thieves.

"Carolina." Austin's voice cut through the silence and made her jump.

She turned to face her sister. Within a moment, years of fractious history came bubbling back into the confined living room and Carolina suddenly felt very claustrophobic. Austin was dressed in worn green sweatpants and a Princeton lacrosse shirt. Green and orange, a fashion faux pas. Although some would consider Austin pretty, she never did much to augment her natural beauty. Her short auburn hair looked like it hadn't been washed in days. The freckles around her nose had faded from lack of sun exposure and, although she was still athletic, she was slimmer than Carolina remembered her. When had she last seen her younger sister? Carolina couldn't remember. Austin invited her to her book signing in Seattle a few years earlier; yet, Carolina had just made partner and couldn't afford to leave the office. She showed up later, but the store had long cleared out.

Just another regret to file away. Another disappointment.

Austin was eating a bowl of newly made macaroni and cheese and the smell of the sulfites made Carolina nauseous. There was no love lost between the pair and Carolina dropped the unopened mail and straightened up slightly.

"No one outside the family calls me Carolina anymore." Carolina tried to manage a smile, but she could just tell from Austin's laissez-faire attitude that the conversation was not going to turn out well.

"Well, since I'm inside the family, I should be allowed to call you by your Christian name, but, hey, Carol works for me," Austin said elongating the vowels so the name sounded almost obscene. She then continued on a Carol riff, "Carol Channing, Carol Burnett, Carole King, Carol Brady, Lewis Carroll ... A Christmas Carol." Austin slowly circled Carolina, like a predator. "You know who else changed her name, well, not really changed it, more like modified it: CCH Pounder. Her name is like a condensed sneeze." Austin faked a loud sneeze in Carolina's face, "Ha ... Cc-cch."

Carolina jumped back, tripping on her heels. "Are you drunk?"

"Not yet." Austin winked. "CCH's real name is Carol Christine Hilaria Pounder. What's it been Carol ... ina, three years?"

"Two."

"—And a half." Austin was always straight to the point and never couched her feelings. It was one of the qualities that made her a good writer; her characters were excessively honest. She was mad at Carolina and she wasn't going to mollify her anger with niceties. It wasn't just because her sister had blown off her big book signing. It was because of everything.

Undeterred, Carolina tried to make conversation; however, her questioning came out more lawyerly than sisterly. The consummate litigator, she had come for answers and Austin remained closemouthed. Austin barely spoke to her on the phone, other than briefly telling her about their mother and insisting that she catch the next plane to Connecticut. Carolina needed the entire picture, not just a few random puzzle pieces. "When's the last time you cooked for yourself?"

"A few minutes ago."

"When's the last time you cooked for yourself that didn't involve microwaving a box?"

"A few years ago."

"Jesus, Austin. If Mother could see you now, she'd be horrified."

"If Mother could see me now, I'd be impressed."

Austin stared at her older sister. She wanted to say a million things to her. She wanted to shake her and scream and cry and just have her be the big sister she had been for most of their childhood. Before Carolina uprooted her life and moved across the country. Before she stopped coming home. Before she stopped caring. Austin just wanted to weep and release all the pain and secrets she had been keeping for so long. Instead, she forced a large smile, her words dripping with irony.

"It is so good to see you."

Carolina opened the window, airing out the stale room. "This place looks like a mausoleum."

"It is a mausoleum." Any chance of connection was lost. The old sisterly tensions had already snowballed into an unstoppable animosity. Austin immediately shut the window. "There's a storm coming."

"So I've been told." Carolina sat at the long table, which divided the kitchen and living room. The oak wood table which the girls had done their homework and played games had been a present from Carolina's dad ... one of the few tangible memories she had of the man who was now sitting in an old age home in Spokane, slowly losing his mind to dementia. She ran her finger over the C in the bench. They had all carved their initials into it. Baltimore did it first, when she was six. Austin and Dallas followed suit. Carolina added her initial when she came back from college. She hadn't realized that she had put her initial at the end, with a few spaces after Dallas's perfectly crafted D. The initials read B.A.D. C. Bad C. Her baby sisters called her Bad Carolina after that. She didn't care. She was living in Seattle, three thousand miles away, married to Matthew. She was building a new life, one diametrically opposed to her old life. A new life where she was the priority. Where she was the good C.

"Where's Baltimore?" Austin interrupted her thoughts.

"In the bathroom."

"Is she pregnant?"

"No! ... Why, is she seeing someone?"

"Pregnant people always rush to the bathroom when they get somewhere."

Austin always talked as if situations were fact rather than fiction. Declarative sentences rather than speculative ones. When they were living in Texas, she convinced Carolina that if she peed in the pool the chemicals from her pee would cause a big spurt of red dye to fill the pool. Even if she leaked a little, the dye would appear. Austin made her so paranoid that Carolina stopped swimming. Even when their mother convinced her that Austin was teasing her, she didn't believe it. It wasn't until Mary sat her eldest daughter down on the edge of the water and peed in the pool herself without any dye repercussions that Carolina finally believed Austin was making it up. Carolina was so mad at her sister, she didn't talk to her for a month. But Austin hadn't cared. She never seemed to let anything bother her. Still, now that she put the seed of Baltimore's pregnancy in her head, Carolina started to wonder.

"No, I mean, she's been on the road for two and a half hours. I wanted her to take the bus from Boston, but she met me in Stony Point and we took the ferry over together."

"You took a bus?" Austin now just wanted to antagonize her sister.

"No, I wanted Baltimore to take the bus. I flew."

"Because you're definitely not a bus person."

"I'm not. I flew... and then took a taxi."

"Oh. Did you have scintillating conversation on the ferry? Baltimore's a scintillating conversationalist."

"No. I was talking to the office. She was talking to Andy." Carolina needed air. She wondered if she should wait for Dallas or just go on a run now. She needed some clarity. What she really needed was a drink, but she was trying to stay sober until she got some answers. Yet, it was Austin, not she who was hurling the questions.

"Why didn't you fly into New Haven, Carol... ina?"

"Will you please stop calling me that."

"Why?" Austin prodded.

"It was half the price to fly into a major airport."

"And Hartford's a major airport?"

"It's more major than New Haven."

"But, you're rich."

"What does that have to do with it?" Carolina was starting to lose her cool.

"Rich people should be able to fly into whatever airport they choose." Austin lectured, "That's why we live in a class-based society; to cater to the convenience of the rich."

"Austin, the rich stay rich because they don't spend their disposable income on last minute airplane tickets flying into New Haven ... and if it makes you happy, I flew first class."

"It does make me happy." Austin pitched her empty macaroni container into the trashcan across the room. A perfect shot. "Did you remember to put in your frequent flyer miles?"

"I remembered. Can we drop it?"

"Sure. Dropping it. No worries. Just making scintillating conversation."

Austin stared at Carolina, willing her to stare back; yet, Carolina was concentrating on controlling her frustration and was breathing in short regulated breaths. With little sleep and no answers, she was close to her breaking point.

The sound of a toilet flushing broke the loud silence. Seconds later, Baltimore bounded down the stairs and looked at Austin curiously.

"Mom's in the tub."

1968

Mary wore a tangerine orange mini dress with a matching headband.

She liked bright colors and was one of the few dancers who favored dazzling secondary colors instead of the requisite black most artists preferred. Mary believed that colors each had their own sentient feelings, a rainbow had its own temperature and depending on her own mood when she woke up, that was the shade she wore. Lately orange had been her color *de rigueur.* It was the color of creativity and of the sacral chakra. The sex chakra.

And Mary was in definite need of some sex. She'd been celibate since Roger had been overseas and nineteen months was too long for anyone. Especially when that anyone was twenty-three. Mary was ready for some changes. And most women's changes begin with the hair. Sure, it was a superficial answer, but it was rebellion in its most dramatic form. Mary had chopped hers off last month. It was easier that way. No fuss. And with her cheekbones, she knew that she could pull it off. She hated the way women hid behind their hair. This was 1968, women didn't need hair to be sexy. They needed confidence. Self-confidence was truly the route to revolution. Twiggy did it. Edie Sedgwick did it and Jean Seberg did it...and she played Joan of Arc, the biggest rebel of all.

Mary gave herself one last look in the mirror and bounded down the stairs where her daughter was playing in the playpen. Mary wasn't a big believer in cages for children, but they were godsends when Mary needed a bit of extra time to make herself beautiful. And today was one of those days. She smiled at her little girl. Carolina was almost one and the best thing that had ever happened to her: Mary was intent on giving her daughter a strong sense of self and the building blocks of self-confidence so that she could conquer the world in any direction it needed conquering. And that began with Carolina's education. Mary was determined that her daughter would be well read and that task began long before she learned to read. Mary had already filled the island house with every classic, especially the ones written by women. She would insist as her daughter grew up that she read every book in the house. So, even though Carolina could barely walk, Mary read her Sylvia Plath and Betty Friedan and Virginia Woolf as her bedtime stories. In a singsong voice, she echoed Woolf's sentiments that men should not socially and physically dominate women.

"You have to be the hero in your own story, Carolina," she'd say. "Empowerment comes from within."

And cutting her locks was Mary's answer to redefining her own femininity. Not in men's terms, but in her own. Plus, *Rosemary's Baby* had just come out and the minute she saw Mia Farrow demurely commanding the screen, she wanted that quiet power. As the closing credits rolled, Mary marched straight from the cinema to the hair salon. She asked her stylist to chop off her hair. No, she demanded it. She had a slight nervous breakdown when he first started to shear the back of her neck like a sheep but she refused to cry or acknowledge her buyer's remorse as her hair was mercilessly hacked away. Yet, when it was over ... when all of her tresses lay dead on the linoleum floor, she felt satisfied.

She felt free.

There was something so neat, so tidy about a clean haircut. And Mary liked clean. She liked tidy. It was why she always matched her bra and panties. She liked to match ... it made her feel more beautiful. Besides, she wanted to be prepared in case she was ever in a catastrophic accident, and she had become obsessed with the idea that if she was unconscious and the paramedics were cutting off her clothes, her undergarments would match. Had she been on the motorcycle with Sammy Gold that day like she was supposed to, the paramedics would have seen her matching pink bra and panties.

And Mary was always ready to take off her clothes.

She wasn't a slut...but she liked to have fun. Being a dancer meant that she lived in a world without boundaries. Roger was overseas and she was a young woman with...needs. So she explored her opportunities. And right now, her opportunity was in a boat heading towards the house with a bed in tow.

She smiled as she watched Carolina playing in the playpen in her orange jumper. Her daughter loved the blue house on Money Island. Her little eyes immediately relaxed when they got off the boat onto the island. It was as if, even as a child, her daughter felt like she was coming home. One day, after Mary travelled the world, she promised herself that she would make this house her permanent home. It was a place where she could put down roots. She had loved it from the minute Roger showed it to her. It felt so...lasting.

She walked over to the playpen and picked up her daughter, hugging her closely, the orange of their outfits blending into one. Sometimes, she would dress up Carolina like a doll, playing matchy match with her little girl. She would cut one of her own flowing maxi dresses into a mini dress to show off her legs and use the extra material to sew her daughter a matching outfit. The one useful skill her mother taught her was how to sew. Without money, Mary had sewn most of her own clothes growing up and she was determined that her daughters would not face the same shame she did. It was horrible to grow up poor. To grow up wanting. To grow up wearing dresses made from the same cheap material that the backwards North Carolina neighbors used to sew their curtains. Not that Mary needed money now, but she liked the stillness which sewing gave her. She liked the combination of the humming whir of the machine and the dexterity her hands felt as they cobbled together an outfit.

She enjoyed sewing out of want instead of need.

One of the reasons Mary married Roger was for the money. Sure, she loved him and the sex was terrific, but she loved his bank account even more. She loved the security it would bring her. Ironic that her mother had named her Mary after the Virgin Mary. Mary was no virgin although she was raised chaste and poor. Mary had spent the first fifteen years of her life being both poor and chaste, and she had more than compensated for both deficiencies.

The doorbell rang and she adjusted her headband, putting down her toddler who was already smiling in anticipation of the visitor. Carolina was such a precocious child and although most mothers were guilty of giving their children false prowess, she knew that her daughter was truly spectacular. "You're my good girl, Carolina," Mary said as she walked towards the door.

Mr. Quinn was right on schedule with Carolina's big girl bed. Her adult bed. Carolina would be able to go straight from the crib to an adult bed. Why waste money with a child-sized bed decorated with roses or racecars when her child was eventually going to be an adult? There were so many more important things to spend money on.

They had found the bed at an estate auction in Branford and Carolina loved the delicate butterflies etched into the hardwood headboard. Well, Mary guessed she loved them. Her daughter couldn't speak yet but when Maude McFeely started waving her paddle, Mary immediately felt a competitive need to beat her neighbor. She did not want to watch McFeely's arm fat swinging back and forth like a full grown walrus. Why did fat people insist on wearing sleeveless muumuus? Mary had no issue with the woman's girth, but she took great offense at her lousy fashion sense. So she made a preemptive bid offering far too much money for the antique four poster bed. After she won the auction, Mary immediately broke protocol and talked the head of the estate sale, Roy Quinn, down on the price. She did this by agreeing to go on a date with him if he'd deliver the bed himself. He was older with salt and pepper hair and a slight limp but he was nice and Mary had a way with nice guys, even though she was usually only attracted to the bad boys. It's okay to wear sheep's clothing, as long as there is a wolf somewhere inside. However, Roy Quinn was all sheep.

She answered the door, pinching her cheeks to flush some color into them.

"Mr. Quinn." Mary smiled, her eyes dilating.

"Mrs. Baxter."

"Mary. Mrs. is such a ... formal title."

"Indeed." Roy blushed, handing Mary the bunch of daisies, which were already wilting from the heat. Apparently it was the only thing wilting as Mary could clearly see through Roy's tight madras shorts exactly how eager Roy was to see her.

Mary tucked one of the flowers behind her ear. She hadn't been attracted to Roy and was not planning on doing anything with him, just give him a little flirt. Yet, there was something about his eyes. Mary was a sucker for eyes and his blue eyes were Paul Newman blue and he even wore the light blue work shirt Newman had in *Cool Hand Luke*. Mary knew she shouldn't be thinking adulterous thoughts; after all, her husband was overseas fighting for America. Yet, Roy

Quinn was right here, in her living room. And she had an itch that needed to be scratched.

Mary turned and looked into the mirror, enjoying the contrast of the lemon yellow of the flower with the tangerine orange of her mini dress. She didn't face Roy as she purred, "Ready to assemble?"

"Not sure that was part of our deal," Roy said, but he had already turned back to the pile of wood he had left on the front porch.

"But Roy," Mary said turning, accentuating and elongating the vowel making his name sound like a pitiful whine, "I'm incapable of building a bed." Her voice was thick and husky and filled with innuendo.

"Bet you're good at using one, though," Roy said boldly.

"Well, you're just going to have to build it for me and then we'll find out." Mary grabbed Roy's hand and gave Carolina a pat on her head as she led the man upstairs.

September 1968
touring with dance co

Dear Daughters,

I am officially a lousy mother.

I promised myself I'd write to my unborn daughters at least once a month and I'm barely cranking out a letter every few years. Guess I've been a little too preoccupied to properly correspond, especially since my first of you has already been born. Carolina. My beautiful, beautiful daughter. I have truly accomplished something magical in you. When they put you in my hands and I stared back at those enormous hazel eyes I couldn't believe it. I couldn't believe I had created something so beautiful. I will never forget that feeling of helplessness. My life will never again be my own because you had me wrapped around your finger from the second you popped out. Before you came, I never understood what it meant when people cried tears of joy. But from the moment I saw you, I couldn't stop bawling. You were crying, I was crying...we were quite the sight to see. Everyone on the hospital floor kept peeking in to see what the commotion was. You definitely needed to express yourself and far be it from me to stop you.

I had no idea how much time a baby takes up and with Roger away and no grandmother to help out – more on that later – I was completely on my own. Well, on my own along with a bunch of dancers. When I hired dancers for my new troupe, I made sure that they were all fine with sharing the babysitting load. And that they weren't perverts.

Some may call it communal living, I call it smart thinking.

I've created my own company, The Womyn Warriors, thanks to Roger's money. He gave me the startup cash I needed to incorporate the business, hire a business manager, buy costumes and afford dancers. Right now, I only have three dancers: Dana, a lanky redhead who is ambitious as hell and fiercely loyal, Wander, a stunning black man with a strong masculine dance energy and Lulu, a gifted mulatto with excellent lines. We're a groundbreaking company because we're racially mixed, but when I look at my dancers, I don't see color, I just see talent. Anyway, they've all signed contracts with me, and Roger's money will keep us in business for at least a year... hopefully my talent will keep us in business after that.

The main reason I started my troupe at such a young age is because I could. The desire had always been there, but now I have money to back it up. After dancing six days a week, sixteen hours a day for the last four years, I was definitely ready to retire. Like I said, dancing is a young woman's profession, and at twenty, I am over the hill. Is that depressing? Perhaps. My shrink tells me that I have mild depression, but that's his job, right? To diagnose... for better or for worse. He gave me a cornucopia of pills, all different colors. Mostly uppers and downers: uppers to dance and downers to sleep. Nothing like a good barbiturate to help me get through the night. But I'm not convinced that I'm mildly depressed. I'm just severely tired: tired of my legs and feet always hurting me. In addition to the shin splints and bloody toes, I've been dealing with muscle tears, tendon pulls, corns, blisters and bruises. I ache every day. Still, I have beautiful legs... gams Roger calls them when he's trying to be debonair and terribly old fashioned, but whatever they're called, they always hurt. And my choreography pays three times what I was making as a dancer and I get to use my mind as much as my body. Instead of following someone else's drumbeat, I get to create my own. I can teach other dancers what to do. Have them execute my vision.

Roger is great but let's be honest, the best thing about marrying rich is marrying rich. With gin and vermouth dribbling down her chin, mother always said, "It's just as easy to marry poor as it is to marry rich." It was one of the only things she was ever right about. I love Roger, and I really appreciate his money. Especially because I have no intention of reliving my shitty childhood on an army base or in an ass backwards town.

After marrying Roger, he thought we'd live on the base in Fort Lewis, Washington. He thought wrong. I told him I was never living on a base again. Good thing too, because he got shipped out to Vietnam right after that discussion. Vietnam: What a fucking waste of lives. I'm not worried about him dying though; he's not on the front line. He's doing something tactical... though really when he talks about it I have absolutely no idea what he's talking about. I just know he's safe. And that's all that matters to me.

We were married just long enough for him to impregnate me before he went on his tour. I hate that they call going to fight in a ridiculous war a tour of duty. I've been on a tour of duty with my dance troupe for the last few years. And they are very different types of tours. The main thing is that Roger is safe and my Carolina will always have a father. Not that he's done one lick of work to help raise her. Not that I need him to.

Women don't really need men to succeed. But they do make terrific bedfellows.

I've always been self-sufficient and I intend to raise you girls that way too. I have a job, I earn a living, I am independent and the best of the best in my field. And the only way to become the best is through experience. Practice and experience. Before you were born, Carolina, my troupe danced our asses off throughout the Southeast and then we did a tour of the Northwest. Talk about crisscrossing the country. I can't encourage you girls enough to travel. See the world. Observe. Widen your perspective. Believe it or not, I think my favorite place on the tour was Palm Springs ... what a wonderful place to retire. There's this dance troupe there that only hires dancers in their eighties. Octogenarian hoofers. Something to look forward to. I can come out of retirement in half a century and then dance until I die. A delicious thought.

The biggest problem with being on tour so much is that I don't really feel rooted anywhere and having some sort of place to call home would be nice. Roger's family has a house on Money Island, which is just off the Connecticut coast. It's gorgeous. A three story ramshackle Victorian with loads of personality. It's a bright cerulean blue with white trim. The color is somewhere between azure and cyan. In case you're wondering why I know my colors so well, it's because I recently choreographed a piece called *Blue,* and I wanted to hit every nuance in the story, including specificity of costume. Did you know there's a shade of blue called Carolina Blue?! It's the color for the Tar Heels at UNC, but I think I'll call it your color, Carolina. Maybe we can paint your new room that color! Anyway, back to the house. There is a porch that goes around the entire house, a backyard with a garden and a front yard with a view of the water to die for. I took you up for two weeks this summer Carolina and you loved it. Now that I can coordinate my own schedule, I will make sure that we have a minimum of two weeks every summer to spend on the island. We'll sail and swim and sun. Doesn't that sound divine? Listen to me, quite the lady. Summering in an island house.

You'd have no idea I grew up in the bowels of North Carolina.

Complete non sequitur, Mama's dead. Dead at forty-four. Christ. Who in the hell dies at forty-four? Well, Billie Holiday, but she died of cirrhosis of the liver. You'd think with the amount of alcohol Mama consumed over her lifetime she'd go the same way, but her exit from this world was quick and relatively painless. Mama had an aneurism at lunch and died. She was halfway through a tuna fish sandwich and a can of Tab when she keeled over. Her boss at Ashley Furniture called me so I went home, buried her and two days later came back to my dance company. Do I have regrets? No. Does that make me cruel and heartless? Maybe. But my mother was the least nurturing person on the planet and didn't seem to care that I even existed. I was far more upset when Miss Tillie died of a heart attack last year. But I know I made her proud. Miss Tillie, not Mama.

That's where you get your middle name, Carolina, from my dance teacher Miss Tillie. Carolina Tillie Baxter. Of course you have my last name. Why would I ever take a man's last name, even if he is my husband? I want my father's legacy to live on. And I want to set an example for you that you can rise to the top on your own merit, without taking a man's name. I reject that patriarchal tradition.

So, my little Carolina, my beautiful girl, I am so glad you are in my life. I promise to show you the world of possibilities that is just waiting for you.

I love you Carolina,
Mom

Four

"Mom's in the tub? Our mother's in the bathtub?" Carolina was apoplectic. If she was waiting for the tipping point to drive her over the edge, this was officially it. She raced up the stairs.

Baltimore flopped next to Austin onto the worn blue upholstery couch and reached into an open bag of barbecue potato chips. "She looks good."

"I thought so."

"A bit too skinny."

"Mom?"

"Carolina." Baltimore smiled and passed the chips. "How've you been?"

"I've been better."

Carolina rushed back downstairs. Her sisters were lounging on the couch as if they hadn't a care in the world. As if it was a completely ordinary day. Except that it wasn't. She glared at both of them. "Mom's in the tub."

Baltimore looked at her innocently. "That's what I said."

"That's what she said," Austin parroted before grinning at Baltimore. If sides were going to be taken, it was fairly clear where Baltimore was pitching her tent.

Carolina looked at her sisters as if they were crazy. She pulled out her cell, but there was no signal. She picked up the house phone and punched zero.

"Can I have the number for the..." Frustrated, she looked at her sisters for help. "Who should I call?"

"911," Baltimore suggested.

"The coroner," added Austin.

Carolina adopted her lawyer voice and spoke into the phone with authority, "Hello, yes, may I please have the number for the police." She covered the mouthpiece and glared at Austin. "You are completely inept."

Austin shrugged and passed the bag of chips back to Baltimore as Carolina continued her diatribe into the phone. "Hello, my mother's passed away and I'm not sure who I should talk to about... What? Okay."

Carolina returned her focus to Austin. "She's transferring me. I thought you could at least take care of this before I got here."

"And miss this drama?" Austin's deadpan delivery incited her sister even more.

Before Carolina could start screaming at Austin, the operator came back on the phone. "Hi... Yes. Who do I talk to about getting a body removed?... 730 North Diversey Avenue... the blue house on Money Island... What? Uh, no, technically, it's not, I mean, I grew up in it, but I don't live here now... It's my mother's house, was my mother's house, but it is my mother's body... What? No, I found her dead... She drowned... Because she's underwater." Carolina bit her lip, preventing her from reaming out the ignorant young worker on the other end. "What? Yesterday... Because I wasn't here, yesterday. I was in Seattle, litigating a case... Yes, I flew. I took the red-eye. American flight #22. Obnoxious stewardess—"

"—Flight attendant," Austin suggested; yet, Carolina put up her hand to stop her from speaking. Her irritation snowballed with every word.

"They showed a Leonardo DiCaprio movie, but I'm not a DiCaprio fan so I didn't watch it."

"Who doesn't love Leo movies?" Baltimore wondered aloud.

"Leo? You call him Leo?" Austin looked at her baby sister incredulously.

"Sure, he feels like someone I could be on a nickname basis with."

Austin started to laugh, but her chuckles were drowned out by Carolina's escalating voice.

"Jesus. Haven't I given you enough details? Can we please focus on my mother's corpse rotting in the tub? ... Thank you."

Carolina grabbed the chips from Baltimore, shoving them into her mouth. "He's transferring me. Is everyone completely incapable?"

Baltimore grabbed the chips back. "Government worker."

"Bureaucracy at its best." Austin laughed as she gave Baltimore a high-five. They were finding perverse enjoyment in their sister's unraveling.

"Hello. Hello ... Yes. My name is Carol Baxter and my dead mother is in the bathtub. I need you to send someone to pick her up ... Yesterday ... Because I wasn't here ... Because I was under the false impression that someone else had called yesterday." She looked at Austin. "Because she's mentally unbalanced." Carolina finally exploded, "CAN YOU PLEASE JUST SEND SOMEONE OVER HERE TO REMOVE THE FUCKING BODY?"

Carolina took a deep breath and tried to compose herself. Baltimore, who never missed a beat, spied Carolina's perfectly manicured OPI Pink Flamenco nails violently digging into her hand ... the pain suppressing the panic.

"Thank you... Wait, what? Two to three hours, are you serious? Yes, I'm aware there's a storm coming, it seems to be the hot topic out here. Can't you come out before the storm?" She glanced out the window. "But it's not even raining yet... Yes, I'm certain busy metropolises like Branford are littered with dead bodies you people need to pick up... 730 North Diversey Avenue... D as in David, I.V.E.R.S.E.Y. The cerulean house on Money Island. What? Really?" Carolina clipped her words as she spit into the phone, "It's a shade of blue. Somewhere between azure and cyan. Thank you."

Carolina slammed down the phone. "Do you have anything to drink?"

"It's noon," Austin said, judgment tingeing her voice.

"I didn't ask for the time, I just need a drink."

"There's vodka in the liquor cabinet." Austin watched as Carolina practically sprinted across the room to the Oriental accent chest that housed the family liquor. It had been a present from one of their mother's lovers, a slight Japanese businessman whom she dated briefly between Carolina and Austin's fathers.

"Thank you, Mommy," Carolina opened the cabinet exposing the vast array of bottles.

Austin tapped Baltimore on the shoulder and the pair silently watched Carolina rummage through the cabinet, inspecting each bottle as if she were a purveyor of fine liquor.

"Do you think 911 operators are equipped to handle hysteria?" Austin asked loudly enough for Carolina's benefit.

"They must take a course," Baltimore replied.

Carolina methodically pulled the bottles out of the cabinet, searching for her brand of choice.

"Smirnoff. Absolut. Absolut Pepper. Grey Goose. Stolichnaya. Findlandia. Popov. Absolut Citron. Belvedere.

It's a vodka cornucopia." She grabbed the half empty bottle of Belvedere and headed into the kitchen.

Baltimore jumped up and surveyed the vodka collection. Most people she knew, especially most older people, kept a small variety of liquor in their house: some gin, bourbon, whiskey, rum, tequila, scotch, brandy. Not two dozen bottles of varying brands of vodka. Most people preferred variety; however, Mary was not most people. "Um, that's a lot of vodka."

"Cornucopia?"

"I sent her a word of the day calendar for Christmas." Baltimore smiled.

"That's a thoughtful gift."

"I thought so."

"Because I would have said mélange or potpourri." Austin considered the options. "Even hodgepodge, but cornucopia: That's a mouthful."

"I didn't know Mom was a boozer." Baltimore put the bottles back into the cabinet, arranging them by height.

"She wasn't. She just liked to 'be prepared' in case she had company. Like today."

"Being prepared is having a bottle, maybe two, not a fully stocked liquor emporium. Like this is the set of *Cheers*."

"Where everybody knows your *name*," Austin sang, directing the dig at Carolina who returned with a very large screwdriver: three parts vodka, one part orange juice. "Besides, Mom always took preparedness to a whole new level. Check the closet; there's enough baby powder and Listerine to disinfect a third world country. Once, I was running low on paper, so I asked Mom to pick me up some. Four hours later, she comes home with twenty different varieties. Bright white. Matte white. Print white. Did you know there are actually different colors of white? I'm still using that paper."

"That's prepared." Baltimore stopped rearranging the liquor cabinet and began to open drawers and nose around the living room.

"That's psychotic. Who needs twenty reams of paper? It's not like we live in the wilderness. There are five Office Depots near Branford. And two Staples." Austin opened up a drawer in the roll top desk and showed her sisters the enormous supply. "Plenty of paper."

Baltimore looked past Austin. "Oh my god, the nesting dolls."

Mary had an impressive collection of Matryoshka dolls. They lined an entire shelf of the living room. The girls used to love playing with them when they were younger. They would arrange the dolls on the shelf, table and floor, both intact and separately. Mary would open the dolls and repeatedly tell her daughters that although they all had different fathers, they shared the commonality of a matriarch. Like the Matryoshka doll, Mary had successively birthed a group of strong women: unique individuals; yet, mirrors of each other. Dependent on each other. The inner layers revealed when the outer layers were opened.

The girls spent their lives trying to find original Matryoshkas for their mother. Dallas had succeeded in finding the most unique set, a hand painted Matryoshka Mother Superior, which housed four novices. She and Peter found it when they were honeymooning in the Seychelles. The irony was delicious as Mary raised her daughters Catholic, despite her own penchant for promiscuity and divorce.

Baltimore opened up a set of Chinese dolls. "I've spent a lifetime looking at these dolls, but if you think of it, they lack originality. Come on. Can you imagine if there was a set of Matryoshka penises? Mom could've assigned one to each of our dads. Though mine would have been the biggest."

"Really? Have you seen your father's dick? That's gross." Austin shuddered.

"It's obvious. I mean, clearly I'm the most virile of the four of us."

"Really, what brings you to that conclusion?" Austin liked to tease her baby sister. She had a sense of humor and didn't take everything as personally as Carolina.

"You're gay, so your virility is in a category by itself. Dallas has been dating Peter since college, hell she probably lost her virginity to him, and Carolina's a divorcee, so—"

"—I don't think you're using the world virility right," Carolina interrupted.

"Sure I am."

"It means sex drive, and it's not applicable to women," Carolina lectured.

"Everything is applicable to women."

"Except virility. That's about fathering children. Each of our dads wasn't virile as he only spawned one daughter. Virility to men is like fertility to women."

"Whatever. I'm probably the most fertile of the four of us as well," Baltimore said.

Austin immediately grinned at Carolina. "See, told you she was pregnant."

"Who's pregnant?" Baltimore was genuinely curious.

"You are."

"No, I'm not."

"You sure?" Austin teased.

"Actually, I'm never sure. But since I'm feeling incredibly PMS-y right now, I'd say I'm almost sure."

A loud taxi horn blared and Baltimore jumped up and looked out the window.

"See, I mention PMS and Dallas shows up, right on cue." Baltimore smiled. "Hey, do you have a cigarette?"

"Only the illegal kind." Austin reached into a secret cubby in the roll top desk and pulled out a joint.

"Do you have to do that?" Carolina asked.

"I do," Austin said as she and Baltimore went outside to greet Dallas.

Carolina silently observed her sisters. Austin was four years her junior, but she might as well be as young as Baltimore. She was certainly as immature. Why couldn't Austin have dealt with Mom before they arrived? She had the time. This would now cut into the weekend and put everything off schedule. Carolina would now have to call the office, there was no way she'd be able to fix this in a day.

It would take at least two.

1970

Mary poured a pound of Epsom salt into the shallow tub before slowly submerging her entire body into the warm water.

She looked forward to the next twenty minutes, hoping that her body would heal, or at least feel a little less uncomfortable. She was just so sore all the time and she was tired of being in pain. It was exhausting to feel like an old woman in a young woman's body. And she was only twenty-three, just a few years younger than Ursula Andress was in *Dr. No*. Mary wondered if Honey Ryder ever experienced her degree of soreness. She probably had a team of masseurs to combat the pain.

Mary sighed. She was almost a quarter of the way through her life. Halfway to her midlife crisis. There was so much more for her to do. So many more dreams to fulfill. Even though she was now choreographing her troupe, she was still dancing all the time. All day every day. The Womyn Warriors were at the tail end of their eight month national tour and her body was feeling the consequences. They had just performed across Texas's panhandle and were heading towards Austin.

Mary closed her eyes and sunk further into the tub. It was a lime green tub, which was barely large enough to cover her tiny body. She could hear Dana and Carolina through the door giggling. Dana had been almost as much of a mother to her daughter as she had. Mary didn't know what she would do without her principal dancer. While Carolina lacked for rigidity, she certainly never lacked for love. And her daughter would certainly let her know if she did. The second Carolina could speak, she gave her mother a litany of demands. There were several things she was unhappy with and she was very clear about her wants and needs. Carolina was someone who knew what she wanted and was not afraid to ask for it. Her little girl had no fear. And at the top of her list was the need to stay in one place. She did not like living like a gypsy and having the sum of her possessions able to fit in a suitcase. Her daughter wanted rigidity.

Carolina wanted her father.

Mary wanted Carolina's father as well; yet, he was nine thousand miles away. And his letters were sporadic. This was mostly Mary's fault because she moved around so much. His letters were sent to a post office box in North Carolina and then forwarded to whatever town she was performing. Sometimes, letters got lost in the mail and she would receive a letter written in January sometime in March. It was frustrating and Mary felt like a war widow and her husband wasn't even dead.

Mary luxuriated in the water; the magnesium in the salts was just beginning to work its magic over her achy muscles. The bath would get cold soon, but the luxury of living in a hotel was the endless supply of hot water. She would just drain a little of the cold water out and fill the tub with more warmth. There was an art to taking a bath and Mary had all but perfected it. Languishing in the bath was such a deliciously selfish event. It was one of the few moments in life where her time was fully her own to do with as she pleased. And when Mary bathed, it allowed her to think.

When she got out of the tub, Mary would craft the daily letter to Roger. She would have Carolina draw him a picture and she'd fill him in on the day's events: the longhorn burger she ate, the racism the troupe experienced in the last tiny town they'd passed through, tidbits from the televised tenth Olympics. She worked hard to send him letters every day no matter how tired she was. Even though she didn't support the war, she wanted to support the troops. She wanted to boost her husband's morale. So she wrote long anecdotes. Mostly about their daughter. Roger hadn't been at Carolina's birth, so Mary had one of the maternity nurses take pictures of their beautiful baby girl. It cost extra money to send the Polaroids in a letter but Mary didn't care. She wanted her husband to feel included in their daughter's life, from her first tooth to her first pair of tiny red running shoes.

Mary manipulated her toe through the plug that covered the drain. As she plucked it from its hole, the water slowly started to trickle out. She would stay in the tub until the water emptied. Despite the constant companionship of her daughter and her dancers, Mary felt lonely. So unbelievably lonely. Having a one-sided relationship was difficult and Mary was someone who needed attention. A lot of attention. She liked to be put up on a pedestal and adored. And Roger was too far away to adore her. Absence was definitely not making her heart grow fonder. It was just making her frustrated.

Emotionally and physically.

February 1970
Austin, Texas

Dear Daughters,

Fucking Roger.

The second he got back from Vietnam, he couldn't keep his dick in his pants. What do they feed our soldiers over there—testosterone filled MRE's? You wanna know why he came back early? The bastard got shot. How the hell can you get shot when you're spending the whole fucking Vietnam War in a Marriott Hotel four hundred miles south of the DMZ. Friendly fire he said, but leave it to Roger to shoot himself in the foot so he could come back. Come back and fuck someone else. Not that infidelity matters that much to me. Clearly by my actions I am not convinced that we're supposed to be monogamous, but the week he gets back? Have a little respect... wait at least two. Only an asshole would kiss his wife and kid and then hire a hooker. I could have given him anything that hooker could... except for an STD. Maybe it was post-traumatic stress. The hooker was Asian. Not that I'm racist, not at all, but come on. There is something psychologically fucked up about traveling halfway around the world to shoot the Vietnamese and then coming home to America to fuck one in a low rent brothel. Fucking Roger. Well, I'm through fucking Roger... I'm on to Mort.

He's Jewish. A Jewish man. An old Jewish man. He's forty. Okay, old by my standards. Although I'm hardly young. At least I don't feel young. I'm twenty-three years old with a three-year-old daughter, hardly the picture of youth. After Roger, I vowed I'd never date a man under forty again. They're too immature, too full of themselves. I need a relationship to be about me. I need to be taken care of.

I want to be the selfish one.

Morty Stone Horowitz. Can't get more Jewish than that. Unless his name was Rabbi Morty Stone Horowitz. Or Sammy Gold. I have to talk to my shrink about that comparison. But Sammy was a boy and Mort is all man. He's delicious. Tall and gangly, with thick black hair and deep brown eyes magnified behind his dark horn rimmed glasses. He is filled with passionate ideas and never stops talking, hypothesizing and deconstructing. We met last week and, I swear, I'm already in love even though I promise that I am going to take this one slowly. Mort's the quintessential intellect: smart, engaging, curious and critical. He graduated from Columbia's School of Journalism and then spent a decade traveling the world as an investigative journalist. I think he's tired of living in tents and not showering, so he's back in the States and determined to be a big time reporter. But to get a desk at the *New York Times,* you have to start small. So, right now when he's not writing anti-Vietnam editorials, he's working the Entertainment beat, doing syndicated fluff pieces around the country. And since my dance troupe just got a year contract to perform at The Paramount Theatre in Austin, he ended up covering me. And boy has he covered me... but I don't want this letter to become x-rated so I'll leave the rest to your imaginations.

I barely gave Mort a second look when he first walked into my theatre during rehearsals. My publicist let me know a reporter would be popping by and interviewing me. Now, by publicist, I mean that one of my dancer's fathers has a small PR company and offered to take on the Womyn Warriors as a pro bono client. Still, it's all how you spin it, so my big time Chicago PR firm called and told me that they got me a syndicated article. A few days later, Mort Horowitz slipped in a side door of the Paramount and made himself comfortable in the tenth row. I didn't really notice him until we broke for lunch a few hours later. I was checking on you, Carolina. Maxine, one of my dancers sprained her achilles last month and is watching you while she recovers. It's cheaper than hiring a babysitter...wow, for a split second I just felt like my mother. Anyway, I was checking in on you and I heard Mort before I saw him. His velvety thick, deep baritone voice with just a hint of a Queens accent. He was all business and wanted to set up a time for the interview. I suggested we do it right then and there, but Mort, after giving me the once over dropped his businesslike approach, and thought it might be less rushed over dinner. It was then I looked into his big eyes. They were smiling at me. I've never seen eyes smile before I met Mort. The chemistry was instantaneous. So, I said yes and that night he interviewed me over dinner. He interviewed me over dessert and he kept "interviewing" me all the way through breakfast the next morning. He is a fascinating man. I've never met someone with such a complex mind. He is focused and direct. He challenges me, which I love as I am usually so busy challenging everyone else. He asks questions, really asks them demanding an answer, even if the answer isn't an easy one to give. I love that he is so interested in my mind as well as my body. We really connected but I told him I wanted to keep it casual and he agreed. Mort's a confirmed bachelor who clearly doesn't want to be tied down by a woman with a kid. And I'm not sure he's great father material as he seems as selfish as I do.

Still, never say never.

So, your Mom's a pretty big deal here. Carolina, I know you don't think so because I keep dragging you to endless rehearsals, but one day you'll look back on these days nostalgically. After all, you're my first. And this will be the only time in your life when you're both my eldest and my baby. You're the darling of the company, you know. The pet. You look like a porcelain doll with your fair skin and long dark hair. Everyone loves you and you have twenty built-in babysitters. Yup, my little troupe has expanded. In addition to Dana, Wander and Lulu, there are seventeen other dancers who cover every ethnicity. Asians, Hispanics, Blacks, Whites, you name it. Last month, we finished a sixteen week tour of Canada and the country's on this big multiculturalism kick right now, so we were in the news all the time. Frankly I think I could solve the race issues in America if people came to see my dancers. Because when the Womyn Warriors dance, it is multiculturalism at its best.

These kids are amazing. They're not much younger than I am, but as the choreographer, I'm the boss. And Carolina, you love the attention. You're independent and bossy. So incredibly bossy. Hey, complete non sequitur, did I ever tell you that your father wanted to name you Beverly, after his mother? Beverly, hmmpft. What a stupid name. I named you Carolina after James's song. James, now there was a wonderful lover. Quite considerate. In hindsight, I probably should have chosen him over Roger. Anyway, I sing James's song to you every night to get you to sleep. I suppose most kids prefer traditional songs like *Twinkle Twinkle*, but you love J.T.'s song because it seems to be about you. *In my mind I'm going to Carolina*... You're three now, practically a young woman. And already independent. So independent. That's why I want to give you some sisters. A support system of women. Not that I don't love men, I do... and your father is a good man, Carolina, when he isn't being such a pig. On the plus side, he is filthy rich and incredibly generous. He put aside enough money for you to go to college... four times. And he gave us the island house in Connecticut. Gave me the deed.

His business is on the West Coast, so he never has time for it. I'll take you there for the entire summer, I promise. Not just a weekend here and there, but a full summer. Just imagine, we now have a summer house. How deliciously bourgeois. It can be our home base when we're not touring.

I love you Carolina,
Mom

P.S. Mort's article highlighted a piece I wrote for the company called Men Suck, Daddy. I wrote it myself. For a high school dropout, I seem to have a flair for poetry.

Men Suck, Daddy

Depression rocks me like a boat hit by a crashing wave.
I tumble out and find myself drowning in my own tears.
Help.
What did Alice do?
She drank from a bottle that said "Drink
Me"... but all I have is beer.
So I drink and I eat and I drink and eat some more.
Now, I am depressed, drunk and fat.
Men suck.
This power that they have over women
to evoke such a complete feeling of utter doom.
What an enigma. I need an enema.
Is there a doctor in the house?
Please, I need something to fix my heart.
No, Daddy, antibiotics and a neon Snoopy
band aid ain't gonna do it this time.
You were a king to me Dad, you could do no wrong.

You were my hero; yet, you never prepared me for the real world.
Men suck, Daddy,
and you didn't warn me.

Five

Baltimore and Austin watched the water taxi approach. In the last half hour, the sky had gotten progressively darker. As the boat pulled up towards the slip, the driver was clearly trying to make the ride smooth, steering the small craft directly into the choppy waves. The boat looked helpless against the churning waters, the white-capped waves lapping against the side of the craft; yet, the driver easily lassoed the rope around a metal stud on the dock as he temporarily anchored.

"Why isn't she bringing Peter?" Austin lit the joint and took a long toke, observing Dallas, in her perfectly coiffed bob, clutching nervously onto her seat for support.

"Maybe Emily Post has rules against bringing one's husband to see one's dead mother."

"Especially when one's so inappropriately attired." Austin handed the joint to her sister.

"Dallas?"

"Mom." Austin laughed.

"You're terrible."

"I know."

Baltimore took a long hit from the joint. "This is excellent."

"This is medical. Only the best for you, little sis."

Dallas emerged from the cab, a bit green; albeit, still without a hair out of place. She wore pearls and a pale pink Ann Taylor sweater set. She was perfectly dressed ... if she was going to a baby shower. But she never knew what to wear on these occasions. She had easily grabbed a taxi from the New Haven train station to the dock in Stony Creek, but when she arrived, she discovered it was mostly deserted. Dallas had to bribe a water taxi driver to take her to the island. He was the only one around; everyone else had packed it in for the upcoming storm. She hoped the weather in Philadelphia stayed clear; her girls never played as well in the rain. Most of them were prima donnas; talented princesses who let the weather affect them. She couldn't believe she was missing the big game. But she had to be here. It was the right thing to do.

And Dallas always did the right thing.

As she walked down the dock, she saw Austin and Baltimore sitting on the porch, waiting for her ... vultures ready to attack their prey. Neither had changed much since she'd last seen them. Austin looked a bit wan, but Baltimore looked vibrant. Youthfully exuberant. There was something off about Austin. She didn't look like herself. And she was smoking. Dallas hated that. Nowadays, people who smoked were idiots. She was about to go into teacher mode and start admonishing her sister, lecturing her on the evils of cigarettes, but she stopped herself. This was going to be a simple trip. In and out. She was not going to stir the pot. She painted on a pleasant smile as she walked towards her sisters in her Tory Burch heels, holding up a large cardboard box wrapped with a twine bow.

"I brought cake."

1971

"Push," the fat nurse screamed for a third time.

Mary wanted to belt her. She had been in labor for over sixteen hours and nothing had prepared her for this. Nothing. Carolina efficiently popped out of her in less than an hour but this baby was taking her good old time. Mary pushed again, feeling her vagina rip as the infant's head made its way through the tiny opening. A part of Mary was glad that her mother had given the birds and the bees lectures a miss. Had she known how painful childbirth was, she probably would have skipped it.

"Just relax, honey," Mort said as he patted her sweaty head.

"You relax! You did this to me, you bastard." Mary originally wanted her husband in the delivery room. It was fairly new for men to be allowed in the sacred space but she'd insisted. Now, she was having second thoughts. Her husband hadn't been carrying nine and a half pounds that was trying to wedge itself through a tiny little hole. And his platitudes weren't helping; rather, they were infuriating her.

As Mary endured the pain of childbirth, she couldn't help but think about her father's death. Somehow, birth and death always intermingled in Mary's mind and throughout this pregnancy she'd been thinking about her dad. Even though he had now been dead for twenty years, not a day went by when she didn't think of him. Too young to remember any flaws he might have had, Mary only remembered her father's attributes: his strength, his loyalty, his love. She talked to him all of the time and was always looking for signs that he was there. That he was looking over her and protecting her. Once, she felt him in the form of a bright blue butterfly that darted around her in the garden. Another time, she was swimming and felt a chill as if he was in the water just in front of her. She didn't question these metaphysical feelings; rather, she embraced them. She wanted so badly to feel the love that her father had given her. His was too short lived and she was determined to find it in someone else. She craved it. It was youthful infatuation with Sammy, primal love with Roger and now she was hopeful that Mort's grownup love could somehow compensate for her father's love. So as she brought another life into the world, she couldn't help but think of her father, wish he was there and hope that wherever he was, he was proud of her.

Seventeen hours and three minutes from the moment she had gone into labor, Mary's second daughter was born. The baby's shrieks wailed through the hospital as her daughter announced her presence in the world. Mary held her screaming daughter, amused that the infant actually seemed put out that she was born. As if she was doing the world a favor by entering it when she would have much preferred to cozy up in the womb a little longer.

"That's my good girl. Let it out, Austin. Let it out." Mary rubbed her daughter's back as her wails softened to exhausted coos.

"You're safe now. You're home. And your Mama will always protect you."

May 1971
Austin, Texas

Dear Daughters,

Hello, baby Austin.

Goodbye, Austin city.

I'm getting too big for this town. Not physically – I mean I can still easily fit into my pre-babies leotard – yes, babies as in plural as in more than one ... but we'll get to that in a minute. The point is, a year is too long for me to stay somewhere: I get antsy. I understand the concept of putting down roots, but flowers wilt unless you deadhead them and after a year in the same location, I feel as if I am wilting. As an artist, I need better energy to draw from to create and this environment is too stale for me. I'm not sure any of the world's greatest artists came from Texas. Okay, maybe a bunch of actors and a few singers and a sports star or three but frankly, I think they were simply trying to escape. Like I am.

I need to escape my past in order to secure my future.

New York is where it's all happening. I'd move there just for the music. Do you know who performed in the last few years at the Central Park Music Festival? Everyone. Positively everyone. Fleetwood Mac, Miles Davis, Joni Mitchell, Van Morrison. It's the musical center of the universe and where music goes, dance follows. Or where dance goes, music follows. Which came first, the chicken or the egg? Same thing with music and dance. Oh, and then there's Mort. I'm absolutely positively crazy about the man. He is the love of my life. Yes, even at twenty-four, I know that he is the one for me. I married him the minute the divorce papers from Roger came through. Poor Roger, he wanted me back the second I asked for the divorce. Typical man. As soon as you officially reject them, they come crawling back. It's pathetic really. Still, he didn't put up too much of a fuss and with his military efficiency, sent me the papers immediately. I went to City Hall the following day. I don't think I was a single woman for more than 24 hours before I became Mrs. Morty Stone Horowitz; although only in spirit because I will live and die a Baxter.

Mort is the one. I am sure of it. I've had more lovers than I can count on five hands and will have many more in the future, but Mort is different. He is my soul mate. A woman can have many lovers, several loves but only one true soul mate and Mort is mine. No matter what happens, he will always be my true love. Always. It's a feeling I can't explain, it's something I just know. Maybe it's the way he looks at me through those horn rimmed glasses. Or it's the smell of his soft skin. Or the way we fall asleep together, first intertwined and then just the slight of our backs and tushes touching, ensuring that we remain connected. Perhaps it's the way he never fails to make me laugh, or the way he insists on wearing Chuck Taylors no matter how dressy the occasion. Maybe it's his uncanny ability to taste something at a restaurant and whip it up in the kitchen the next day. Maybe it's because I've been searching my whole life for a father figure... not for my girls, but for me. Yes, I realize Freud would have a field day with this, but I don't care.

Because Morty Stone Horowitz is my soul mate.

Carolina, you were the flower girl at the wedding. Not that people who get married at City Hall need a flower girl, but you insisted. I wanted you to be the witness, but apparently four and a half is too young to bear witness to a wedding. So, you were the flower girl. You even picked out a white dress at Kmart... not for me, for you. I wore maternity jeans which barely held in my belly and a XXL Tar Heels tee shirt, which you told me was inappropriate wedding attire.

Even though it was Carolina Blue.

"That is completely inappropriate marital attire, Mother," you announced assuredly. "I've read all the Bride magazines. One does not get married in jeans and polyester blend cotton." Ha. You actually said those words. Marital attire. I didn't know you were such a fashionista or up on your wedding etiquette. Frankly, I didn't even know you could read, but who was I to argue? Although Emily Post does say that the bride should be the only one in white. Still, you are the boss. You always have been and you probably always will be. I did follow one tradition though. I did the *four somethings*. Kind of. *Something old* was Mort, although he wasn't too happy to be labeled in that category. *Something new* was the enormous baby inside of me fidgeting to get out. *Something borrowed* was a diamond and garnet studded hair clip Dana lent me. *Something blue* was my Tar Heels tee shirt.

I've always wanted a big wedding. I didn't have one with Roger and I certainly didn't have one with Mort... perhaps I can do the whole nine yards on my next one. I imagine it being a mix of traditional and contemporary. Walking down the aisle to the theme song from *Goldfinger*, watching my dancers do a tributary copulation dance, serving pink champagne, hiring The Band as my band ... anyway, another time. This wedding was a fairly ordinary affair... until my water broke halfway through the ceremony.

And that's when the ordinary became extraordinary.

Carolina, you were mortified and pretended like you didn't know me. The witness, a waitress who was about to pull a double shift at the diner across the street, looked sick. But Mort took it all in stride and calmly insisted that the Justice of the Peace finish before we went to the hospital.

He really wanted to be able to fill in the "father" line on the birth certificate. Texas is such a repressed state; they would have probably made me leave it blank if I wasn't officially hitched.

So, the Justice finished in double time and we grabbed a taxi and got to the hospital in six minutes. Not that we needed to rush. I thought you were going to slide right out of me like your sister did. But you were intent on keeping us waiting. It took almost an entire day for you to arrive. You entered in classic Gemini fashion, constantly changing your mind: vacillating between wanting to stay in the womb and entering the world...and almost killing me while you made up your mind. Kid, I was in labor with you for seventeen hours. Seventeen hours!

Finally, you deigned to bless us with an appearance. And, like most babies, you screamed like a banshee when you entered the world, yet after a few minutes, you quieted down and looked around completely nonplussed...as if you were doing the universe a favor by gracing it with your presence. Talk about a kid with attitude! You are going to be one special woman. There is a world out there just waiting for you to conquer it.

And you'll start conquering it in the center of the universe, New York City. As soon as I finish out my contract here, we're moving in with Mort in the West Village. He has a cozy walk-up and there's room for all of us...just barely. It's a one bedroom, but there's a tiny balcony and the living room-slash-kitchen-slash-dining room is unusually large. It can easily convert to a second bedroom-slash-playroom-slash-living room-slash-kitchen-slash-dining room. Okay, it may be a little cramped, but it's located on the corner of Bleecker and Cornelia and you know what they say about real estate...location, location, location!

The Womyn Warriors are moving as well. I got us a temporary rehearsal space in Times Square and once we take up permanent residence, I'm sure a theatre home base is soon to follow. No one protested about the move. Hell, it's my company and the dancers will follow me wherever I lead, although half of them are getting too old to dance for me. I have the draconian age limit of 29, but the demands I put on my dancers can only be handled by the very young and the very committed. Their muscles are stronger, their tendons more flexible and their energy more joyous. The older we get, the more the life gets sucked out of us. We'll use our reputation to find a new space and we'll expand and give both Alvin Ailey and another up and comer on the scene, Twyla Tharp, a run for their money.

That's why, as women, we must constantly search for what makes us happiest. Where our deepest passion lies. Mine lies in my dance, my men and my girls.

Not necessarily in that order.

I love you Carolina and Austin,
Mom

Six

"You look like Adidas threw up all over you."

Carolina ignored Baltimore's quip as she sat at the old redwood picnic table, lacing up her running shoes. The bright yellow laces and purple and aqua shoes provided a strange contrast to the fading bench with the wood knots, peeled paint and weathered bleaching. Mary used to be so diligent about keeping up appearances and refurbished the table yearly, giving it a deep clean and stain. When had she stopped caring? Maybe around the time she stopped caring about living. Carolina sighed. She needed information and Austin had been closemouthed from the minute she got there, glibly deflecting all of her questions.

Carolina finished lacing her shoes and looked at the table. Three plates were filled with chocolate crumbs from the half devoured cake: The plate next to Carolina still boasted a moist slice. The girls had wolfed down the German chocolate cake, well, the three youngest sisters had, but Carolina resisted. Maybe she'd have it a little later if she felt her run was good. There was coconut on the cake and Carolina was trying to up her coconut intake, especially coconut oil which her nutritionist said had unlimited health benefits. It was supposed to ward off Alzheimer's. Of course, running was too and she was more than diligent about that. She looked at the tempting slice and tried to remember how many calories were in a bite of cake. There was an application on her phone that broke down her daily caloric intake; yet, she wasn't getting a signal here. Maybe she'd find one on the far side of the island.

Carolina looked across the yard. Baltimore and Austin were swinging on the antiquated swing set, each pumping their legs as hard as they could to outdo the other. The rusted swing set was probably a health hazard, but they looked like they hadn't a care in the world and their laughter annoyed Carolina to no end. She had no idea how it affected Dallas, because her sister had barely spoken since she arrived.

No one wanted to be in the house so they picnicked outside, despite the looming storm. As soon as she finished her cake, Dallas hadn't been able to sit still and with the lawn covered in leaves, she went to the old vinyl shed where she got a rake and went to work trying to tidy the lawn. The shed had stood there as long as the girls could remember. Mort used to store his clippings there, important articles from newspapers which he'd promise to refer to "at a later date;" yet, with the advent of the internet, he never looked at the clippings and they sat in the stacked up boxes in the shed, yellowed with age. Along with the rake, Mort's clippings and Mary's gardening equipment, the shed stored various discarded sports equipment: Baltimore's skates and rackets, Austin's lacrosse sticks, Dallas's field hockey sticks, Carolina's basketballs. There was a graveyard of cleats piled high in one of the corners. All four girls had excelled in a sport, Mary made sure of that. She encouraged each girl in a different athletic discipline to dissuade competition. The oldest girls all played team sports, whereas Baltimore played tennis. They had all made their respective teams in college and Austin had been a three time All-American her freshman, junior and senior years.

The Baxters' backyard was also filled with memories. Besides the swing set which Mary put up for Dallas and Baltimore when they permanently moved to the island house, there was an old lacrosse net where Austin used to polish her shots and a torn basketball hoop and a small patch of cement where Carolina used to practice her jump shot and layups. In addition, there were a few old croquette wickets, which had survived several decades stuck in the tough soil. On the small deck was a barbecue where the family used to enjoy Sunday cookouts... until Baltimore declared herself a vegan and shared her beliefs a bit too dramatically with the rest of her carnivorous family. Mary's garden, nestled in the corner of the backyard, was a bit overgrown, but she always preferred her garden to be unruly. Just like her life, with possibilities in every corner.

No one else felt the compunction to join Dallas in raking up the yard so, still in her Ann Taylor outfit, she attempted to organize the chaotic lawn on her own. It was inundated with fall leaves and the wind was picking up, disturbing her neat little piles. In the tranquility before the tempest, the sky was a turbulent deep charcoal grey; the fast moving clouds gathering like soldiers ready to wage war.

Finally, Carolina stood up, ready to go on her run, but she couldn't let the charade continue any longer. "Are we going to talk about it?"

"What?" Austin grinned, swinging wildly on the child sized wooden swing.

Baltimore turned to Austin. "It's the pink elephant in the room."

"Pink?"

"Isn't that the expression?"

"I thought it was just an elephant, I didn't know it had to be pink."

"Although, we're outside, so it's not necessarily in a room—"

Unable to control her frustration, Carolina screamed at Dallas, who was furiously raking, "Will you please stop that?!"

"Why are you yelling at me? I didn't do anything." She went back to her raking and muttered to herself, "Cleaning calms me down."

Baltimore giggled. "Such a Virgo."

Austin continued to swing as she looked at Carolina. "What do you want to talk about?"

"You know what."

"I do?" Austin said innocently. "Hmmm, well, earlier we covered paper and alcohol. That's earth and water. All we have left are fire and air and we've exhausted conversation on the four elements."

"Carolina flew in on the red-eye," Baltimore offered.

"That's air, fire anyone?"

Baltimore shrugged. "I still wouldn't mind a cigarette."

"—Mother's suicide. I need to talk about it. Can we please talk about it?"

Austin jumped off of the swing, landing close to Carolina. She looked up at her. "Why? You weren't present during her life, why should you give a shit about her death?"

"That's unfair."

"Suicide is personal."

"I talked to Mother at least once a week."

"Once a week?" Austin had difficulty hiding her disdain.

"Okay. Maybe every other week."

"Biweekly."

"Whatever." Carolina defensively folded her hands over her chest. "Look, she didn't indicate any symptoms of unhappiness."

"*Symptoms of unhappiness?*" Austin rolled her eyes. "You really need to let the legalese go when you're out of the courtroom."

"Fine. Did she indicate any fucking signs of unhappiness?"

"What do you think, Carolina?" Austin growled.

"Well, was she upset?"

"I don't know, counselor. Do people generally commit suicide if they're not upset?"

"How can someone who isn't in pain suddenly kill herself?"

"See, there's your misconception." Austin clipped her words as she spoke in a low, angry voice, "One does not suddenly kill one's self. It is a systematic, methodical event. Mother did not just slit her wrists with an old Bic shaver from the Branford Walmart. She went under ... sank ... drowned ... in a civilized and ladylike fashion. No mess."

Carolina, Dallas and Baltimore didn't move. Dallas stopped raking and Baltimore stopped swinging. Carolina simply stared at her sister in disbelief.

"You're joking."

"We saw it in an old black and white movie." Austin returned to the swing, focusing her attention on Baltimore. "Hey! Complete non sequitur ... Guess who I saw last week?"

"Who?" Baltimore started swinging again.

"What's her name? Your friend. That prom queen—"

"—Lori Braithwaite?" Baltimore grinned. "Let me guess. That bitch has three kids. She lives down the street from her mother. And she's fat. She's very fat. Am I right?"

"An A+ to young Baltimore Baxter. Three kids, two blocks and ... she's enormous."

"Enormous or ENORMOUS?" Baltimore couldn't contain her glee.

"Well, she's not 'lose a few pounds' at Jenny Craig chubby or 'watch yourself change' Weight Watchers fat. I'd say, she's ... 'my husband doesn't touch me, I hate my life, give me another muffin' enormous."

"It's poetic justice." Baltimore sighed. "The prettiest, most popular girl at Our Lady of Lourdes High School is now obese."

"Clinically obese," Austin corrected her. "But she's still really pretty."

"Sure. Pretty face. They never lose the pretty face." Baltimore jumped off the swing. "Beat that."

Austin swung higher and jumped farther than Baltimore, tackling her on the ground. "Hey, where's my hug? I haven't seen you in months. Why didn't I get a hug?"

"Because you smell." Baltimore giggled as she rolled away from Austin, disrupting a pile of recently raked leaves. "You know I have a thing about body odor."

"How can I shower? ... Mom's in the bathtub."

The sisters started laughing hysterically, their high shrieks infuriating Carolina. She turned to leave.

"I'm going on a run ... can I get you intellectuals anything?"

"Vodka!" Baltimore and Austin shouted in unison, which sent them into another fit of giggles.

"I'm thrilled. Really thrilled that my sisters are handling the suicidal death of my mother so damn lightly. Maybe, when I get back, we can have a grown-up conversation about how to handle this."

1972

Mary walked through Times Square devoid of fear.

She'd lost her first love at a young age, her father at a younger age, mothered two babies and survived a divorce. She could handle pretty much anything, including the group of hoodlums that hung out in front of her rehearsal space. It was prime real estate: There was trash in the street, graffiti on the wall and homeless people in the alley.

The Crossroads of the World was a complete dump.

"Excuse me." She brushed shoulders with one of the prostitutes who frequented the corner where the Womyn Warriors rehearsed. The woman's name was either Amber or Jade. Some kind of crystal she'd heard the Pimp call her.

"No harm, honey," the hooker said in a deep voice, which made Mary realize that she was probably a he. "And you just let me know when you want to switch occupations and I'll be sure to set you up." The hooker winked at her and went back to primping her afro, which added another three inches to her already tall frame.

Mary climbed up the stairs and opened the door. She hated how the old buildings were all overheated. There was nothing between freezing and boiling. No nuances. She started flinging off layers as she climbed the seven steep flights to the studio. First Mort's large brown winter coat with the faux fur hood, next the cable knit sweater Mort's sister Shoshanah made her for Chanukah, then the cranberry turtleneck she picked up on sale at Gimbel's. By the time she entered the studio, Mary was down to her black leotard, sheer skirt and yellow snow boots.

"Let's get to work," Mary announced as she wriggled out of her boots.

Everyone was already there. Twenty dancers in different stages of warm up stretched across the floor and at the barre. As she put on her dance shoes, Mary looked around the room at the young expectant faces. It reminded her of going to Mass with her mother back in North Carolina. How eager she would be for the priest to start the service. She now wielded that position of absolute power and she loved it. This was her church and these kids were her parishioners. She nodded to the accompanist, a bearded effeminate gay named Cal, and she began to lead the company through a series of exercises.

As Mary walked up and down the line of dancers, she made small corrections. A better turn out, a longer neck, a fuller rotation. She demanded excellence and her dancers delivered. As Mary stopped to work with Maxine to better hold her extension, she nodded to Dana to take over the class. Both Dana and Wander had been with Mary since the beginning. Lulu had as well, but she fell in love in Texas, left the company and was now pregnant with her first child. But Wander and Dana were lifers and Mary appreciated their loyalty. She'd met them during the Roger days and had known them longer than Mort and the girls.

They were as much her family as her own blood, maybe more so.

June 1972
New York City

Dear Daughters,

All men lie.

I wish I could tell you otherwise, I wish I could soften the blow of pain when you're older, but I'm afraid my warnings will fall on deaf ears. Because when you love someone, you stop listening to your instincts. That's what the expression "love is blind" must mean ... it blinds you from all sense of reality. So, you can't see the lies coming. You only recognize them in your rearview mirror, when it is too late.

I was putting you girls to bed and Carolina, you were going on and on about these oatmeal creme pies called Little Debbies. You made me promise I would buy them. So, I went looking for a scrap of paper to jot it down. I rummaged through Mort's desk and grabbed the first piece of paper ... which was a letter. A love letter. A love letter from Linda. Now girls, I don't know anyone named Linda. Except Linda Lovelace who is currently starring in *Deep Throat* which Mort and I both thoroughly enjoyed ... but I'm fairly sure it's not her. This Linda, I have since discovered, was Mort's college girlfriend from twenty-odd years ago. An intellect, just like my husband. And although I have no idea what Mort wrote to her in his letter, I'm fairly sure I can catch the drift by her flowery response. Maybe it's just a flirtation. Maybe it's a matter of never letting go of your first love. Hell, if Sammy Gold were still alive, maybe I'd still be writing to him. But whatever this thing is, it's a betrayal. Mort and I promised to be honest to each other and this betrayal has obliterated our trust.

I'll never be able to eat a Little Debbie again.

Then, I put you girls to sleep and I dug a little deeper. I found an advert Mort put in the newspaper. The fucking newspaper. What about the expression "don't shit where you eat"? He placed a personal ad. He's married and he placed a personal ad. What kind of person does that? The things he said in his profile ... the kind of woman he is looking for ... the person he wants to spend time with ... go traveling with ... he's describing me. It doesn't make sense. Why go looking for what you already have? I'm having A LOT of trouble digesting all of the emotions I'm feeling right now. It is incredibly painful. What is wrong with me? I had come to terms with the fact that he was having less and less sex with me and that he had some deep-seated need/addiction/desire to sleep with other women. Fine. Sex is sex. But what he wrote on his profile ... wanting that companionship ... WHAT THE FUCK AM I? How dare he place a personal ad and look for another relationship when he is stringing me along, making me feel like I'm his life partner. Ironically, I had to see those words 'life partner' on my health insurance form yesterday when I got x-rays taken after I slipped on the ice and thought I broke my wrist. But is he my life partner? Putting a personal ad in the newspaper to start dating is not being my life partner. What the fuck am I doing? Maybe we need to 'officially separate' ... FUCK YOU MORT. FUCK YOU FOR HURTING ME SO MUCH. I can get over you having sex with other people, but how dare you go looking for companionship. I don't know if I can get over that. The hurt is just way too deep.

Roger lied and I just discovered that Mort lied. My Morty. Well, my Morty is a fucker who, like Roger, can't keep his pecker in his pants. The short of the long of it is that all men lie. It's how you choose to deal—or not deal—with those lies that defines who you are as a person. So I have a decision to make. And whatever the outcome of that decision is, remember one thing that will never ever waver:

I love you Carolina and Austin,
Mom

P.S. The one good thing about discovering the lies is that it has fueled this amazing creative output. My choreography has evolved in unexpected ways because I am so raw and beat up. Somehow, I've been able to translate my pain into the choreography. I can't stop writing. Mostly expletives about Mort, but once in a while a poem or three sneaks in there. Poems that express my hurt. I'm going to incorporate the spoken word into the dance. I'll start with the troupe in all red, bodies entwined and pulsing in unison... like a beating heart... I'll start with a low drumbeat and keep the dancers in that pose for five minutes, their only movement a slow undulation. This will give the audience time to see each intricate vessel and chamber that makes up the human heart. This takes remarkable discipline and strength for the dancers to execute the exact moves repeatedly with extreme precision, but they can handle it because I trained them. The drumming will then fade and as the spoken word begins, the heart will slowly rip apart.

A three-dimensional heart attack.

Each dancer will have a brief solo as they leave the group... and die. The music will continue until every dancer on stage lies there... lifeless.

Wander, with his deep baritone voice, will perform the spoken word poetry.

And the lies continue.
New always trumps old.

queen of spades beats queen of hearts
the new is always more exciting
The heart beats until it flatlines...
Time of death: Valentine's Day 1972
He is in love with her:
She has fallen in love with he.
No love left for me.
And the pain continues.
There is no longer a laugh track in my story
Just silence where giggles should have been.
The world is upside down and nothing makes sense.
When the King of Hearts lies
you are forced to play with an uneven deck.
Unbalanced, unstable, unfair.
The spades, clubs and diamonds pair up
but you are alone
A queen navigating through the chaos.
And you try to dilute your pain, know-
ing that behind closed doors
they are unhappy:
The Spades are racist
The Clubs are violent
And the Diamonds are blood dia-
monds which no one should wear
yet you still wear yours
and remember the day he proposed
and the now completely irrelevant cut
and karat of your blood diamond
blood
so much blood
when we're born we bleed
and when someone we love lies we bleed

yet our heart beats on, even though
we feel like we're flatlining.
A heart which loved
fully, wholly, completely
An enormous heart, which is now lac-
erated down the middle
I'm bleeding out
and I think it's almost too late
to stitch me up.

The Womyn Warriors have been invited to the Edinburgh Fringe Festival this year. I'm going to have the troupe perform this. A world premiere of the pain that Mort has caused me.

SEVEN

Carolina sprinted down Diversey, the main street on Money Island. Even as a child, she loved the feeling of running as fast as she could. Like there was no gravity. She passed all the boarded up houses on the street. Old Mrs. McFeely, who was old even when Carolina was a teenager, lived two houses down in a green Victorian. Most of the ramshackle houses were colorful Victorians and Carolina loved the way they reflected on the water, like an architectural rainbow. There was no rainbow today as the sky was becoming progressively darker. It would storm any moment. Finishing her jog around the island, Carolina looked at her porch, loath to go in.

"Carolina, where are you running to now?"

She heard her mother's voice in her head as she remembered the summer when she was twelve years old, sitting on the bottom step of the porch, a large suitcase beside her. It was the first of many times she had tried to run away from home.

"Not that you're interested, Mother, but I'm going to the West Coast."

"Ah. That's the whole... other coast," Mary had said patiently. "Well. If you're going to fly, you'll need—"

"—I have money, Mother." But Carolina had double checked her small purse just to be sure. She unhooked the brass clasp and showed her mother the five twenty-dollar bills she had saved from babysitting.

"You're practically a millionaire. What about a passport?"

"You don't need a passport to fly. I happen to know that." Carolina smirked. Her mother underestimated her resourcefulness.

"Well, you need identification."

That had taken Carolina by surprise.

"In case you haven't noticed, you're underage, young lady," Mary continued.

"Then I'll take a bus. Or I'll hitchhike."

"Carolina." Her mother's voice was firm.

"Carol." She was tired of her name. She wanted a normal name like Debbie or Lisa... or Carol.

They had sat in silence for a long time before her mother spoke again. Her voice was softer, kinder. "Your father's a good man, honey... But he doesn't have time to raise a daughter the way a daughter needs to be raised. We don't need men."

"Why not?" It didn't make sense to Carolina. Her mother had married her father, Austin's father, and would soon become pregnant with her third husband's baby. For someone who didn't need men, Mary got married a lot. All of a sudden, Carolina broke down and started to cry. Her mother held her tightly even as Carolina tried to shrug her away. Mary's strength won as Carolina eventually surrendered to her mother's hug.

"My girls can rise to the top without a man." Mary wiped her daughter's tears.

"Do you promise?"

But Mary hadn't answered her; instead, she stood up. "Why don't you come inside?"

"Austin doesn't care if I go."

"She does. She just doesn't know it yet."

Carolina stood up just as the water taxi pulled up to the slip. "Fine, but you should probably pay the driver and tell him I won't be needing him today. In fact, I may never need a man again."

The memory was so fresh, as if it had happened yesterday rather than three decades earlier. She looked up at the darkening sky and guessed she could get in another lap before the rain started.

The problem was, Carolina had needed a man. She had needed Matthew. She ran past the rocks where Matthew proposed to her. He was a romantic who insisted upon meeting her mother and asking permission for her daughter's hand. Carolina thought it was ridiculous; however, Matthew was insistent and Mary was charmed both by the arcane concept and by the lanky, bespectacled intellectual. They visited the island after Carolina's graduation from law school. It was one of the most wonderful weekends of her life. She was twenty-four. Only two years younger than Baltimore was now. And it felt like a lifetime ago. When everything was perfect. Before her fairytale marriage was plagued with an unhappy ending.

Carolina never suspected him of having an affair, but it made sense. It made so much sense. They barely had sex anymore and when they did it was perfunctory rather than passionate. Each time they did it, she made a notation in her calendar and, one day out of curiosity, she counted up how many times they had made love over the course of the year. Four. She asked her girlfriends if they still had sex. Most of them, who had also been married for a while, said that the sex certainly became more sporadic; however, they were talking fifteen or twenty times a year. Not four. Yet, it was more than that: The lack of sex was just a symptom.

The root of the problem was Matthew's jealousy.

As Carolina rose in the firm, Matthew became increasingly jealous. She didn't blame him; most men had a jealousy gene inside of them especially when it came to success. And she was succeeding much more rapidly than he was. Why wouldn't she? Carolina had been an A+ student from kindergarten through graduate school and the one quality she mastered in life was succeeding: She was good at it.

Trying to get as far away from her family as possible, Carolina went to Stanford and then, in classic Carolina fashion, straight into law school at Hastings. Matthew Shaw was her TA in first year law. He had gone the less traditional and more outside the box route to law school: Berkeley undergrad, two years abroad doing volunteer work in India with American Friends Service Committee, four more years doing pro bono social work in San Francisco before matriculating into Hastings. Matthew was a lanky thirty-year-old with a classic grad school scruffy beard and a photographic memory. He was seven years Carolina's senior and she fell in love with him instantly, both with his green eyes and his passionate determination when explaining the mechanics of the law. Because he had so much more world experience than she did, Matthew represented the father figure she had been invariably looking for her entire life.

They dated through law school, moved in together in the Castro and married in a quiet civil ceremony downtown. The early years were wonderful; they both worked as public defenders and were extremely poor, albeit happy. Trying to pay off student loans, they rarely ate out, and managed to cook their way through the entire Moosewood vegetarian cookbook. They became avid bikers and runners and spent their spare time advocating for gay rights and women's rights and always rushed to join forces with the underdog against *the man.* Yet, as they got older, Matthew was tired of simply making ends meet. He applied for and got a job at a top corporate firm in Seattle. The firm really wanted Matthew and offered Carolina a job as well. With both of their salaries quadrupled, they bought a renovated Victorian overlooking Puget Sound. They ran 10k's together. They were happy.

They were happy until Carolina made partner before Matthew.

At thirty-seven, she was one of the youngest people ever named partner at Schaefer, Gallagher & Muskin. At forty-four, Matthew was considered a strong asset to the firm; however, he was not partner material. When Carolina thought about it, the fissure started then: the small cracks that start to break up a solid relationship and, over time, turn into unfixable fractures which rock the entire foundation of a marriage. Once she was made partner, Carolina's work increased tenfold. She and Matthew had never wanted kids, so the only thing that suffered from her long hours was Matthew.

Carolina had learned about Rika exactly a year ago.

It was one Friday in the fall, and Carolina finished in court early. She won her case. Hoping to get in a celebratory run, she stopped home to change and found them: Matthew and Rika in the mahogany antique sleigh bed he bought her three years earlier for her fortieth birthday. She thought she'd scream or slam doors or cry; instead, she grabbed her running shoes and went on a ten mile run. Later, Matthew explained it "just happened." Yet, Carolina knew things don't "just happen." Especially in her antique bed.

Matthew was turning fifty, he wasn't partner and he was searching...for what, she wasn't sure. Perhaps for his lost youth. Rather than have a typical midlife crisis and buy a Ferrari or go bungee jumping, Matthew found Rika. She was a gorgeous twenty-two year old law clerk who worked for Old Man Schaefer. Carolina saw her around the office, but they worked on different floors. Although Carolina enjoyed a large enough salary to afford an expensive haircut and enough Botox to keep her forehead taut, she could not afford the price of her lost youth. Youth was priceless and with pert little breasts and a flat stomach, Rika enjoyed the consummate twenty-two-year-old's body. More importantly, Carolina guessed that Rika made Matthew feel young. She looked up to him the way Carolina used to, filled with doe-eyed awe and she gave him confidence, whereas Carolina's success had somehow emasculated him.

They tried to make it work. Carolina was a fighter and she had no intention of quitting the marriage. Matthew agreed to end it. To stop seeing Rika. And Carolina believed him. Yet, the one thing she hadn't figured into the equation was Rika falling in love with her husband. One Sunday afternoon, when Matthew was taking the rare nap and Carolina was doing some light cleaning, she saw a text message flash through Matthew's phone. Months earlier, she would have ignored it; however, the trust had been broken and she was suspicious of everything. She looked at her husband's phone and there was a picture of Rika with her mouth stuffed with cock. Carolina squinted at the picture, she wasn't convinced it was her husband's penis; however, the bitch was still sexting Matthew, which probably meant she was still seeing him as well.

It took six months for the divorce to go through. Matthew moved out of the house and Carolina hadn't yet bothered to hang pictures on the still empty hooks or move some of her wardrobe into his closet. When she got back home, she would take a day for herself, maybe two. Two days to reclaim the house as her own. The senior partners told her to take as much time as she needed to grieve for her mother. Yet, Carolina didn't need time to grieve, simply time to make all the necessary arrangements.

Then she would take a few days for herself back in Seattle and redo her closets.

1972

Mary peered through the curtain. Another packed house. The greatest thing about performing at the Edinburgh Fringe was that dance broke the language barrier better than any other form of performance, so the seats were always filled. While the critically acclaimed dramas were half empty every night, her show was a commercial hit. Her dancers told stories through movement: sagas and histories conveyed through the flick of a wrist or the extension of a toe. Specific tales filled with sound and fury signifying everything.

Mary's core troupe, five dancers including herself, spent their sixty minutes on stage dissecting the heart. Their program included a medley of movements with titles like heartbeat, heartache, heartbreak, heartburn and heart attack. And the audiences went crazy for it. Artists express pain so that civilians don't have to and Mary gave her audiences the heart-rending release they needed ... without venturing into the dangerous emotional area themselves.

The energy of Edinburgh reminded Mary of New York. The small Scottish city came alive during the month of the theatre festival. There were over a thousand different shows one could choose from between ten in the morning until well past midnight. Even at three a.m., the streets were packed with performers and patrons all looking for a good time.

And no one liked a good time more than Mary Baxter. On her day off each week, she went exploring. She visited castles and took trains to some of the outlying islands. She went shopping in Glasgow and even caught a screening of *Diamonds are Forever.* Mary loved the film, especially the campy Jill St. John.

The routine in Edinburgh was simple. Tuesday through Sunday: Wake up midday, perform at the Gilded Balloon every night from 6:45 to 7:45 and then go to the Performers' Bar for the rest of the evening. Everyone who was anyone at the festival ended up there and Mary often plunked herself down at an outdoor table where she smoked and drank and socialized with the coming and going patrons who sat at her table as if in a game of musical chairs. Mary was a practiced drinker, but she had never seen anything quite like the amount of alcohol people consumed in Scotland. The evening started with a few beers to quench the thirst of dancing for an hour, followed by a couple of whiskeys and then a bottle... or two of wine. It didn't matter that she mixed her liquor; she could sleep it off until noon... or two and then repeat the day.

The audience was often packed with appreciative seniors, intrigued travelers and available paramours. Mary had a string of admirers who came to watch her work with the troupe. She settled on one for companionship, a Scottish comedian whose show was on just before hers. Ginger-haired, Frazier was shy, polite and attentive and promised to adore her for the month.

And Mary was someone who needed to be adored.

It made sense for her to take a lover. After all, her husband had cheated, and in Edinburgh, Mary was a free woman. No husband and no children. Mort's spinster sister was staying at the apartment for the month of August to help him with the girls. Mary always suspected Shoshanah Horowitz loved her brother a little too much. Whenever he beckoned, his zaftig older sister came running. Still, she was a nice woman and incredibly convenient as her availability allowed Mary a month to figure out what she was going to do about Morty Stone Horowitz. She loved the cheating bastard, more than she had ever loved anyone in her entire life. And she had to decide if that love was enough to stay with him. To put up with his shit. To risk more pain and hurt than she deserved. But she loved him ... she loved him enough to put up with the bad. After all, she had promised for better or for worse. Carolina had witnessed it. So had Austin, in utero. Wasn't her vow and her love enough? Mort was bright and funny and charming and both a terrific companion to her and a surprisingly good father to her children.

But Mort had a sex addiction, which meant that she had to come to terms with the fact that she was not enough to satisfy him. He needed more, a lot more. Part of Mort's sickness was that he could never be satisfied with the same woman because he was wired to always be in search of something different. It was the way his brain worked. And while he dutifully came home to Mary and the girls every night, they were not enough to complete him.

As she looked at her ginger-haired companion wrapped in the sheets next to her, his pale white skin almost comical when she compared it to Mort's Ashkenazi coloring, she asked herself the question again: Did she love him enough to stay with him?

Mary sighed because she knew the answer and it would cause her nearly a decade of pain.

December 1972
New York City

Dear Daughters,

Love is enough. For now.

Mort and I have come to an understanding. He can fuck everything on two legs and so can I. It's called an open marriage; apparently everyone is doing it these days. Welcome to the seventies! Not that I necessarily believe in open marriages, but right now my priority is my dancing and my girls. So if Mort wants to redefine the parameters of our marriage, it's fine with me. Plus, the odd fuck is quite fun. And different partners add a certain spice to the equation so I never have to worry about getting bored.

We go to key parties every weekend.

It's the latest thing: Everyone throws their keys in a bowl and when it's time to leave, the ladies pluck out a car key that doesn't belong to their husband. Although, in the city few people have cars so they throw in apartment keys instead. So far, I've fucked a pot-bellied guy named Johnny, an extremely hairy guy named Paul and a gorgeous black guy named George.

All I need is a Ringo and I can boast that I've fucked all four Beatles.

Mort looks forward to the parties a little too much. He's turned out to be a certified asshole, but I love him. I think I'm an asshole magnet. First Roger, now Mort. I guess if you think about it, all men are assholes and all women invariably become assholes for putting up with them. It's frustrating, but it's reality. Apart from having a sexually complicated marriage, our relationship is quite wonderful. We get along and really enjoy each other's company. We especially love exploring the mélange of ethnic restaurants in the neighborhood. A new one seems to pop up each week. Every food I can imagine is within walking distance: Indian, Thai, Indonesian, Chinese, Ethiopian, Turkish, Japanese, Italian ... the list goes on and on. New York City is the greatest city in the world and I never plan to leave. Granted, we don't have much space and the fifth floor walk-up on Bleecker is tiny, but the energy of the city is contagious. At night, one of my dancers will watch you ladies and Mort and I will go to the theatre or to a movie at the art house around the corner. Mort may be a lousy husband, but he is an excellent friend. Plus, he is a really good father to both of you.

Complete non sequitur. Your Mama was almost a movie star. Almost but not quite; the story of my life. They're filming the new James Bond film right here in New York City. Harlem to be exact. I heard about the shoot from one of Wander's friends so he and I hopped on the A train up to 125th and, sure enough, there were trucks and cameras and loads of movie people. I didn't see the new guy playing 007, a Brit called Roger Moore, but I got Yaphet Kotto's autograph. Talk about a sexy man. Anyway, Wander and I kept trying to walk past the exteriors where they were shooting so we could get into a shot. Eventually, a production assistant came up to us and politely told us that Wander could be in the shot, but I couldn't. I asked her why and she told me because I was White and this was Harlem. I told her that I didn't have a problem with it so why should she. Things then might have gotten a little out of hand when I called her racist and she asked me if I needed to be escorted out of the area. There were two fairly scary security guards who looked like Black Panthers and I didn't really want to mess with them so I didn't press the issue. I suppose since they're apparently going for this whole Blaxploitation cliché, a White woman would be out of place. Makes me want to give the movie a miss. But knowing me, I'll probably see it anyway... especially since one of the Beatles is doing the theme song. It's genius. Speaking of geniuses... back to my husband.

I love Mort, but I don't trust him.

I think one of my problems is confusing trust and love. I continue to trust people even though I shouldn't. One of my favorite Shakespearean quotes is "*Love all, trust a few, do wrong to none.*" Okay, I know you're thinking, how can a high school dropout know Shakespeare? Mort persuaded me to get my GED... which I did and I passed with flying colors. I love to read and devour as much literature as I can. Especially the new feminist writers.

But the point about trust, I think the only person you can trust is yourself. Trust your instinct and know that things will work out but don't put the power in the hands of others. I think the two words "trust me" are the two most duplicitous words in the world. If someone tells you to trust them, they are already worried that you don't. I'm saving you years of pain girls.

Don't trust men. They will all lie to you.

And if you can start a relationship without trust in the equation, there may be hope. I take that back. You can trust someone other than yourself. You can trust each other. There is no stronger bond than that of a sister. No matter what direction you head in your life, your sister will always be someone you can count on. Someone you can trust. You may lie to your lovers. You may lie to your parents. You may lie to your kids. But never lie to your sisters. There has to be someone in your life you can trust. You don't have to like them, but you have to trust them.

I love you Carolina and Austin,
Mom

P.S. I'm starting to rack up a few awards for my work. Our work. The Womyn Warriors' work. Though, I am the head warrior, so I'm the one who gets to bring home the trophy. Although, frankly, I should give it to Mort, as he is my unsolicited inspiration.

You used to read my mind when I was hurting
Why can't you read it now?
Just a hint of a tear in my voice and, like Superman,
you'd fly over and comfort me
Why did I award you these superhero qualities?
You don't look like Superman or Batman or Aquaman
But you embraced their excellence
as you used to embrace me
Long passionate kisses with balloons of
emotion expanding in each kiss.
I miss your kisses.
Warm, soft, gentle, passionate.
I guess there's only one Superman and
Lois Lane got him before I did.

Eight

"*Somehow, just because you despise me, you are the only one I trust.*"

Peter Lorre's character Ugarte was on the television, confiding in Bogart's Rick, and Austin knew exactly how he felt. She felt like she barely knew her sisters, she wasn't convinced that she even liked them; yet, somehow, she felt like she could trust them with her secret. With her secrets. As *Casablanca* played on the television, she told Dallas and Baltimore that she was ready to talk; yet, Dallas insisted that they wait for Carolina to return from her run. So, she had to wait. Just a little bit longer.

"Every time I watch this, I pray she lets Laszlo get on the plane by himself," Austin murmured. She'd seen the film over a hundred times. She practically knew it by heart. She and Mary watched it a week earlier when Mary was in a Bergman mood. They watched *Casablanca, Joan of Arc* and Austin's favorite *Cactus Flower.*

"It wasn't Ilsa's choice. Rick told her to go." Dallas was matter of fact when analyzing films. If she were in Ilsa's position, she would have gone as well. No questions asked.

"He tells her to go, so she goes. Sit, Spot. Stay, Spot. Go, Ilsa."

"She goes because she understands the bigger picture," Dallas explained. "She realizes that politics are more important than love. Besides, if she stayed, the movie wouldn't have caused emotional unrest and probably wouldn't have won an Oscar."

Austin turned to look at Dallas, who still hadn't changed out of her travel clothes. There was something uncomfortable about curling up to watch a movie with someone who was wearing pearls and pantyhose. Next to her prissy sister, Austin felt oddly underdressed. "Yeah, but her role sucked. Both Claude Rains and Bogie got nominated, but Bergman didn't. Not even a nomination. Why? Because she's just a pawn in the whole thing. Sit, Spot. Stay, Spot. Get on the plane with Laszlo, Spot. No red carpet for you, Bergman."

"Is there a dog in this movie?" Baltimore was annoyed by her sisters talking over the movie. She cranked up the volume.

"The fact that you've never seen *Casablanca* explains so much about you, Baltimore."

They watched for a few more minutes before the conversation sunk in. Baltimore turned to her sisters. "Wait, Ilsa and Laszlo get on the plane? She didn't stay with Bogie? She chooses duty over love? Did you just totally give away the ending?"

"It's not like I told you Rosebud is the sled." Austin giggled.

"What? What does that mean?" Baltimore looked from Austin to Dallas.

"Never mind." Austin shook her head. For one of the smartest women she knew, Baltimore was a solipsistic product of her generation... clueless about a past much older than her own. "Baltimore, you know that *Casablanca* is a classic, right?"

Dallas snorted. "Baltimore considers *Sixteen Candles* a classic."

"Hey." Baltimore abruptly turned off the television. "Molly Ringwald did some of her most definitive work in the eighties! I defy you to name a movie that defines teen angst better than *The Breakfast Club*."

"Movie, or film?" Dallas asked.

"There's a difference?"

Austin thought about it. "*To Sir with Love*."

"I've never heard of it."

"Sidney Poitier. Lulu ... the tampon?"

Baltimore looked at her and shrugged. Austin knew she was fighting a losing battle trying to educate her sister.

Dallas jumped in, "Films don't have titles like *Pretty in Pink*. There's a cliché. Why can't you be pretty in a color other than pink?"

"Alliteration," Austin offered. "You wouldn't say pretty in maroon or—"

"—Pretty in purple, why couldn't she be pretty in purple?"

"Is anyone pretty in purple?" Austin and Dallas high-fived over Baltimore who looked at them incredulously. She was wearing purple. A violet tee shirt from the Alzheimer's walk she did the last weekend in September. She was always doing walks for charity, her small contribution to raising money for seemingly hopeless causes. She loved her purple shirt. She looked good in it. Damn good. But of course, her sisters refused to acknowledge this.

"Well, Mom was. Mom was pretty in purple." Baltimore put a moratorium on the conversation by mentioning the taboo subject. Quickly realizing that she was being the downer, she continued, "So, what happens? Do Ilsa and Laszlo make it to America?"

Austin immediately brightened up. "Sure. They move to Darien, Connecticut and have 2.5 kids—"

"—And a white picket fence." It was rare for Dallas to be on the inside of a joke and she was fully enjoying herself.

"—And they open a bar. Call it Laszlo's Place. Hire a black piano player."

"Speaking of which ... " Baltimore jumped up.

"A black piano player?" Dallas was almost giddy.

"A bar. What's your poison? Vodka or vodka?"

Dallas followed Baltimore to the Oriental chest and looked at the massive variety of vodka bottles that were now displayed by height. "I'm going to go with the vodka, thanks." Dallas hesitated, "Although ... I don't usually drink before five." She corrected herself, "Unless it's a Bloody Mary at Neiman Marcus with my mother-in-law on a Sunday afternoon."

"We have tomato juice," Austin offered.

"Stoli works for me." Dallas stared at the bottles. "There's a lot of vodka here."

"A potpourri." Austin grinned.

"A hodgepodge," Baltimore added.

"A cornucopia," they both exclaimed together.

Dallas looked at them strangely. "Tabasco sauce?"

"Kitchen. Hey, will you throw some pizza bagels into the microwave while you're there. I have pepperoni for us and Amy's organic for the vegetarian."

"I eat meat now," Baltimore announced.

"Since when?"

"Since I discovered how amazing hamburgers taste." Baltimore wiggled her left foot in Austin's face, begging for a foot massage. She'd demanded them ever since she was a baby and her sisters usually capitulated since it was easier than having her constantly pushing her feet in their faces.

Dallas grabbed her vodka bottle and went into the kitchen.

"Hurry up, I'm starving," Baltimore called after Dallas, kicking off her socks so she could enjoy the full benefit of the massage. She looked up at Austin. "I can't believe she brunches at Needless Markups."

"I can't believe you eat meat."

"It's a woman's prerogative to change her mind." Baltimore closed her eyes and relaxed for her massage.

Austin massaged her sister's foot. "You know, I have thirty-two varieties of beef in a box."

"Do you ever cook for yourself?"

"No. Do you?"

"No. That's why I date men who can cook."

Austin smiled. "Because why do it yourself when—"

"—men can do it for you." Baltimore giggled. "The third commandment in Mom's biblical philosophy."

"Sandwiched in between 'Marry for love' and 'Divorce for money.'"

"And, 'Name your children after the cities in which they're born.'" Baltimore pushed her other foot into Austin's lap. "Dallas is in trouble."

"Why?"

"She'll have to name her kid Philadelphia."

"She's not pregnant."

"How do you know?"

"It's Dallas we're talking about." Austin rubbed her sister's feet. "The second that Peter's sperm connects with her egg we'll receive calligraphed invitations to the baby shower."

"On Papyrus stationary," Baltimore added.

"Yellow, so that it isn't gender specific, because she won't want to know the sex of the baby."

Baltimore laughed, "You're probably right, but Dallas is a little puffy. And if she's not pregnant now, she will be soon. She and Peter are always going on and on about having a family. Like there aren't enough unwanted children on this planet already. I'm just glad Carolina didn't have kids before the divorce."

"Because she'd be a terrible mother?"

"Because she's too skinny. Skinny people never have good pregnancies. Carolina and I take after our fathers, whereas you and Dallas both inherited Mom's childbearing hips."

"Baltimore, you shouldn't insult the person giving you a foot massage."

"Touché. Hey, was she always this uptight?"

"Who? Dallas?"

"I don't think Dallas is uptight. I think she's fun." Baltimore nodded to their sister who returned with a large glass of tomato juice.

"Who's fun?" Dallas sipped her Bloody Mary through a straw.

"You are," Baltimore assured her.

"I know." Dallas smiled, joining her sisters.

"Austin thinks you're uptight," Baltimore goaded.

"Thanks a lot." Austin dropped Baltimore's foot and jumped up from the sofa. She looked out the window. It was about to pour any second. She should have boarded up the windows, though the idea of sitting in a boarded up house with her sisters and her dead mother wasn't terribly appealing.

"What are we talking about?" The liquor immediately relaxed Dallas.

"Carolina. Whoever's not in the room is fair game."

Ever the peacekeeper, Dallas tried to defend the absent sister. "Give her a break. Her husband just left her. She puts up this ridiculous veneer of stoicism, but she's really just as confused as the rest of us. She just hides it better."

"Yeah, I'm not sure she's hiding it." Austin looked through the window as Carolina sprinted up to the house and stopped just outside, obviously loath to come in. Austin stepped behind the curtain, observing her older sister without being seen. Carolina looked as if she was hyperventilating; yet, she was in terrific shape. It wasn't from the run. She was having some sort of panic attack.

Dallas joined Austin behind the curtain, spying on Carolina. "She works fifty-two hours a day."

Baltimore joined them, looking through her sisters at Carolina who was bent over, trying to catch her breath. "Yeah. Someone in our family needs to perpetuate the myth that women can have it all. Husband, family, career."

"She doesn't have a family." Austin wondered if Carolina was having a heart attack. One death a day was about all she could handle.

"Or a husband." Dallas couldn't help the dig. She was the only one who was happily married. She came in last in every competition growing up, but she fell in love and stuck with it. She won something. She won Peter.

"Okay. Career." Baltimore sighed, "Look, when Mom graduated high school, her two options were to become a secretary or a teacher."

"So, she got married. Four times." Dallas had always been judgmental of their mother's promiscuity.

"Yes. Marriage was also an option. But, I'm talking career."

Austin was irritated. "So, Carolina has made up for Mom's lack of academic fortitude and marital ineptitude by schooling herself through a law degree and ignoring her family in favor of her career?"

Dallas poked her usually zen sister. "Is Miss Never-Get-Uptight tightening?"

"Observing," Austin shot back. "What's the point of a successful career if you can't share your life with someone?"

Dallas chuckled. "Okay. And I don't mean to be morbid or accuse you of being hypocritical or anything, but who's the one with the successful career still living with her mother?"

Austin looked into Dallas's blue eyes and spoke very quietly, punctuating each word, "Technically, I'm not living with her anymore."

The microwave bell rang and Austin went into the kitchen. Dallas shouted after her, "Jeez, Austin. You'd think after your novel came out, you'd, I don't know, move at least next door to Mom, rather than be her roommate."

Austin returned with a plate of pepperoni pizza bagels and put them in front of Baltimore. "In college when your roommate dies, you get an immediate 4.0."

"I thought that was just a rumor." Baltimore popped an entire bagel into her mouth. "Ow, hot."

"Fact." Austin smirked at Dallas. "Besides, I pay rent. Paid rent."

"C'mon, Austin. You and Carolina aren't that different." Dallas nibbled on a bagel.

"Really? Well, I didn't ignore my family," Austin boasted. "I've spent countless hours on your couch, Dallas. I've even visited Baltimore at Harvard."

"It's true. She has," Baltimore mumbled through a mouthful of pizza bagel.

"Family is my priority. Carolina has the career, I choose the family."

"Dallas has the husband. So, where does that leave me?" Baltimore wondered aloud.

"With the potential," Austin comforted. "That's the nice thing about still being young. You can do anything."

"I can't do that many things." Baltimore shoveled in another pizza bagel and went over to the window.

"Yes, but your youth perpetuates the illusion that you're capable of infinite possibilities."

"I'm getting a master's in sociology," Baltimore said, rapping loudly on the window and beckoning Carolina to come inside. "I think my possibilities are pretty finite."

1973

Mary walked away from the Rivoli Theatre on Broadway and 49th. She'd just been to see *Live and Let Die* and she needed a drink. Roger Moore did a stand up job replacing Connery and she liked the humor that he brought to the role. Mary had a tradition after seeing James Bond films that she'd always walk into the first bar she saw and order a drink. It was cheesy, but it was a tradition. And she liked traditions. As she headed west, Mary promised herself that she'd never be a practiced drinker like her mother, even though she recently discovered a penchant for vodka. Mostly because it had the fewest calories. She ducked into a bar in Hell's Kitchen, slid into a seat at the bar and motioned to the bartender.

"Vodka martini, shaken not stirred," she purred in a fake British accent as she surveyed the room. She was the only woman. The rest of the patrons were a mixture of working class Irish and Italian mobsters. Mary laughed. She loved the Catholics.

"Buy you a drink," a roguish man with a thick brogue said as he approached her.

"Or even two." Mary grinned. Even though her husband had stopped finding her attractive, other men clearly hadn't gotten that memo.

The young man sidled up next to her at the bar and within minutes he was making her laugh. It was a harmless flirtation, but it felt good. It made her smile.

And Mary couldn't remember the last time she had smiled.

June 1973
New York City

Dear Daughters,

Happy Birthday Austin. You're two! A real milestone. Your sister carries you everywhere, like you're her doll, so you can imagine how furious she was with me when I explained to her that she couldn't bring you to kindergarten with her for Show and Tell. Carolina, you started to throw a tantrum, so I gave you my NOW button, the one you're obsessed with, and that seemed to placate you. Thank goodness Roe vs. Wade passed 7–2 or you would have been impossible to live with! My little feminist. My little suffragette. My little pro-choice advocate. Now, just a heads up that Catholics do believe abortion is murder. I'm not sure how I personally feel about it, but I've never been in a position to have to make a choice. I wanted both of you so badly and I never thought twice about it. But not everyone is as committed to motherhood as I am. Not everyone is ready to be a mother. It is a big responsibility and certainly a life-changing event and I absolutely believe in a woman's individual right to choose. It is a personal decision and I am proud that my girls are on the forefront of the revolution for women's rights.

Either you girls are getting bigger or our apartment is getting smaller. When we moved in, it felt quaint but now it's feeling a bit claustrophobic. Luckily, we're right down the street from a park, so you have somewhere to release your energy. I swear Mrs. Paborsky downstairs hits her ceiling at least twice a day, trying to quiet us down. But how can you quiet down life? Poor lady. I tried to bake her some cookies, to quiet *her* down, but you know your Mom is a lousy cook, so it was a completely ineffectual form of bribery.

Mort's busy with the paper. He got a promotion and does the whole nine to five thing. Nixon's in China now and Mort begged the paper to send him there to cover it, but they're keeping him on Entertainment. He grumbles a lot about it, but hey, we get to see shows for free! Even though you slept through *Pippin* and didn't quite understand *Grease*, Carolina you loved dressing up. And Austin, when you're bigger, I promise I'll take you to tons of theatre as well ... though I have a feeling you'll go more for the straight plays than for musicals. You're such a serious little girl.

Mort and I are doing ... fine. It's not a word I'm proud of ... fine. What does "fine" mean? Its actual meaning is deceptive. If you look it up in the dictionary, fine means "of superior or best quality" yet, in colloquial language it means "okay" and I swore I'd never settle for okay. But that's what we are. We are okay. I realize it sounds like I have to convince myself of that fact, but it's true. I mean, I love the man, really, he's the love of my life ... but he also makes me sad all the time. His father passed away a few months ago and it's changed him. It's changed his relationship with me. When someone dies you are supposed to mourn. I cried for weeks after Sammy died and Shoshanah has cried daily since their father passed ... but Mort just closed up. Never cried, never said a word. He just bottled up his emotions and, subsequently, withdrew even further away from me. I kept telling him I could be a good resource for him. Sure, my father died when I was five but the feelings are still relevant. The emotions are still raw and I'm definitely still grieving. Only, now I'm grieving both for the past loss of my father and for the present loss of my husband. Girls, I'm so tired of being sad. Of feeling unwanted. Of feeling unloved. I remember reading once about absent-presence ... the notion that you can physically be with someone; however, your mind is elsewhere. Even when Mort is physically with me at dinner, or a show or seeing music at The Bitter End, his mind is always somewhere else. Honestly, I have never felt lonelier. No offense, girls. You are wonderful... but you're just children: It is hardly appropriate for me to confide my pain to you.

I initially thought his behavior was because he's having a midlife crisis, but he saw an analyst who told him he's fine. Naturally, he believes the shrink, whom he sees five times a week... don't get me started on that... so I'm the crazy one. Shit. I just have to accept that the problem isn't him or me... it's us. Something is happening with us. With Mort and me. I miss him so much; but I can't force him to feel things he may not feel anymore. Hell, the reality is that I'm twenty-six, which is probably too old for him.

Mort used to make me laugh. Now, he just makes me feel bad about myself. It's like I'm dancing on this emotional minefield. I have to accept that we're drifting apart. And I'm just as guilty. I have wanderlust... I want to travel. And going to the house on Money Island in the summer isn't enough of an adventure for me. I want more. Well, I don't know really what I want... but I feel like something's missing. Like I'm searching for something, but I don't really know what I'm searching for. Does that make sense? You girls are my saving grace. I love you so much. Not that I get to see you as much now that The WWDT, the Womyn Warriors Dance Troupe, has a permanent residence on 23rd. The job is keeping me busy. We keep our little theatre packed every night and it's challenging to come up with new choreography every six weeks when we change shows. We work in rep, so while one show's up, we're rehearsing the next. It's fulfilling though. Busy, but fulfilling.

Whatever you girls decide to do with your lives, whomever you decide to be ... make sure you're fulfilled. And that you're happy. Life is too short not to be happy. Dream my little daughters, dream. Anything is possible.

I love you Carolina and Austin,
Mom

Nine

"I'm back," Carolina announced as she swung the door open and breezed in.Other than a few raindrops splattered on her jogging suit, she looked surprisingly refreshed. Whatever was going on outside had passed and she was basking in a post run glow. Yet, her good mood was short lived as she spied her sisters gobbling down pizza bagels.

"Dairy, artificial preservatives and white flour. How healthy can you get?"

"They're actually pretty good," Dallas said.

"So good," Baltimore echoed. She was sitting on the floor surrounded by Matryoshka dolls, opening them all up and arranging them in rows.

Austin smiled sweetly at Carolina. "But if you need to enhance the flavor, you could always take one and dunk it in some vodka."

Carolina glared at her and went into the kitchen, returning with a large glass of water. She rummaged through her purse and pulled out a green packet and poured it in.

"What's that?" Dallas made a face at the disgusting looking green concoction.

"A protein detox drink. Alfalfa leaf, kale, organic barley grass, chlorophyll, chlorella and spirulina. It's good for you."

"Ah, good for me." Dallas returned to her pizza bagel.

"Did the coroner call?" Carolina demanded.

"Was he supposed to?" Baltimore asked.

Austin looked at her. "Why do you assume it's a he? Coroners can be a she."

"Nope, it's a he. Definitely a he. A tall, cute, muscular he."

"Really, how do you know?"

"I was right about Lori Braithwaite's body composition." Baltimore smirked. "It's a gift. No, he didn't call. Do coroners call? I thought they just appeared."

"It's been an hour." Carolina went over to the phone.

"Maybe he's *running* late?" Austin joked.

Carolina picked up the phone. It was dead. Already knocked out by the wind.

"Shit."

"Relax." Austin smiled sweetly. "It's not like Mom's going anywhere."

"WILL YOU PLEASE START TAKING THIS SERIOUSLY," Carolina exploded.

Everyone quieted as Carolina walked over to the vodka bottles and poured a healthy shot of Grey Goose into her protein detox drink.

"That can't be good for you," Dallas said.

"Gross." Baltimore made a face.

"You drink a lot for a lawyer," Austin observed. "Do all lawyers drink so much?"

"Do all writers act with complete disregard for their family in times of crisis?"

"I don't disregard my family. I visited Baltimore at Harvard."

Baltimore echoed, "It's true. She has."

"And you." Carolina turned on her baby sister, "You just instigate her. Having one of you is bad enough, but two, I think I'm losing my mind."

"Have some more vodka, that'll help you find it." Austin was about to say something else; however, she changed her mind and ran up the stairs. Her sisters watched her go.

"What is her problem?" Carolina poured herself another drink.

"You mean, today or always." Baltimore watched Carolina inadvertently grab a pizza bagel. "Whoa! I thought you didn't put artificial things in your mouth."

Carolina threw the rest of the bagel down.

"I think grief hits people differently." Dallas looked at an 8 x 10 framed picture on the wall. It showed a pregnant Mary sitting on the piano bench surrounded by her three oldest daughters. Everyone looked so happy in it. So innocent. "Carolina, when's the last time you saw Mom?"

"I spoke to her biweekly," Carolina murmured.

"But when's the last time you saw her?" Dallas persisted.

"I don't know, Christmas?"

"You guys were in Hawaii at Christmas."

"Right. The 'maybe-THIS-will-save-the-marriage' vacation. He shagged a stewardess, I got shingles." She took a long swig of her green concoction. "Easter."

"You had the O'Hagan case."

"Why do you know more about my career than I do?" Carolina was surprised. She didn't think her sisters paid attention to her life, let alone could name her cases.

"Come on. You're the second most famous person to come out of this family, we all have your clippings ... somewhere."

Baltimore added, "I do ... somewhere."

"The point is, you haven't seen Mom in over a year." Dallas looked at Baltimore. "Have you?"

Baltimore shook her head.

"And I haven't since ... last Christmas ... Wow." Dallas let the information sink in. "Then I guess none of us have really seen her ... except Austin. And we're not the ones who found her."

"Yeah, and that whole drowning thing." Baltimore imitated Austin, " 'She went under, sank, drowned in a civilized and ladylike fashion. No mess ... ' God, that's really fucked up." Baltimore sat up. "She obviously really planned this."

Carolina was furious. It wasn't right. It was completely out of character for Mary. "You cannot make me believe that Mother planned this."

"I'm just saying, we don't know the particulars."

"That's what I'm trying to find out."

But as Carolina, Dallas and Baltimore sat silently, they wondered if they ever would find out the truth about what really happened.

1974

Mary sat at the tiny formica kitchen table as she ate her Wonder Bread toast and drank her second cup of Folgers coffee. Mort had taken the girls to the Met and she was enjoying a rare morning to herself. She picked up the Times, which Mort had dutifully laid out for her. As usual, he had circled his op-ed in red flair pen. Men were so fucking needy. It was a dull piece about the growing conflict between Turkey and Cyprus. She wasn't particularly interested; however, she knew that Mort would quiz her later so she read the didactic article. But it was a piece a few pages later that really caught her attention. A picture of an attractive brunette around Mary's age was splashed across the page. Unlike Mary, the brunette didn't make headline news because she was aiming for fame, but infamy. Newscaster Christine Chubbuck was doing a live report one inconsequential day in July when she pulled out a gun and committed suicide on air. Mary was flabbergasted. Why would anyone kill themselves, especially in public?

Suicide was a private affair.

Mary read further. Unlike the last several people who had all publicly killed themselves, mostly by setting themselves on fire to protest some fascist government's wrongdoing, Christine was a respected Floridian newscaster who was only three years older than Mary. The aftermath of the on air suicide blamed Christine's depression for the desperate act.

Hell, who wasn't depressed?

There was rampant crime, economic stagnation and New York City was on the brink of fiscal disaster. Mary was always mildly depressed, but she'd never stoop to killing herself. She dropped the paper in the trash as she cleaned up her breakfast. And if she ever did kill herself, she certainly wouldn't do it publicly. That was just a cry for attention and what is the point of needing attention if you're dead.

Attention is for the living.

Still, shooting oneself in the head is a quick and, Mary supposed, painless way to go. There had been so many public suicides in the last decade. Mary blamed it on the monk. In '63, a Vietnamese Buddhist monk sat down in the middle of a busy intersection in Saigon, covered himself in gasoline, ignited a match and set himself on fire. Mary shuddered; she couldn't imagine anything more awful than burning to death. She'd rather drown than burn. Yet, there were several protesters in the seventies who followed the monk's example.

If Mary wanted to protest something, she wouldn't kill herself. She'd protest through her art, through her dance. Several artists whom she respected had done the same thing. Although three of them were dead. Jim Morrison and Jimi Hendrix and Janis Joplin had all died at twenty-seven. The same age she was now. They'd all overdosed, but they'd made beautiful music first. What had Christine Chubbuck done, other than report other people's news? Had she ever made any news of her own, Mary wondered. Well, Mary wasn't planning to die and she still had a lot to accomplish before it was her time: more art to create, more daughters to procreate.

Life is for the living.

She wondered, briefly, if Christine Chubbuck had any daughters.

September 1974
New York City

Dear Daughters,

Last month Nixon resigned from the presidency.

Last week Mort resigned from this marriage.

And your mother, in her infinite genius, was able to combine both betrayals. To use Mort's behavior as a metaphor for Nixon's betrayal. I have officially put the WWDT on the map.

I was so angry at Mort's last dalliance, I locked myself in the bedroom for a weekend and didn't come out. I just wrote and wrote and wrote—don't worry, you were both safe, Mort took care of you. It was the least he could do after breaking my heart and sleeping with the babysitter, I-won't-wear-a-bra-Genevieve, the chain smoking actress/model who is now no longer in our employ. Yes, Carolina, I know you liked her, but the bitch slept with my husband.

The sad irony is that she looks a lot like I do. Except for that fact that she is twenty-five, slightly mousy and a definite social climber. She defines wannabe: a trust fund baby who has spent her entire life desperately trying to win approval from her absent daddy whose great claim to fame was that he had an insignificant part in a fairly significant movie half a century ago. Without even delving into the mind of this young slut, I'm pretty sure that there wasn't a chapter in the "Parental Approval Handbook" which advocates sleeping with your employer's husband.

I keep vacillating between anger and sadness. I know I deserve better than all of this shit that I am drowning in and I know that there is a silver lining somewhere and one day I will look back on this and smile at the memory of the pain. There is someone out there who will love me in a way that I deserve to be loved, but I need to let go in order for that to happen and I'm having a really hard time letting go because I still really love him.

Girls, what Mort and I have is special, incredibly special, and I am willing to fight for it. But because he keeps lying to me, he's pushing me away, and one day he will push me so far that I will not be able to come back. I guess sadness trumps anger because I know how lonely he will one day be and that I was the best that he could ever have. And that he will see that in hindsight, which is, unfortunately, too late.

Anyway, I used my combination of sadness and anger to choreograph a new dance. Another spoken word piece, which has gotten us almost as much press as Twyla. Her company is doing the *Bach Duet* while mine is doing *Betrayal.* I think I definitely have her beat in the title department. Content too! We've been offered a national tour because I was able to successfully put my pain on paper. I used all of my pent up frustration towards Mort's unfaithfulness as the storyline, which the troupe performed. The audience thought they were seeing an interpretation of a country's betrayal, when in truth, it was a woman's betrayal. My personal betrayal.

People just see what they want to see.

You both came to the opening night, in matching purple polyester pants suits. Austin, you fell asleep immediately and Carolina, I'm not sure you understood it, but I was thrilled to have your support. My dancers were completely naked, their bodies speckled with red, white and blue paint to illustrate the bleeding heart of our country.

Here is an excerpt from the spoken word piece I recorded over the performance.

The Cover Up Was Worse Than The Crime.

Betrayal.
An eight letter word, for the eight years you should have
been in office. Should've. Would've. Could've. Didn't.
Fucker. Fucker. Fucker.
How dare you.
You betrayed me, tricky dick.
Not by falling in love with someone else,
but by not giving me the courtesy of telling me.
Not after it happened, but while it was happening.
So we could talk about it.
Like friends/lovers/confidantes do.
The cover up was worse than the crime.
I voted for you. I voted for us.
I never knew hurt could feel like this.
I never knew what betrayal was until now.
What being completely blindsided and shell
shocked by foreign information.
By a foreign concept.
You pulled us out of Vietnam, but you
pulled us into your web of deceit.
When did you lose your moral authority?
You opened good relations with China, then
served her dinner on my good china.
As the days pass, and the pain fades,
I will be able to rebuild our friendship, but not my trust.
I don't trust you.
I believed in you and you stuck a spear through my heart
and through the middle of my hope.
You cried that others may hate you,
but those who hate you don't win unless you hate them,
and then you destroyed yourself.

I forgive you for the crime. I don't
forgive you for the cover up.
But I will fight. I will win.

Because I am a survivor.

Okay...intense, I know. But your father is a fucker, Austin. He is a hotheaded fucker with the maturity of a gnat. And I'm sticking it out because I still love him, despite the pain he has caused me...and yes, I realize I am capitalizing on my pain but such is the life of an artist.

I love you Carolina and Austin,
Mom

P.S. I went to put away a pair of Mort's tighty whities in his underwear drawer and I found a pair of Genevieve's size small yellow panties in there. I think I'm going to be sick. Although...in all fairness...it's giving me EXCELLENT material to write about.

Ten

Austin slammed the door behind her. Her sisters had no fucking clue what had been going on in the house. She didn't know which one was the most selfish: Carolina with her obsession to know every detail or Baltimore with her complete lack of curiosity. Which was worse...wanting to know, or simply not caring? Dallas was somewhere in the middle as she always was...almost non-existent. Invisible.

Austin plopped down on her bed and pulled her iPad from underneath her quilt. She loved her patchwork bedspread which was one of the best presents her mother had ever given her. Austin had accumulated tee shirts throughout her life: shirts from various lacrosse camps, 10k runs, music festivals. She had so many she couldn't count and most of them were crumpled up, forgotten in various drawers. Three years ago, just before she moved back home, a large package arrived at her apartment in the East Village from Campus Quilts. The card read "36 memories for my beautiful thirty-six year old." Mary had sent away Austin's old tee shirts, which the company had sewn into a beautiful quilt.

It comforted Austin to envelop herself in her memories: the Turkey Trot she and Sarah ran a few Thanksgivings ago, a Princeton lacrosse shirt which reminded her of her glory days on the field, a picture of a black cockerel – the symbol of Chianti – when she had backpacked through Italy and Greece. Thirty-six memories from happier times. Austin often fell asleep wrapped in the quilt, listening to an audiobook, podcast or music on the iPad. Even though her bedroom overlooked the water and the sound of the surf, she preferred to fall asleep to the sound of voices. It made her feel less lonely.

Last night she hadn't slept at all.

Austin scrolled through her emails. There were three from her New York editor, Janis Stein. Austin was hesitant to open them. She knew they were going to be either angry, "Your manuscript is three months late" rants or, even worse, passive aggressive, "Was just wondering when you were planning to send me the manuscript." They were equally disconcerting. Lately, she neither had the time nor the inclination to write. She tried... her mother nudged her to work, but Austin couldn't focus. Not with everything going on.

Her last visit to Janis left such a bitter taste in her mouth, she hadn't been back. Austin knew the manuscript wasn't up to par, but she was long past her deadline and had to hand in something. Anything. Austin loved going back into the city; yet, when Janis called and asked to meet her in person, Austin was wary. Usually after she sent in some chapters, her editor emailed her enthusiastically, begging for more. This time, she had requested an in-person meeting.

Austin hadn't been to Janis's office since the launch party of her *New York Times* Best Seller five years earlier. It was a big deal and Mary and Dallas had been there for her. Baltimore, understandably, couldn't make it because she was traveling abroad and Carolina simply hadn't bothered. Typical. Still, it was a wonderful party and Austin reveled in the adulation from her first book, *Keys To Pandora's Box.* The building was pulsating with energy: There had been adoring people, expensive champagne and hundreds of books to be signed.

When she was next summoned to her agent, the energy in the waiting room was different. It was cold and imposing.

"Ms. Baxter," a handsome androgynous man, who looked no more than twenty, said as he entered the room, "Ms. Stein will see you now."

Austin guessed the boy, whose name was Atticus, naturally, would be running the publishing company in a few years. It seemed like young people were running the world and Austin had never felt so old.

Austin followed Atticus down a series of corridors, whose walls were adorned with oversized posters of their client's greatest hits. Just outside Janis's door, Austin allowed herself a small smile as she saw the framed poster of *Keys to Pandora's Box.* The artist had chosen a Pulp Fiction art which was usually reserved for science fiction or mysteries. Her book was a historical romance and the poster showed a strong, attractive redhead in the foreground wearing a key around her neck, her red stilettoed heel resting on an antique burnished metal box. Somehow, the bizarrely provocative cover art and the actual content of the book combined to become a best seller and Austin had spent the better part of the year touring the country and promoting her book. Everyone was excited for the follow up and she had finally delivered the first draft to her editor.

Taking a deep breath, Austin said goodbye to Janis's assistant and walked through the chrome door.

Janis, dressed in an expensive Armani suit, was on the phone. Pacing in front of the full picture window overlooking Broadway, she nodded hello before resuming her conversation. "You're joking. Look, this isn't just pulp chic lit, it's screaming Pulitzer. Okay, maybe not Pulitzer, but she's friends with Dr. Oz. Do you know what that means, Dr. Oz?!"

Austin guessed Janis to be about sixty, though she had clearly been nipped and tucked in the right places because there wasn't a wrinkle on her face. What Janis lacked in facial lines, she made up for in height. Six feet tall without heels, and Janis always wore four inch heels: It was hard not to be intimidated in her presence.

"You have her agent call," Janis said before clicking off her bluetooth and coming around the desk to greet Austin. "Look at you. You look great. Just great. Have you lost some weight? Here, have a seat."

Austin looked at her editor without sitting. "Oh god. You hated it."

"Austin—"

"Have a seat? Is that a euphemism for, get comfortable before I kill your dreams?"

"Don't be so overdramatic, darling. There's no need to get paranoid." Janis motioned for Austin to sit in the leather chair across from her as she rummaged through the pile of manuscripts on her desk. "How's your mother?"

"She's fine," Austin said cautiously.

"How's Sarah?"

"Fine."

"Fabulous." Janis finally pulled out Austin's manuscript. "I hated it. Although I can't quite define what 'it' is. This isn't a manuscript, it's... a diary. What's going on Austin? These are scribblings, fragments... I gave you, the company gave you, quite a sizable advance."

"Picasso used to scribble on napkins."

"Picasso's agent didn't have to pay for two kids at Spence and a greedy ex-husband." Janis looked for the right words, trying to soften the blow of her kill. "*Keys To Pandora's Box* was…it was transcendent. Some of the best writing of your generation. Of any generation. But this… " She dropped the manuscript on the desk, creating a chasm between them. "I have a reputation to uphold."

"So do I," Austin mumbled.

"I'm sorry. You have to do better than this," Janis said matter of factly. "You've raised the bar too high to fail."

Austin squeezed her eyes shut, trying to erase the memory. She heard her sisters clumping up the stairs. Why couldn't they just leave her alone? She listened to Baltimore's padded shuffle as she lumbered past her door, then the more exact steps of Carolina. Finally, the sound of Dallas's designer shoes clicking on the hardwood floor. They stopped just outside her room and Austin felt her sister's hesitation as she wavered whether or not to knock. After a minute, the steps moved on and Austin breathed a sigh of relief.

But she knew she couldn't put off the inevitable much longer.

1976

Mary got the call at 2pm.

At first, she thought the polite voice belonged to a telemarketer, however, it was someone doing a Gallup poll. Mary thought she should tell the researcher that since she was married to a Lefty who worked for the paper, her opinion was probably skewed... but she was curious to hear what the man had to say so she agreed to participate.

"Do you agree with the Quinlan verdict?" the man asked.

Mary was nonplussed. She thought he'd ask about Patty Hearst's bank robbery or the success of the new Peter Frampton album... not about the right to die. Frankly, she didn't care. She'd read about the case; who hadn't? Karen Ann Quinlan was a twenty-one-year-old who slipped into a coma after taking drugs. She had remained in a vegetative state for several months and her parents wanted to unhook her from the life support. Her brain was fried. There was no life waiting for her if she recovered. Yet, the state forbid it. So, the parents had to petition the court.

"I do," Mary eventually responded.

Even though the girl had done drugs and had made her own choices, Mary empathized with her parents, fellow Catholics who were intent on stopping their daughter's suffering. Apparently, even in Karen Ann Quinlan's vegetative state, she was uncomfortable: thrashing and moaning and unhappy. No one should have to live like that.

"I mean," Mary added, "I think it's the individual person's choice."

Mary remembered Sammy in his coma. He was so still, so peaceful, but even though he looked like the boy she fell in love with, she knew that his mind was gone. Had he woken up from the coma, he would not have been the same person. He would have wanted to go. If the roles were reversed, she would have wanted to go.

"But she's in a coma," the voice at the other end of the phone prompted in his practiced monotone objectiveness. "She doesn't have a choice."

"So, it's her parents' choice. I mean, who the hell would want to live like that? Who wants to endure the unendurable? Life is for living."

Mary hung up the phone, highly disconcerted. She hated politics and tried to stay away from them. Luckily for the Quinlans, the New Jersey Supreme Court rendered a unanimous decision appointing Karen Ann's father as her Power of Attorney. He was given the right to determine her medical treatment, including the right to discontinue all extraordinary means of life support.

Mary wondered who, if she were in a similar situation, she would appoint as her medical Power of Attorney. Certainly not Mort. He was Jewish and had God issues. He'd think it was unethical. Not Roger. He would think like a Catholic instead of a compassionate ex-husband. Miss Tillie would have been an obvious choice; however, she was already dead. That left Carolina and Austin. A fourth grader and a kindergartener. No, they were too young. It'd be unfair to ask them.

At least, not yet.

She could ask Dana or Wander, but society was so racist they probably wouldn't accept a black man as the one responsible for pulling the plug on a white woman. Which left Dana, whom she loved... but there had been something off with Dana lately. Her principal dancer had been pulling away... both personally and professionally and Mary couldn't understand why. Was it because Dana was approaching thirty and she knew she'd have to leave the troupe? Well, Mary would make an exception for her. Dana was her right-hand woman, her co-choreographer, her best friend.

She could be a Womyn Warrior forever.

May 1976
New York City

Dear Daughters,

You're both growing up so quickly, which means I am getting old. America is almost two hundred and I am almost thirty. And while America is getting a big bicentennial celebration with balloons and bands and parades, I'm just getting old...and bitter. I thought I'd be more influential by now. My work is touching people...but it's small scale. Twyla Tharp is already a household name and I'm just a name in my household. She's gone on to work with the Joffrey and the American Ballet Theatre and I...well, I have two daughters and you take up a lot of my time. Look, don't get me wrong...it's not your fault; it's the choices we make as artists. And I chose to have children. I choose to have children. And I couldn't be prouder of you. Carolina, you're already in fourth grade and, of course, the smartest girl in your class and the most popular. Who knew there were class presidents in fourth grade. What is your political agenda? More milk? Sorry, I know it seems like I'm mocking you, but I'm really quite proud of you. In fact, I even offered to help you with your campaign speech, but you were very clear that if you were qualified to be president, you were qualified to write your own campaign speech. Wow. And Austin, even though you're in kindergarten, you just made an announcement to the family that you are going to be a writer like your father. Another artist in the family. Although with your gene pool, you didn't really have a choice. A dancer and a writer would naturally produce a creative genius. And if that's what will make you happy, then that's what you should pursue. Although, hopefully you'll choose not to be a political writer, like your father. Because he's never home.

Mort's been spending most of the year covering the election. Carter's the front-runner. Thank God. I'm ready for a Democrat and especially an outsider. I'm sick and tired of our government. Not that I'm dissuading you from your political ambitions, Carolina. I think you'll make a marvelous president. On the fourth grade level. But our government...well, it sucks. After Watergate, Mort jumped to the political desk and has been gone all the time so it's just us girls. I miss him, but we've been fighting...a lot. Probably because of his nonstop string of bimbos. I know, too much information, but it's true. Truth is important girls. Lies will make your lives far more complicated than they need to be. Because they spiral out of control.

I love the man, but he refuses to be monogamous and although I decided to participate in this open marriage, I just want to feel special. I want to be adored. I want to be the most important person in someone's life and I'm not sure that can ever be possible with Mort. He tells me I'm special, but I believe actions speak louder than words and his actions prove otherwise. He comes home later and later and while I seem to be the person he dumps his shit on, he doesn't balance it with joy. I want to be adored; yet, I am barely even liked. So, I get the sad, angry, frustrated and tired Mort while his tramps, harlots and hussies get the charming Lothario I first met.

I guess what sums it up is that I don't feel safe.

I feel like Mort is ready to leave the relationship at any moment. I think he doesn't appreciate me nearly enough. He hasn't tried to satisfy me sexually and that is an important part of a relationship. I often feel trapped. Like I'm stuck under Sylvia Plath's Bell Jar. Trapped...and suffocating because there is no air left. How do I escape? How can I protest this relationship? Where is the burning monk when I need him? I am pissed off that he invested so much time in the fucking babysitter, when she lacks talent… talent that I have. It makes me disappointed in him. I hate that he calls his girlfriends late at night when he should be making love to me. I hate feeling like a stranger in my own home. Girls, Mort and I need therapy if we are going to survive. But I don't know that he wants us to survive.

I see the end of the rainbow; I just need to find the courage… or at least a sign to show me the way.

When I was a little girl, my mother told me that people are either farmers or sailors. They either prefer to stay in one place, or they like to let the wind push them from port to port. Mort is a farmer. He's a New Yorker and never wants to leave the city. Even in the summer when we go up to the island house and it's humid and sticky here, Mort stays. It's ridiculous. Half of the city empties out in August, but Mort stays. We go to paradise, and he stays in hell. Not that New York is hell, but it's dirty and congested and dangerous. The island house is a nice reprieve, but Mort is disinterested in amnesty. He claims he can only be creative entrenched in the city's frenetic energy. Bullshit. A writer should be able to write anywhere. After all, a dancer can dance anywhere.

Speaking of which, my troupe was offered a trial residency in Texas. The Palladium Theatre is gorgeous, ten times bigger than the one I'm in now. And my salary will double. Take that Twyla Tharp. Okay, I'm sure she's a lovely woman… but she's my dance equal and has already surpassed me, so I'm bitter. Maybe her mother was more supportive than mine was. I do believe that in order to succeed, in order to be the best of the best, you need parents to push you. To adore you. To believe in you. And although my mother failed in her role of nurturer, supporter and believer, I am still on the road. I am still on the journey to self-discovery and success. And, my darling girls, I will be your biggest cheerleader, your biggest fan. Because I believe in you. And moving isn't a big deal. Besides, you girls need to travel more. I'm sure you'll protest Carolina, because you're a farmer too. You like to stay put. But Austin, my little sailor, you'll be fine with it. I just have to find a way to tell Mort. I'll tell him when he gets back, after the election. Hey! Procrastination is different from lying, it's just... prolonging the necessity to tell the truth.

Reach for your dreams girls, you can never dream too big. The sky is the limit for you. Gotta set the bar high to have something to reach for.

I love you Carolina and Austin,
Mom

P.S. This is my piece that got us accepted in Texas. It's called *Lack*. I had my dancers naked... yes, I like naked dancers, sue me. They started the piece in a huge writhing orgy (choreographed with grace and style of course) that slowly dwindled down dancer by dancer. As the group dissipated, the dancers became progressively clothed. Until it was just one couple on stage. A man and a woman way too overdressed in puritanical garb replete with Victorian lace collars. Admittedly, the principal dancers Dana and Wander may have looked a little like me and Mort... bitter, you think? Here is an excerpt of dialogue that went with the piece. At least Mort still fuels my creativity!

Don't mind the lack of sex if you still have the intimacy.
Don't mind the lack of intimacy if you still have the kisses.

Don't mind the lack of kisses if he still holds your hand.
But when he stops holding your hand—mind.
Mind the lack of kisses,
The lack of intimacy,
And the lack of sex.
Because settling for nothing...
Is unacceptable.

Eleven

"Do you ever have foreplay before sex?" Baltimore smiled wickedly at her oldest sister, before rummaging through her closet.

"That has nothing to do with anything." Carolina pulled off her sweaty tee shirt. "It's none of your business."

"Says the woman who taught me how to give a blow job with an unripe banana."

"Yes," Carolina growled, "I have foreplay. Your point?"

Baltimore found a worn Mariners tee shirt at the bottom of the closet and immediately ripped off her own top. Braless, she stood in front of the long oval mirror and admired her pert breasts. "With Austin, you have to enjoy some light banter and witty repartee and then ease into the more intense stuff. A conversational seduction of sorts."

"When did you get so smart?"

"I go to Harvard." Baltimore grinned.

"What's that got to do with anything?" Dallas said as she peeked into the room. "Why are you naked?"

"Um. It has everything to do with everything," Baltimore insisted. "If you go to the best school in the country, you should say it. So, I'm saying it. I go to Harvard. It's a huge pet peeve when people from Harvard say they went to school in Boston. That's like being totally arrogant."

"You are like being totally arrogant," Dallas mimicked her.

"No. I'm just stating the obvious. If you go to Harvard, be proud of it. Of course," she baited, "if you didn't go to a college you were proud of, you could just say you went to college in Boston ... or New York."

"I'm proud of my alma mater," Dallas insisted.

"Sure you are."

"Will you please put something on."

"Why? Am I making you uncomfortable?" Baltimore asked before finally putting on the Mariners shirt.

"Is Austin still in hiding?" Carolina interrupted. She hated when Baltimore needled Dallas about college. Dallas was the only one of them who hadn't gone to a top tier school. Carolina went to Stanford, Austin to Princeton and Baltimore to Harvard. Only Dallas had opted for a smaller school and Baltimore never let her hear the end of it.

"Yeah. She's still in her room," Dallas said.

"So, what are we supposed to do?" Carolina looked out the window. The rain was practically horizontal. No one would be coming or going until the storm let up.

"We have to relax. We have to try to relax," Dallas said, still standing in the doorway, wondering if she was convincing her sisters or herself.

"Relax?" Carolina tried out the word. She hadn't been relaxed in years. She couldn't afford to let her guard down, because when she did she was burned. Best to stay in control ... even if it always meant being slightly uptight.

Baltimore tied her shirt at the waist, showing off her taut stomach. "Yeah. Holly Hobbie's right. Take your hair down."

"What?" Carolina was already exhausted and needed some quiet time. She wished her sisters would leave her room. It was still her room, her space. She just wanted to shut the door and be alone. Process. She couldn't do that with Dallas's constant questions and Baltimore's persistent pestering. Carolina pulled off her shorts and went over to the bureau to find a pair of pants. She would have loved to take a shower, but the Victorian only had one full bathroom and her mother was presently occupying it.

"I want you to take your hair down," Baltimore pestered. "Literally. It's not just figurative speech."

Carolina glared at her sister and Baltimore glared right back. Sometimes it was just easier to appease Baltimore than to fight with her. It took less energy. Finally, Carolina deliberately undid her tight ponytail. "This is ridiculous."

Baltimore appraised her sister, slowly walking around her. "You're really beautiful, when you don't try so hard. And you've got great legs."

Carolina shrugged as she stepped into a pair of cargo pants. She hadn't dressed this casually in a long time and it felt good. "I run six point two miles every morning before work."

"No wonder. If I ran that much, I'd have great legs too."

"You do have great legs, Baltimore."

"I know." Baltimore smiled. "I just wanted you to say it."

"Point two?" Dallas finally settled on the old rocking chair in the corner of the room.

"What?" Carolina looked surprised. Sometimes it was easy to forget that Dallas was there...especially when Baltimore sucked so much air out of the room. "It's a 10k."

"I know what it is. It just seems like a lot of running."

"It's not," Carolina said with a hard tone, intending to end the conversation.

"Before work?" Dallas kept nudging.

"Yes."

"Why?" Dallas asked innocently.

"What do you mean, why?"

"Why do you run that much? It's ... excessive."

"It keeps me fit. At the top of my game. On point." Carolina pulled open a drawer and rummaged through, looking for a pair of socks.

"Oh. On point," Dallas said knowingly, even though she had no idea what her sister was talking about.

"Don't listen to her, Dallas," Baltimore said. "She runs because she thinks that's the best way to relax."

"It is," Carolina insisted.

"It absolutely is not," Baltimore said, moving behind her eldest sister as she put her hands on Carolina's shoulders. "The best way to relax is to have sex. Or masturbate. Have an orgasm or five. Activate your second chakra. Your sacral chakra. Your sex chakra. That's the best way to relax." She started to massage Carolina's shoulders, trying to loosen the tight knots in her neck. "But in a pinch, you can always get a massage. In Boston, they have loads of Korean places. It's twenty bucks for an hour. Amazing. Feel this? Loosey goosey, free flowing ... This is what it feels like to relax."

"Okay. I get it. I'm relaxed," Carolina said, although she stood rigidly.

"I'm relaxed, too," Dallas said.

Both Carolina and Baltimore looked at their sister sitting primly on the edge of the rocking chair.

"What? I am," Dallas insisted.

"Uh huh." Baltimore ignored her and glanced over at Carolina. "Let's play Scrabble and make grilled cheese sandwiches."

"Now?" Carolina panicked.

"Why not now?" Baltimore grinned. "Are you suddenly lactose intolerant?"

"Because our Mother is in the other—" Carolina made the mistake of taking the bait. She would not let her little sister screw with her. She was already bickering with Austin. She took a deep breath. "Sure why not, I'm relaxed... I can be relaxed. Grilled cheese and Scrabble, sounds delightful. Let's see if Mom has a nice smoked gouda we can grill up."

"That's the spirit," Baltimore said. "And onions, nothing better than grilled cheese with grilled onions."

Dallas smiled nostalgically. "Remember the tournaments we used to have?"

"No." Baltimore went to the hall closet, which was just opposite Carolina's room. Sitting on her knees, she pulled out game after game. "Wow, Chutes and Ladders, I could totally get money for this on Ebay." She looked at Dallas who followed her to the closet. "You guys never used to let me play in your tournaments. I was always stuck with Mom making cookies in the kitchen."

"That's because you were a child."

"Well I'm gonna kick your butt today. Who has the Harvard degree?"

"Technically, you don't have it yet." Dallas smirked. She was tired of Baltimore's holier than thou attitude.

"But I got in. Getting in to an Ivy League school is far tougher than staying in. I'll get the degree. Piece of cake."

"I still think you should have stayed closer to home. Connecticut or New York."

"New York? Right. Cornell is too depressing, NYU is too big and the rest of the schools are too preppy."

"Vassar is not too preppy," insisted Dallas.

"You're dressed head to toe in Ann Taylor." Baltimore rolled her eyes.

"That just means I have impeccable taste."

"No. It means that you're conditioned to dress to please others. It's not a big deal, it's learned behavior... Pavlovian. I'm studying it right now. Mom was pseudo-preppy and you wanted to please her so you dressed pseudo-preppy. The only reason you even went to Vassar, which is a good school, although inferior to fellow sister schools Wellesley and Bryn Mawr, which I happen to know you got into, is because Mom wanted you to stay close to home." Baltimore stood up and whispered in Dallas's ear, "And I guarantee your bra and panties match."

"What?"

"Your panties. They match your bra. I'll bet money on it. Mom's matched, so my guess is yours match too."

"They don't." Dallas walked back into the bedroom, where Carolina was pulling on a pair of black Uggs.

"Oh please. It takes work to be perfect, Dallas. We get it. Never a hair out of place. Matching your purse to your toe nail polish."

"I don't do that," Dallas said defensively.

"Sure you do," Baltimore insisted. "You're a matcher. Miss matchy match."

"No... I'm..."

"Look, I'm coming from a place of deep knowledge rather than pure speculation when I say that your bra and panties match." Baltimore snapped Dallas's bra.

"Ouch. Stop that."

"Am I right? Come on. Your panties match your bra. I'll bet money on it. Mom's matched, so my guess is yours match too."

"Leave her alone," Carolina warned.

"No, they don't." At thirty, Dallas still felt bullied by her little sister.

"Show me," Baltimore taunted.

"I'm not going to show you." Dallas went to stand by Carolina, who was now comfortably dressed in cargo pants and a white ribbed tank top which showed off her toned arms.

"Show me your panties," Baltimore badgered.

"No."

"Come on. Take off your pantyhose."

"No," Dallas whined.

"Pantyhose are an antiquated torture device created by men to give us the equivalent of a tie."

"I'm not going to—"

Baltimore jumped over the bed and tackled Dallas, savagely ripping her shirt, exposing her pink bra. She then straddled her and violently pulled up her skirt revealing pink underwear.

"Ha! Pretty in pink!" Baltimore started laughing hysterically, ignoring the squirming Dallas underneath her.

"Baltimore!" Carolina yelled.

"Get off of me," Dallas fumed as she tried to push Baltimore off of her. "You ripped my favorite sweater."

"I thought you said you were relaxed." Baltimore grinned, still straddling her.

"I said to leave her alone." Carolina yanked Baltimore up, surprising them both with her strength.

Red faced, Dallas laid on the floor and started screaming at Baltimore, "Are you happy now? You caught me, I match. I've always matched. Take a good look, I'm the mother-pleaser whose bra and underwear always match."

"Don't get your knickers in a twist. I bet you five bucks Carolina's match too. And your tits are better than hers."

"Thanks a lot," Carolina growled. "Don't take the bet. Guilty as charged. How could they not? Remember Mom's commandment—"

Baltimore joined in Carolina's singsong rhyme, "Always match your bra and knickers, else the police will give you snickers."

"That is one of my more disturbing childhood recollections." Carolina chuckled as she helped Dallas off of the floor. "I can't believe she was actually mortified at the thought of the police finding our lifeless body after whatever catastrophic accident we were in, and judging our poor upbringing by our uncoordinated underwear... Talk about misplaced priorities."

"Did Mom have any priorities?" Dallas asked.

Carolina thought about it for a minute. "No."

"Can I please borrow something to wear?" Dallas was the only sister who didn't still keep her stuff at the island house. When she married Peter, she pulled everything from her childhood home, wanting to solidify her new life rather than nostalgically looking back on her old one.

Mary had turned her bedroom into the exercise room.

Carolina rummaged through the drawer for a change of clothes for Dallas. She was several inches taller and about ten pounds thinner than her sister. She finally found a light blue tee shirt dress which would probably fall to her sister's ankles and a cut up Stanford sweatshirt from her Flashdance fashion period. She tossed them to Dallas.

"Peter makes fun of me," Dallas confessed. She gingerly took off her pantyhose and Ann Taylor outfit as she put on the tee shirt dress. "I get completely neurotic if I try to mix it up a little and go blue with red or purple with grey or lilac with jade or fuchsia with—"

"We get it," Baltimore interrupted.

But Dallas was unable to stop. "—teal. Or mauve with yellow, or apricot with rose, or tan with beige or pink with... white." She was on a roll, almost hyperventilating, speaking frenetically and way too fast, "It's pathetic. I can't feel good on the outside unless I feel good on the inside ... I was the only person in my gym class whose bra matched her underwear."

Carolina grabbed her sister, her nails digging into Dallas's flesh, immediately calming her down. "Dallas. Stop."

Dallas sank onto the bed, trying to breathe. "I have to match."

"I know. It's okay," Carolina said, gently putting her arm on her sister's shoulder.

Baltimore stuck her head out of the room and leaned on the doorjamb. She looked towards the closed bathroom door at the end of the hall. "Mom's ingrained herself in us. Permanently. Ironic that she decided to kill herself in the buff."

"Baltimore," Carolina cautioned.

"Well, she did. After all these years, I bet she's collected some pretty nice lingerie, but no ... We've got to see her distended boobs and grey cootchie."

"Baltimore!"

"What?" She turned back into the room towards her sisters. "I'm only saying what you're thinking. And, FYI, I never listened to Mom's dictum." Baltimore ripped off her torn jeans, revealing men's tighty whities beneath.

"What are you doing?" Dallas was dumbfounded.

"Whose are those?" Carolina wondered.

"I don't give a shit if a cop sees me in matching underwear." Baltimore sauntered over to the bed where she winked at Dallas. Affecting a deep southern accent, she wiggled her ass, posturing, "S'cuse me, Ma'am. You're in possible vi-o-lation of the Matching Bra and Panties Act. D'ya mind straddling my car so I can frisk ya?"

Dallas opened her mouth and closed it again, annoyed by her sister's behavior. Baltimore started to grind on her, as if giving her a lap dance, and lifted her shirt up. "Why yes, Officer, Sir. Forgive me for my possible vi-o-lation of the law. But, as you can see, it doesn't really matter what the color of my panties are, 'cause I never wear a bra ... so, academically speaking everything I wear matches my underwear. But you can still frisk me if you wish."

"Jesus, Baltimore," Dallas sputtered, "you are such a ... slut."

"If you've got it, flaunt it." Baltimore, still in her underwear, grabbed the Scrabble game and bounded down the stairs.

1977

Mary walked out of *The Spy Who Loved Me* filled with conflicted emotions. The film was fine, but it was the music that really affected her. Marvin Hamlisch, who had created the greatest musical ever, *A Chorus Line*, composed the titular song, which Carly Simon had sung. Carly Simon, who had married Mary's James five years earlier.

Mary wondered how her life would have been different had she married James instead of Roger. Not that James had asked her. Still, it might have veered in a different direction. She might be a huge star instead of a minor celebrity. But life is too short for regrets and what ifs. She had made a choice. Several choices, in fact, and she would stand behind them. Plus, if her life had gone down that alternate route, she would not have her beloved daughters.

And she wouldn't have Mort.

July 1977
NYC

Dear Daughters,

The silver polish hadn't come.

I'd ordered it several weeks earlier. I went to a rundown hardware store in Chinatown, sandwiched between a restaurant that hung dead ducks in the window and a meat market that hung pig carcasses in the window. Trust me, it sounds as revolting as it looked. Holding my breath, I ducked into the hardware store where the proprietor informed me in his unintelligible accent that he had to special order the polish...from China I presume. So I waited. And I waited some more. And it never came. If I were a more superstitious person, I would have known. I should have known. Another sign. Why was I so blind to signs?

I needed the polish. Over the years, Mort had given me silver. So much silver. And it was beautiful. Exquisite. Small intricate M's.

Our sign.

Each day, I'd hunt through my white jewelry box, the musical one Miss Tillie gave me years ago with the coiled ballerina who springs to life and dances to Beethoven every time the lid opens. From the tiny compartments, I'd choose the perfect necklace for my ensemble. A bakers dozen of beautifully designed necklaces with love and forever in mind to choose from. His gifts were never bracelets, they were never rings, only necklaces. My favorites included a long shiny rectangle with a tiny M at the end for dress up occasions. A funky shaped M for daily wear. A hammered silver one with tiny M's that I'd wear to interviews. It always brought me good luck.

M. Mort and Mary. Mary and Mort. M&M. I wish I had some M&M's.

I treasured that jewelry as I had treasured him. And then he finally gave me a ring. I suppose it's every girl's dream. *Diamonds are Forever.* Jill St. John taught me the fine appreciation of a well-cut diamond. This was my first diamond from Mort. When Morty and I married it was an impromptu affair and he fulfilled societal conventions by picking up a grape ring pop in an Austin candy shop. It cost twenty-five cents.

I would have preferred strawberry.

But this time he gave me his mother's ring. She was dead and it was part of his meager inheritance. Shoshanah wanted the heirloom, but I got it. Mort wanted me to have it. And hot wife always trumps spinster sister. It was a ring that would solidify our eternity together. Too small for my finger, I wore it on my keychain. I looked at it several times a day when I used my keys to enter the apartment and the dance studio. It was a constant reminder of our love. Of his devotion to me. I thought we were going to go the distance, grow old together and look back on our lives and laugh. But the deeper we got into our marriage, the more superficial our laughs became. They weren't deep belly laughs. And a troubled relationship can only be saved by belly laughs. But I still had the ring. I still had his commitment. And then the silver began to tarnish and I ordered the special silver polish. The special polish from China that never came.

I should have known. I should have guessed.

I wonder what jewelry he'll buy for her. Will it have a "D" on it? Elegantly etched in a Cooper Black or a Tango font. No, he'd probably go for something pretentious like a Glaser Stencil Bold. Fucking Dana. He's fucking Dana. Talk about a double betrayal. Dalliances with strangers, I can handle. Even the big boobed braless babysitter Genevieve didn't bother me as much. But Dana? And the bastard actually thinks he's in love with her. Men. Fucking men. She cooked for him so he's suddenly in love with her. She whipped together some borscht recipe that reminded him of his childhood and now he's smitten. Let's see how long that will last.

I've tried, gosh I've tried, to fight and claw for this relationship to work. But I think it ultimately comes down to Mort or us. MORT meaning my husband dating who he wants and me being a part of that world or US meaning Mort throwing his energy into us, what we've had, what we could be.

I was fine having an open relationship when it meant just sex... but him loving someone else... loving fucking Dana... and spending so much of his energy, conflicted by that love... it's not fair to me. I deserve more. I deserve the vacation he took her on, I deserve him wanting to sit fifth row center on my opening nights, I deserve him wanting to be my plus one at Wander's wedding.

I asked him to choose either him or us. Because his sexual addiction, his newfound love of Dana has become a cancer to our relationship. We won't fly if he still wants her. He can't focus his attention on both of us and I am the one suffering.

It's a sad fact, but it's true. I'm not blaming her... she's just a kid. I'm blaming him for not figuring out how to prioritize me. I also guarantee that he is not telling Dana everything. He may be telling her that we're not sleeping together... Why aren't we? Why doesn't he want to fuck me? He won't tell me the answer to that... does he tell his analyst? I pray he tells someone, but the person he should be telling is me.

I want to be with someone who puts my picture in his office. Who boasts that he is in a relationship with me. Who is proud to be my other half. That hasn't been Mort for a long time as his focus has been on philandering.

I want a partner, an equal, a friend.

He has to talk to his analyst about the possible plan of me taking the girls and moving back to Texas. And I'm not being histrionic... it is simply me responding to the repeated fact that he seems to be choosing himself instead of us. I am not a psychologist. I do not have any ability to diagnose, assess, judge. But I have been his partner for the last seven years... and the seven year itch is more like a rot in our marriage and I need to cut it out before it gets infected and kills us both.

Plus, if Mort's ultimate infidelity isn't enough, the Son of Sam has made me never want to live in a big city again. The stress is giving me anxiety and the Chlorpromazine from my shrink isn't working. I'm tired of the dirt and the crime and the noise. Someday, Walt Disney should come in and clean it all up. I'm done with this city. If Mort doesn't get his shit together ASAP, we're moving permanently to Dallas. There's a company there who's been trying to poach me and I might just let them. Bring the best, leave the rest... including Dana. You are ten and six, old enough to understand that Mama isn't happy. Old enough to want better for me.

Old enough to want better for you.

I love you Carolina and Austin,
Mom

P.S. Poetic justice or perhaps just cruel, you girls decide... When I found out about Dana and Mort, I changed the spoken word piece minutes before curtain. The rhythm and measures beat out the same so it didn't confuse the dancers, but boy oh boy did I enjoy watching Dana dance what she thought was "The Queen's 25th Jubilee" piece which was renamed "The Trollop's 25th Whoopee."

Dana played Queen Elizabeth and the dance was a relatively fluffy costumed piece celebrating the Queen's reign. Yet, as the conflicting, angry words were read over the seemingly celebratory work, the dancers became progressively confused. When they walked off stage, Dana was red-faced. She demanded to know what had happened. I smiled politely and told her she was fired.

She asked if it was for fucking up the dance. I said no, it was for fucking my husband.

After he broke her heart, i was there
pushing away cigarette smoke as she
bitched
and whined
and cried and yelled
at he and he and he and he.
i, whom she hated, listened
... because that's what people do when others are in pain.
and for the next few years, i continued to listen
as she drank too much
and smoked too much
and talked too much
and crushed everyone golden who came in her path:
her toxic energy crushing them with
her evil words
and ugly sentiments
and cruel energies.
only her dance kept her alive. kept her relevant.
and even though she disliked me and envied me, i listened

... because that's what people do when others are in pain.

and when you came into my life like a
bright burning sun, radiating heat and life
and energy and good, she took steps
first position – baby steps
second position – unobtrusive steps
third position – innocuous steps
fourth position – closer and closer
fifth position – and with a pas de deux and pirouette,
she stole what was not hers to steal.
she took what was not hers to take.

and when she reveals her true colors to you and you
eventually see the ugly truth underneath the painted veil
and you come to your senses and her heart breaks
I will not be there for her.
I will not be there for you.
i will no longer listen ... because i am no longer a fool.

For the first time, I realized, I am not going to grow old with this man with whom I have invested so much time and love.

And it breaks my heart.

Twelve

"Does anyone have a cigarette?" Baltimore sat at the old oak table and turned over the Scrabble tiles.

"Will you stop asking." Carolina looked out the window again.

"When you start answering." Baltimore smirked.

"I'm out." Carolina felt like she had cabin fever. She had only been back home two hours and she was about to explode. She powered up her iPad. She needed to check the weather and see when this storm was planning to let up.

"You smoke, Balt?" Dallas was disappointed. Baltimore was looking extra skinny and she supposed her little sister was substituting nicotine for food. Plus, it was what everyone in grad school did and Baltimore was never one to spoil a group's fun.

"No," Baltimore snapped. "I'm asking for a cigarette to make conversation. Yes. I smoke. Infrequently. When I'm either drunk or under duress. I am currently under duress. Later, I plan to be drunk." She rolled her eyes. "I know all about the death stick lecture so save the sob song."

Dallas opened a jar of green olives and popped three of them into her freshly made Bloody Mary. "I think Mom smoked."

"She so didn't seem the type," Carolina said.

"Really, so what's the type?" Baltimore was tired of her know-it-all sisters, especially Carolina who seemed to have an answer for everything.

Carolina turned from the window and cleared her voice as if preparing to give a deposition. "There are three types of people who smoke. One: pre-pubescent children who think that smoking will elevate them to the unattainable echelon of cool. Two: fucked up twenty-somethings without a clue, who use cigarettes like procrastination props..." She smiled at Baltimore, who flipped her the bird. Carolina immediately returned the gesture. "...hoping the five to seven minutes of ingested cancer will give them some remarkable insight into their unfocused lives."

"Go fuck yourself." Baltimore picked up a Scrabble tile. "A, I go first."

"And three: lonely older women." Carolina sat back down and picked up a tile: N.

"Is that what category you're in?" Baltimore smiled sweetly at her eldest sister, who glared back.

Dallas sat down with her drink and reached into the pile of tiles, turning over the letter F. "My students definitely fit into the first category. And I have to say it Baltimore, you're a classic number two. But Mom, she didn't strike me as a lonely woman. I mean, she had Austin around all the time and she had her men."

Everyone suddenly quieted. They all knew about "the men." There could have been five men or five hundred men who wandered in and out of the island house while the girls were growing up. Mary didn't discriminate: If they had a pulse, they were potential sexual partners. No one really knew how many men Mary had slept with...except Mary who ceremoniously bedded them and unceremoniously disposed of them.

"Do you think they'll start coming out of the woodwork now that she's dead?" Baltimore wondered.

Dallas shrugged. "My father won't. He's dead too. Mommy and Daddy are dead." She giggled. "Sounds like a Country Western song." She looked at Carolina, who had gotten up to refill her drink. "Is yours still in Vancouver?"

"No, I just moved him to Spokane. Alzheimer's. I'll tell him about Mom, but he won't remember her. Shit, he barely remembers me."

"I guess on the Richter scale, you're worse off. I mean, I'd rather my parent be dead than suffering in silence."

Carolina grimaced. "He's not exactly silent. He has visions, which I don't think he likes because he's always yelling at them. At first, I thought it was personal, but when he started screaming at me about cheating him out of forty bucks at a celebrity poker game in Vegas, I realized that it was one of his imaginary friends. That, and the fact that he called me Mikey."

"Who's Mikey?"

"No clue. He had a cat once named Mike. Maybe he thinks I'm the cat. It's a horrible disease. The body works, the brain doesn't. All of his memories gone... or so fuzzy they might as well be gone. Hopefully, he'll get pneumonia and die before he realizes what his life has dissolved into."

"That's cold." Dallas could never understand her oldest sister's severity. For Carolina, everything was black and white. There was no softness. There was no grey.

"That's fact," Carolina retorted. "I don't wish it on anyone. Watching a strong, vibrant intellect waste away. It terrifies me. He led such a full life and now it's all gone. Disappeared somewhere in the deep recesses of his mind. His passion. His enthusiasm. He just sits there, all day every day, in that depressing room and tries to conjure memories which may or may not have happened." She struggled to laugh. "He won a purple heart, you know. A fucking purple heart for saving half his troop in Vietnam. He was a hero. Last month, when I was visiting, he asked me what it was. He had no idea he'd even been in the army. What a waste. It's hereditary, you know. I've memorized the statistics."

"You'll be fine." Dallas ate the third vodka-drenched olive and suddenly remembered that she hadn't had any breakfast. Just chocolate cake. Cake and olives. How quickly she had fallen back into the bad habits she had worked so hard to overcome.

"Easy for you to say," Carolina said. "We all have the same mother and she's not sick, just suicidal, which is sick in its own right. Dallas, your father died in a car accident. That's not hereditary."

"He died because his blood alcohol content was point twenty two and he thought hitting a tree was the same as hitting the brakes." Dallas lifted up her drink and toasted her sister. "Alcoholism. Hereditary."

"Mort is around somewhere. The city, I think. I barely keep in touch with him anymore. Just the odd Christmas card. I wonder if Austin still sees him. They used to be so close." Carolina bit back the familiar jealousy. Of course Austin's father was nearby. She never had to feel the loss Carolina did. Mary married and divorced her father in the space of two years and Roger spent most of her childhood on the West Coast, only seeing his daughter on the occasional birthday or July 4th long weekend. Mort was more of a father to her than Roger was. Mort had been a mainstay in all of the girls' lives, even after he and Mary had divorced. He remained her mother's best friend through her aborted marriages to both Dallas and Baltimore's fathers.

It wasn't fair.

"Well, I'm not dying of Alzheimer's or drowning in a bathroom," Baltimore announced. "And I only drink on special occasions, so alcoholism's out of the question. When my time comes, I'm going to a leper colony to help sick children." She rearranged her tiles. She already had a twenty-four point word and because she was going first, it would earn a double score. She grinned. She was leagues ahead of her sisters and the game hadn't even begun.

"Do they still have leper colonies?" Dallas refilled her drink. She was definitely not going to be able to get through this day sober. She couldn't remember the last time she had more than one drink... college, probably. The sorority party when she had experimented with her Kappa sister, Debbie Mandlebaum. They were both wasted on grain liquor and had a blast. The following day, Debbie wanted to pursue the relationship, but Dallas wanted nothing more to do with her and had been uncharacteristically cruel in curbing her advances. She wondered where Debbie was now. Probably somewhere more healthy than she was. Probably not on a cocktail of Klonopin and Xanax.

No, Dallas definitely was not going to be able to get through the rest of this day sober.

"Whatever," Baltimore snarled. "I'm going to help the kids."

"You can do that before you die." Dallas took a long sip of her fresh drink. The alcohol was definitely fueling her courage.

"But then I might catch it. I'm still young. And virile."

"That's terrible."

"That's fact. I can do a lot more good work from my desk in Boston than in the middle of a leper colony."

"You're being ridiculous. That's like saying a teacher can teach better outside of the classroom away from the students."

Baltimore cocked her head and looked at Dallas. "So you're comparing your students to lepers?"

"Lepers is politically incorrect."

"How do you know?"

"Because it's not appropriate," Dallas stammered. "It's like the N word or the F word."

Baltimore threw her head back and laughed incredulously. "You're comparing the word fuck to the word leper?"

"You know how much I hate that language. Why do you insist on using it around me?"

"Are you going to wash my mouth out with soap and send me to the principal's office?"

"I just don't think people use that word anymore."

"Fuck?" Baltimore smiled mischievously.

"If you google lepers, the last reference will be sometime in the Middle Ages. People just don't get leprosy anymore."

"Don't you teach history?"

"Social Studies," Dallas corrected her. "They're fifth graders."

"Then they should be socially conscious." Baltimore insisted, "Recycling, global warming, lepers."

"They're studying the presidents." Dallas was exasperated. Why did Baltimore love to harp on about a subject? She needed to let it go.

"Reagan barely mentioned the word AIDS in his eight years as president. Are you teaching them that?"

"The world is painful enough, they don't need to know about AIDS and leprosy." Dallas found herself raising her voice. Her sister was working her last nerve.

"They need to wake up and face reality," Baltimore said matter of factly.

"THEY'RE ELEVEN!" Dallas was done. She couldn't stay in this madhouse. As soon as the storm passed, she was getting off the island and going home. She should have never come home in the first place. She should have known better.

Carolina scrolled through her iPad. "Recently, 738,284 cases of leprosy were identified worldwide; ninety-one in the United States. Between one million and two million people are believed to be permanently disabled by the disease."

"Ha!" Baltimore victoriously fist punched the air. "Twenty-first century. Still lepers running around. Seems your curriculum is a tad outdated, teach."

"Ninety-one cases in the United States. Oh, I'm sorry Baltimore. I guess I have failed as a teacher for not knowing that there are fewer than a hundred lepers living in the United States."

"I thought lepers was politically incorrect." Baltimore grinned, knowing that she'd won that round.

1977

Mary pulled the station wagon into a small gas station outside Harrisburg and consulted the map while the gas station attendant filled up her '77 Chevelle.

"Heading west?" he asked.

"Uh huh." Mary didn't even look up. "Girls, go get some treats." She handed them each three dollars and went back to her map.

"Need any advice?" the attendant asked.

Mary looked up at him. He was young and attractive. He was also a gas station attendant in Pennsylvania. "If I do, I'll be sure to ask you, but I think I'm going to have to take this journey solo."

Mary felt a migraine coming on. Her headaches were few and far between but the last few days had been chaotic. After learning about Mort's affair with Dana, Mary was through. She'd reached her breaking point. Mort had officially crossed the Rubicon and she was done. Within a few days, she packed up all of her belongings and the girls' belongings, bought a car and headed west. The tension in the car had been thick as both girls were stunned by their mother's seemingly sudden actions. She'd have to do something special for them, but she wasn't sure what. She could have stopped in Hershey to get them candy at the chocolate capital of the United States, but she wanted to get as far away from New York as possible. Plus, she had to organize a place to live and enroll the girls in new schools.

"Shotgun," both of her girls screamed interrupting Mary's thoughts as they raced to the passenger door.

"You had it last time," Carolina said.

"I'm the co-pilot," Austin said, pulling the handle.

"I'm older."

"I'm smarter."

"Girls!" Mary shouted. There was no way she was going to avoid this headache. She'd have to pop a few Tylenol, stop at a hotel when it got too bad and then take something stronger. Much stronger. She wished one of her girls could pick up some of the driving slack, but ten was too young to take the wheel and the last thing Mary needed was to get arrested. "I'm trying to figure out where to stop for the night."

Carolina finally pried open the door and was about to get in, when Austin beat her. "It's 78 to 81 to 140 to 130," Austin said as she ducked under Carolina's outstretched arm and slid into the front seat. Austin held her Coca-Cola and potato chips in one hand as she maneuvered on her seat belt with the other. "We have five hundred and twenty-six miles to go on 81 before we switch to 140. I memorized it Mother, you don't need a map when you have me!"

"I hate you," Carolina grumbled as she got into the back seat.

She wasn't sure whom she hated more, her annoying know-it-all little sister or her clueless mother who hadn't even consulted her about the move. It wasn't fair. Carolina picked up a book and tried to lose herself in it, hoping to forget that she was leaving everything she knew behind. Life was unfair, her mother told her when Carolina tried to protest the abrupt move. But her mother wasn't class president. She didn't have loads of friends. She didn't know that Andy Shenker was planning to ask her out on the first day of school. Carolina was giving up a political position and a potential boyfriend. What was Mary giving up? Carolina wished she could stay in the city with Mort, but apparently it wasn't an option which was even up for discussion.

"Well, at least we're moving closer to my dad," she needled Austin.

"And further away from mine," Austin groaned. She was also sad she was leaving. The West Village walk-up was all she had ever known. She didn't remember Texas and now she was moving back there.

"Farther," Carolina corrected her.

"Shut up."

"You shut up."

"Make me."

"I will."

Carolina reached for Austin's hair, but her little sister was faster than she was and tried to bite her. Mary's strong arms pried the girls apart.

"Girls! Stop it," Mary screamed again as she handed a wad of cash to the attendant who gave her a piteous look. "We've been through this. It's not up for discussion. We have to move. There's a wonderful dance company out there that desperately needs the world's best choreographer."

"You?" Austin asked.

"That's what I told them." Mary tickled Austin, who immediately started to giggle. She then looked back at her eldest daughter. "Come on Carolina, give me a break. I'm doing my best."

"Have you even thought this through, Mother?" Carolina scolded. Sometimes she felt as if she was the mother in the relationship. "I mean, you just plucked us out of our home exactly three weeks before the school year begins and you expect us to just start over in Texas?"

"Yes," Mary said. "You love Texas."

"I don't remember Texas and besides, we lived in Austin not Dallas. It's an entirely different town. Do we even have a place to stay?"

Mary hesitated for a moment. When had their roles switched? When had she become the daughter in the relationship? "Not yet, but I'm working on it."

"Thought not," Carolina harrumphed and went back to her book.

"Don't be such a bitch, Carolina," Mary snarled.

"Yeah. Don't be such a bitch, Carolina," Austin echoed before Mary slapped her.

Austin jerked back and held her hand to her face, trying not to cry. "What was that for?"

"I am the mother," Mary insisted, the tension between her eyes throbbing. "I am in charge. I don't like you girls bullying each other. Now, we're moving because your father is a schmuck and I had to get out to save myself. You girls may not like it, but it's how it is. And you'd better wake up and notice that the only thing you each have is each other. So stop acting like little monsters and be nice to each other." Mary willed away her encroaching migraine, turned on the ignition and floored out of the gas station, heading westward on the monotonous highway.

Carolina grimaced in the back seat. She'd rather take her chances with strangers than with her sister and her mother. She felt like a stranger in her own family and was tired of being the sane one. When was it going to be her time to relax and do what she wanted to do?

When would she finally be able to break free?

In the front seat, Austin was quiet as she bit her lip and counted the passing telephone poles. She was determined not to cry even though her mother's slap had hurt her, both physically and emotionally. She was determined to be positive. She idolized her mother and believed her.

If Mary said it was going to be better, it was going to be better.

Because after listening to all of the yelling and name calling and drama over the past few years, it couldn't get any worse.

Feb 1978
Dallas, TX

Dear Daughters,

Sometimes you don't know what you are missing until it is gone. And sometimes you do.

We got out in the nick of time. A huge blizzard has completely closed down NYC. The city which never sleeps has been snoozing for three days. Mort says it's unrecognizable. The Village is like a ghost town. Huge snowdrifts, no public transportation and stranded commuters. It reminds me of that line from *Willie Wonka and the Chocolate Factory*: "Nobody ever goes in and nobody ever comes out." That movie gave you nightmares, Carolina although Austin you were quite fascinated by it, especially the Oompa Loompas. You really are quite a strange little girl. Wonderful, but strange. Anyway, it's a nightmare in New York and apparently Rhode Island and Boston are worse. Much worse. New England's been declared a Federal disaster area. It snowed for thirty-three hours straight with record snowfall over twenty-seven inches and lots of flooding along the Eastern Seaboard. I made Mort promise to check on the island house as soon as he can get out of the city.

Let's see if it's a promise he is capable of keeping.

Yet another one of the many reasons I'm glad we're in the Lone Star State where it's over seventy degrees nine months out of the year. This place is fantastic. The Dallas Cowboys won the Superbowl and the fan fever is contagious. Everyone is so excited about everything, the complete opposite of New York where cynical and jaded are the attitudes of choice. Everyone in New York seemed to pop pills in order to cope and I was definitely at the head of the line when people signed up to drink the Koolaid. Every time my shrink prescribed a pill ending in -zine or -zac, I took it... no questions asked. So, when we packed up and moved to Texas, I stopped overmedicating.

I am so glad that life is behind me. Behind us. It's not healthy when someone needs pharmaceuticals in order to function. Life is for living, it's for feeling the ups and the downs: Humans are not meant to walk around in a neutralized daze. Besides, who needs a shrink when I have the sun. Vitamin D is the cure for any ailment and it always seems to be sunny here.

Not only is it warm, it's friendly here as well. Two big plusses. You can't put a premium on positive energy. It's the Southern hospitality I had growing up in North Carolina in a far more sophisticated town. Dallas isn't filled with back city hicks, instead there are real men here who wear suits and cowboy boots and smoke cigars and hemorrhage money. Have I mentioned that Texan men are extremely generous... both in front of and behind closed doors. Bigger is definitely better if you know what I mean. Well, since neither one of you has hit puberty yet, probably not. But we're talking enormous. Girth, length, diameter. Mort was my first circumcised penis and he will definitely be my last.

I prefer traction.

I am currently dating an enormous amount of men. And by enormous I'm talking ENORMOUS. Why not? I'm thirty-one and I wasted my twenties primarily having sex or, in my case, *not* having sex with Mort. I have a lot of intercourse to make up for. We're in the middle of a sexual revolution and I am standing on the front line, proudly doing my duty. You girls are annoyed that I'm not home as much as I used to be, but a girl's gotta live. Since there isn't Mort to help take care of you, you're kind of stuck with some of my younger dancers as your babysitters. It could be worse. If Mama were still alive, you might have to deal with her and that would be a nightmare.

Sometimes not having a mother is better than having one. I speak from experience.

I promise that I'm not committing to anyone. You girls are my priority. I love you and I want to focus on you. I want to focus on you and on my troupe. I am not looking for a long term relationship, I just want to have fun. Okay, there is this one man. Sully. He's richer than god and never comes to the house empty-handed. Maybe house is a grandiose term for the shitty apartment we live in, but it's near the studio and the school system is pretty good... so I can't complain. He worships me and bends over backwards, literally and figuratively to satisfy me. Sully knows how much I love Saturday Night Fever (I've seen it five times), so he took me to a Bee Gees concert. Wore the white suit and everything. My own sexy John Travolta. He's loaded and is quite the lover. Does everything Texan style... big and loud. I don't know if I've ever had more fun in bed. Talk about Night Fever! Bad Bee Gees pun? Who cares. It's true. Sex with Roger was hot but Sully takes it to a whole new level: He was a Boy Scout and has an intimate understanding of knots. Too much information? Fuck it. I'm tired of our puritanical society. Did you know they were shocked when I tried the naked dancer routines here? Called me prurient. Like they even know the meaning of the word! (Though they are right, I am prurient.) There is nothing more beautiful in the world than a dancer's body and they—the right wing Republicans who run this town—want to see it covered up. Frankly, they're just pissed that a Democrat is finally in the White House. All politicos are hypocrites. You know, deep down, they are all prurient nymphomaniacs who have sex dungeons in their basements but on the surface they appear all prissy and upstanding. Still, they pay me a lot so I guess I can't complain. But nudity is beautiful. Especially women's bodies. So why do they want us to cover it up? The Dallas Cowboy cheerleaders barely wear any clothes and they're just jumping around. My dancers are creating art.

Girls, no matter what size you are 6 or 16, show off your body. There is nothing sexier than a woman who is confident in her own skin. Do not let anyone dictate how you feel about yourself. There is nothing more important than loving yourself and knowing how special and valuable you are. Remember my fifth commandment: Love your body, love each curve, attract the attention you deserve.

I love you Carolina and Austin,
Mom

P.S. Apparently, the only thing which gets Texans' knickers in a twist more than nudity is language. I show boobs and butt and audiences are "appalled" but they still pack the houses; yet, the minute we perform a piece with the C word, the theatre is boycotted. These Republicans are going to be the death of me. This was the offending piece, which I had to pull after only one performance.

A Response to Society's Diatribe

The decade of the woman.
Empowerment. Acknowledgement of Backlash.
Equal Pay. Pro-choice. Pro-woman.
Taking off the blindfolds of ignorance.
We can teach you, but many times
you do not want to learn.

Is it too painful?
The era has come. The era is now.
ERA. NOW.
veni, vidi, vici
I spend my time championing women's rights
voicing my discontent with the establishment
A member of the unsilent minority.
I am called bitch, butch, he-woman and cunt.
yes, cunt.
Gee, what an intelligent put down.
Perhaps you refer to me as cunt because
vagina has too many syllables for your limited vocabulary.
I am not angry at you.
I pity you.
You pathetic man, how dare you con-
sider yourself on the same level:
conversational, intellectual and spiritual,
as I am.
We speak a different language.

open your ears and find a piece of your
mind to imbibe some of my
milk and honey
until then, you cannot begin to understand me.

The irony is that the piece was really important. The national board of NOW just voted unanimously to declare the ERA state of emergency because the ERA needs to be ratified state by state. I was simply trying to make a statement through my art, to set a strong example for my girls; yet, these Republicans... and by the way there were mostly women boycotters, figure that out... have put an end to my educative dance.

THIRTEEN

"Are we playing strip poker?" Austin's voice was bright and cheerful as she bounded down the stairs and spied her baby sister wearing only men's tighty whities. Austin had changed into jeans and a multicolored checkered flannel shirt and looked refreshed.

"Do you want to?" Baltimore teased.

"Not particularly."

"Then how about Scrabble," Baltimore said. "We're waiting for you. Wanna play? I'm going to need some competition."

"Sure."

"Paper?"

"What kind? Bright white, matte white or print white?" Austin joked and nodded to the closet in the corner of the room. "Where's Dallas?"

"Fixing her eleventh Bloody Mary." Baltimore gestured to the kitchen.

"Eleventh?"

"Eleventh. Third. It's all the same." Baltimore plunked a key on the piano as she passed by. Remembering something, she sat down on the piano bench and played Hot Crossed Buns. "Do any of you still play?"

Carolina and Austin shook their heads.

"What a waste. Remember all those lessons Mom made us take?"

"She didn't make me take any," Austin said.

"Me either. We didn't grow up in this house like you did," Carolina said bitterly. "We got to move nineteen times."

"Nineteen?"

"Nineteen, six. It's all the same."

"Oh. Well, I hated them. The piano lessons. It took breaking my finger playing capture the flag to get me out of taking them."

"How do you break your finger playing capture the flag?" Carolina asked. She missed all of Baltimore's childhood and really didn't know any of the details surrounding her sister's life.

"You don't want to know, but I did." Baltimore smiled wickedly. "I remember two songs. They're like parlor games. I go to a party and play Beethoven's 'Moonlight Sonota,' like this." Baltimore proceeded to play the entire song by rote. "I even use the pedal so I look professional." She laughed. "Then, when someone wants to hear something else, I play 'Brahms' Lullaby.'" Baltimore played the lullaby Mary routinely played and sang to her daughters.

Carolina and Austin listened as Baltimore played the dulcet chords. Dallas entered the room from the kitchen, put down her Bloody Mary and joined her sister on the piano bench. She played a complicated counter melody that complemented the song. It was hauntingly beautiful. When their younger sisters finished the duet, Carolina and Austin clapped.

"Where'd you learn to play that?" Baltimore demanded.

"I teach piano. I've played my entire life," Dallas said.

"Really? You kept it up? How come I didn't know that?"

"Because you never asked. Do you really know anything about me?" Dallas asked earnestly.

"No. No I don't," Baltimore said as she got up and went to the closet in search of paper. The closet was just beyond the piano and behind a plant which looked like it hadn't been watered in weeks. The closet was a hoarder's paradise: The top shelf was home to a wide assortment of hats, scarves and gloves, while the clothing rod was jam packed with mismatched plastic hangers holding wool coats, down jackets, fleeces and parkas. Baltimore sat down on the floor and started to rummage through the junk. "Jesus, we have even more games in here. Mousetrap, Careers, Mork and Mindy... oh she saved my old Spirograph. Mom was sitting on a goldmine. Everything is classic seventies. Vintage is so in right now."

"Vintage?" Austin looked at Carolina.

"In her mind, everything before 1990 is vintage. Hey, do you happen to know where Mother's address book is?"

Austin walked to the secretary desk at the opposite corner of the room and pulled open the single drawer. She removed an old leather-bound book stuffed to the brim with scraps of paper and plunked it down in front of Carolina. "Try to decipher that."

"I will. Thank you." Carolina hesitated before broaching the next subject, "We do need to call people, Austin."

"Of course we do."

"I'm taking these back to Boston if no one minds." Baltimore sat cross legged and stacked up the games. "Risk, Payday, Perfection... do they even make these games anymore?"

"They still make Risk," Dallas said, who was playing a classical piece on the piano, but everyone ignored her.

Baltimore shrieked, "Tell me that's not who I think it is." She spied a patch of brown hair on the closet floor peeking out from underneath a stack of worn Betty and Veronica comic books and got on her belly in order to shimmy her hand underneath the stack of worn comics in order to reach it. She slithered out and triumphantly held her prize aloft. "It's my Ken doll!" She rested on the floor, hugging the naked plastic doll replete with synthetic brown hair. "My Ken doll! This is my Ken doll! I love this doll!"

Baltimore suddenly let out a loud shriek as she bolted upright, "Oh my god!"

"What?" Carolina leafed through the address book. Was there something else dead in the house?

"My Ken doll is a eunuch," Baltimore said, clinically examining his penisless crotch.

"Huh?" Dallas wondered.

"He's missing his penis. Was he always missing his penis?"

"Mattel was never a big fan of genitalia on dolls," Carolina said.

"Yet they had no problem giving Barbie 36 D's." Austin picked her tile: G.

Baltimore sat down, stroking her beloved doll. "I can't believe it. Ken. Unable to procreate. Why didn't you guys tell me?"

"We were trying to protect you." Austin picked six more tiles.

"From what?"

"We wanted you to think that all men were like that. This way your expectations weren't so high," Carolina said not looking up from the address book. There were so many random names whom she had never heard of. Mostly male. How was she supposed to know the ones she should call?

Baltimore plopped back down on the piano bench next to Dallas. "Did you guys ever make your Barbies have sex in the bathtub?"

"You're disgusting."

"I did. Lots and lots of sex." She looked at Ken, contorting him into various sexual positions. "You got laid a lot! Barbie, Skipper, Francie, black Barbie ..." She bent him over. "G.I. Joe ... for a eunuch, you did really well."

"Better than most of us." Austin laughed.

"Speak for yourself, I am extremely sexually active," Baltimore boasted.

"Do you practice safe sex?" Dallas asked innocently.

"Safe sex? You sound like an after school special. No, I'm actually a big fan of the rhythm method."

"Grow up." Dallas moved to the middle of the bench, knocking Baltimore off.

Baltimore picked herself up and looked at Austin. "You changed."

"I was starting to smell. Can I get my hug now?"

Baltimore crossed the room and sat down on Austin's lap. "You smell like baby powder." She gave her sister a big bear hug.

"I doused myself. Just for you."

"How come Mom doesn't smell?" Baltimore looked up.

"You smelled her?"

"No. I didn't smell her, but I happen to have ultra-sensitive nostrils. Remember when old Mrs. McFeely's dog died? I knew three days before she did. And she lived two houses away."

"I loved that dog." Dallas joined her sisters at the table. She looked at her tiles. X.A.A.A.N.P.I. She couldn't see any words in there other than 'pan.' She wished she played more

Words with Friends. She was already out of her league and the game hadn't even begun.

"Who knows?" Austin said, arranging her tiles. "The water's probably blocking the odor. Who's going first?"

"I am." Baltimore sat down and put down her first word. "J on the double letter, plus O.Y.O.U.S. is joyous for twenty-four. Doubled 'cause I went first, forty-eight points."

"We should divvy up by letters," Carolina announced.

"What?" Baltimore looked confused.

"Mom's friends," Carolina said as she held the address book up. "I'll take A through G. Although, I can barely read her handwriting. Dallas you can do H through ... " She counted through the letters. " ... Through M. Baltimore, you can do N to R and Austin, you can take care of the rest." she moved to the oak wood table and sat next to Austin. "Obviously, you'll have to call Mort."

"Obviously."

"When's the last time you talked to him?"

Austin didn't answer her as she pushed Baltimore off of her lap and looked out the window at the swings raging against the wind. She had just seen her father last week ... and since then she had aged a lifetime.

1979

Mary nailed the cross to the wall over her bed.

Religion was the norm in Texas and she was determined to fit in with the Dallas society ladies with their big gold crosses and even bigger golden hairdos. She'd all but forgotten her religion when Mort was around. In New York, it wasn't hip to believe in anything, but Texas demanded a religious loyalty. All of the clubs, schools, and even doctors' offices had a check box for religion. And Judaism wasn't even on it. Once, when Mary was waiting for Austin at the pediatricians, she had to check off a box stating her religion. The choices were limited to Catholic, Protestant, Lutheran, Baptist, Methodist, Presbyterian and Other. Mary was so shocked by the audacity of the question, she checked Other in defiance. But she was 100% Catholic and wanted to raise her daughters that way. It was one of the few things she held onto from her childhood and even though her belief was lost, it didn't mean it couldn't be found again. And, suddenly, she was determined to keep it up. She wanted to raise her daughters as Catholics since as far as she could tell, they were both leaning towards Atheism. That's what Catholic schools were for she decided. They could indoctrinate her children so she didn't have to.

She put a bit of spit on a handkerchief and wiped off the miniature wooden Jesus who was stretched out on the cross. He did not look happy. Poor guy, he died so young. Mary shuddered, realizing Jesus had died at thirty-three. She had just turned thirty-three. Well, that's just great she thought as she plopped down on the bed and stretched out, spreading her hands like the savior. The Son of God had died at thirty-three making a solid name for Himself, a real contribution to the world. She had barely done anything.

It was time for a change. She would reinvent the Womyn Warriors and earn the company, and herself, the necessary fame. First, she would need to work on a new piece. Mary swung her legs off the bed and went over to the small Secretary desk in the corner of the room. She pulled out a few pieces of matte white paper, determined to write a spoken word dance piece on religion. She would start with a bunch of hypocritical church going ladies in their Sunday finest with their pantyhose pulled up, clutching their white latticed pocketbooks in one hand and their beloved bibles in the other and then—

"Mom!" Carolina's cry pierced through the air.

Mary braced herself. Within seconds, Carolina came storming into the room, followed by a recalcitrant Austin.

"What is it this time?" Mary looked at her daughters.

"She took my Cabbage Patch doll," Carolina accused.

"Did not."

"Did too."

"Girls," Mary said.

"She's my doll too," Austin insisted.

"Only during the day," Carolina said. "You get her from breakfast to dinner and I get her from dinner to breakfast. It's after dinner and she's mine."

"I didn't take her."

"Yes you did."

"Time out." Mary got up from the desk. She wouldn't be getting to work on her next big idea any time soon.

"Austin, why would Carolina say you took Judy?"

"Julie, Mother," Carolina corrected her. "Her name is not Judy, it's Julie. Julie McCoy. Geez."

"Right. Sorry. Julie." Mary tried to stifle a giggle. Carolina should have grown out of the doll stage already, but Julie was like Linus's blanket to Carolina. She couldn't sleep without her. "When's the last time you saw her."

"I don't know, Mother. She's not my responsibility during the day." Carolina rolled her eyes and left the room. Mary watched her daughter flounce away. Carolina would become a teenager next year and Mary was convinced her daughter would then officially hate her. She walked over to Austin and studied her defiant face.

"You know where she is, don't you?"

Austin looked down at the floor and nodded.

"Okay. If you don't want to tell me, maybe you can show me," Mary said gently and held out her hand. Austin put her small hand into it and led her mother out the front door, down the outside steps of their second floor apartment and to the playground in the back of the complex. She pulled Mary past the swing sets and the slide to the sandbox where a cherubic doll's head was peeking out from under the sand.

"You buried her?" Mary looked at her small daughter incredulously.

"She can still breathe," Austin said. "I didn't mean to do it. I just kind of started and couldn't stop. And now I can't get her out." Austin proved her point by tugging on the doll's ropey ponytail to no avail.

"Hold on," Mary said. "You stand guard, I'll get supplies." Mary rushed back upstairs, past Carolina who was already curled up on the couch, engrossed in *Mork and Mindy*. Mary went to the closet where she pulled out a small shovel.

"What are you doing?" Carolina asked.

"Educating," Mary replied before leaving again. She returned to the sandbox and handed the shovel to Austin.

"What are you doing?"

"Giving you a tool to fix your problem."

"It's not my problem," Austin said.

"Hmm. Well, that's where I'm afraid we're going to disagree. You made an agreement with Carolina to give her Julie McCoy at night. Right now, it is night and Julie McCoy is still in your possession. You can't break a promise once you make it. Especially to your sister." Mary watched as Austin digested the reasoning.

"I'm too little. You do it," Austin finally said.

"Oh no. You got yourself into this mess, you get yourself out of it." Mary guided the shovel, with Austin's hands attached, towards the sand. "And I'd recommend not coming back upstairs empty-handed." Mary walked away, willing herself not to look back. She climbed the stairs and entered the apartment where she joined Carolina on the couch.

Half an hour later, Austin trudged up the stairs, dirty and tired with a very sandy Julie McCoy clutched in her chubby hand. "Here's your stupid doll." She hurled the cabbage patch at Carolina and ran to her room, sobbing.

"Mother. She had her all along. You have to punish her," Carolina said as she stripped down her beloved doll, trying to get out all of the sand from her crevices.

"I'm pretty sure she's already been punished enough." Mary smiled and turned her attention towards the television. That Robin Williams was a talented man. She grimaced. He was four years younger than she was. Between Robin Williams and Jesus, Mary felt like the least talented person on the planet. At least, as far as she knew, Jesus had never married ... or had children.

And those were arenas in which Mary could continue to explore her potential.

July 1980
Dallas, Texas

Dear Daughters,

Let's hope three's the charm!

It was the wedding of the century, at least my century. Sully pulled out all the stops and gave me everything I wanted: the dress, the venue, the flowers. It was a fairytale wedding and I got to play the part of the princess. It's amazing how fast and how easily I transitioned from pauper to princess. My wedding bouquet was filled with vibrant pink Crape Myrtle and it was enormous. So was my dress; enormous, not vibrant pink. And the Jessica McClintock dress needed two of my dancers to carry the train. Of course, I was hiding a tiny baby bump ... so there was loads of extra material swathed in there. But more on that later. Speaking of flowers, they were everywhere at the Joule ... the swanky hotel where the three hundred and fifty person wedding extravaganza took place. Now, I personally know maybe thirty people, mostly my dancers and my ex-husbands ... but Sully has a huge family with ancient aunts and balding uncles up the wazoo. Plus, with his business contacts, there were about a hundred Texas bigwigs whom he felt obligated to invite.

Since we didn't want to exclude anyone, we invited everyone.

We practically rented out the entire hotel, which you girls loved ... especially because they had a huge pool and you swam right up until the wedding. Well, Austin swam, Carolina you wanted to have your hair and makeup done with me. Austin, my little tomboy, you just pulled yours back into a wet ponytail and went au natural. That's my girl. Carolina, you were promoted from flower girl at my last wedding to maid of honor at this wedding and you did your duty marvelously. Tall and graceful, you took attention away from the bride, but I didn't mind. And this time it was you who was wearing the Carolina blue. You all were. Austin, my little rebel, since you refused to stand next to your sister, you were bridesmaid number three ... instead of two. It was a sight to see ... Carolina in the first position, then your zaftig Aunt Shoshanah ... yes, I realize it's weird that Mort's sister and I stayed friends but I really love the fat old broad ... and then my Austin. Two children flanking a 250 pound Rubenesque butterball. It was nothing if not comical. And although I didn't have The Band perform, Sully got me REO Speedwagon who is the new big thing. As I walked down the aisle, they performed *Keep on Loving You.* It was an enormous affair with half of Dallas society coming out to witness the spectacle.

So, I married Sully four months ago, and I'm never planning to divorce him. He is everything I want in a man. Well hung, well preserved, well educated, and he owns wells. Many, many oil wells. And clearly, from the amount of crisp hundred dollar bills his business associates kept handing me at the reception, he does very well. It literally felt like a scene out of The Godfather, with people handing me stuffed envelopes. I should have brought a bigger purse. But money is just one plus to Sully, who has many wonderful traits including very promising daddy potential. He spoils you girls rotten. Carolina you talked about going to basketball camp and he got you one-on-one coaching with a Dallas Maverick. A real professional basketball player! He and Brad Davis play golf together, so Sully convinced him to come over to the house and give you some pointers. You were in heaven. And Austin, when you wanted to go to

Howard Zinn's book signing for *A People's History of the United States* (seriously, what ten-year-old wants that?), Sully set it up. He wants to make me happy and he knows that when my girls are happy, I'm happy.

Money is lovely girls, especially when there's love to go with it. And I love my Sully. He's everything Mort wasn't...which means he treats me like I am a goddess. He properly adores me and lets me know that I am the most important person in his life. I am special. You should always be special, girls. You should always be adored. And Sully adores me. Oh, and did I mention he's loaded? Maybe that makes me shallow, maybe I am. But after living like a pauper with Mort, I am going to enjoy being filthy rich.

I promised you a pool and we have a pool. Of course, every mansion on the block has a pool...but not every person in the world has a mansion. We do! We have a mansion. And you each have your own room! Carolina, you're thrilled with the space, especially after the crowded walk-up in the West Village where you shared the pullout couch. I think your bedroom is bigger than our entire West Village apartment. You jumped three economic brackets in one move. Thanks to my Sully. Think of the biggest mansion you've ever seen. For me, it's Hugo Drax's mansion in Moonraker. Guess what girls? Sully's is bigger. Which means your home is more impressive than the home of a James Bond villain. It might not seem like a big deal now, but trust me, after you've seen and appreciated the movie, you'll get it.

Bigger is definitely better.

You girls are thriving here. Carolina, my straight A+ student, you are the captain of every team and president of every club; you have so many friends. Every week you're sleeping over at someone else's house: You are extremely popular. And Austin, you're quite the athlete...already the star of your soccer team and you've started to write some good poetry. I may even incorporate one of your poems into my next dance. Since leaving Mort, I haven't been as creatively inspired. I hate to say it but I'm inspired by pain and since meeting Sully, my life has been devoid of pain. Not that I'm complaining. It's so nice to finally be happy. Creatively constipated, but happy. But my Austin, my serious girl, you can mine creativity from anywhere...you are just that talented. And I promise that you will have your first professional writing gig before you reach your teens. Because somehow, even as a kid, you know how to tap into your inner angst. Whereas I am feeling nothing but joy...speaking of which...

The absolutely best gift Sully's given me is my Dallas. I am seven months pregnant with you, baby girl, and you have been nothing but perfect. My easiest pregnancy yet. Sometimes when I sit at our baby grand, and play for you, I can actually feel you dancing in my belly. Sully is your daddy, baby girl. Mr. Sullivan P. Vanderline III. Not quite sure who one and two are, but my Sully's number three.

There's a new show on television called *Dallas* and I swear it could be about Sully. I love the show so much. It's about JR and Sue Ellen Ewing and the soap opera of their lives. I watch it religiously and I'm going to name you Dallas Sue Ellen Baxter...maybe you'll be an actress or some sort of performer. There is show business in your blood, my darling.

Austin, I know you still want Mort and me to get back together. It's not going to happen. He's a good man, but not a good husband. We are better friends than lovers. I even invited him to the wedding, but he's working the campaign trail. Believe it or not, he jumped political ship, hopping from Carter's posse to Ronald Reagan...yes, the actor. An actor is actually running for President. Like that could ever happen. Ha. Mort is a good reporter and a great father and, admittedly, he's probably still my best friend... but I'm with Sully now, so you have to respect Mama's need to be happy.

I love you Carolina, Austin and, in utero, Dallas,
Mom

Fourteen

Austin's visits to her father were rare.

She and Mort were so similar, that sometimes when she was with her dad, Austin felt the uncomfortable feeling of having to look too closely into herself. A mirror that showed not only the external features but the flaws, inadequacies and limitations beneath the surface. And she hated it. But her mother had given her the ultimatum a week earlier and Austin didn't have anyone else to turn to.

Weaving her way through the stream of college students crowding the English department hallway of NYU, Austin spied her father's old wooden door which sported a neat metal sign: Professor Mort Stone Horowitz. Journalism. She knocked twice before a gruff voice called from the other side, "Be with you in a minute."

Ignoring her father, Austin opened the door to find a slight blonde buttoning up her powder blue oxford shirt.

"Shit," the blonde said. Neither Austin nor her father spoke.

The girl's cheeks turned red as she gathered her backpack. "I'll, um, look into that research, Professor Horowitz," she mumbled as she ran out of the room.

"Ah, research," Austin repeated, shutting the door behind the fleeing girl. "She's younger than your usuals, Dad."

"It's good to see you too." Mort ignored the dig and hugged Austin. "To what do I owe the honor, favorite daughter?"

"Only daughter." Austin smiled. It was their running gag. She smelled the wafting scent of vanilla on her Dad's corduroy blazer. Probably belonged to the girl. Mort usually smelled of licorice and whisky. She looked around the messy office. Stacks of papers filled the room from floor to ceiling. There were worn books, newspapers and pictures everywhere. When she was little, she used to study the pictures carefully, fascinated that her father had interviewed some of the world's most influential politicos. She knew those pictures by heart: Gaddafi, Princess Di, Ronald Reagan, Margaret Thatcher, Anwar Sadat. The list went on and on.

"You want to get lunch? Some falafel, maybe?"

"I hate falafel." Austin wondered if her dad missed being in the field. Probably.

"You were always a picky eater."

"How would you know?" Austin shot back. She immediately felt bad, but she couldn't help being snarky. Mort often put her in that position.

Mort looked at her for a moment, weighing his answer. "Your mother told me."

"It's a convenient way of parenting, isn't it? Report cards, periods, proms. You got all the pivotal points of my adolescence via phone ... or snail mail."

"Did you come here to talk about your mom, or about you?"

"Is there a difference?" Austin was pissed off.

Mort sat down. "You're here. Talk to me ... Austin."

Her mother had just given her a disturbing ultimatum and Austin didn't know where to begin.

"Did she talk to you about what she wants?" Austin began.

"Yes." Mort reached into his bottom drawer and pulled out a bottle of Highland Park Whisky. A fairly frugal man, Mort splurged on scotch and the thirty-year-old single malt was his favorite. A bottle cost him $300, but he didn't care. He skimped in other areas... like falafel lunches from a street vendor for three dollars. Mort held out the bottle towards Austin, but she shook her head. He poured the amber liquid into a heavy tumbler on his desk and drank a long shot before giving Austin his full attention.

"It's illegal," Austin said.

"Some laws are meant to be broken." Mort sighed as he poured himself another shot. "Why hasn't your mother told any of your sisters that she's sick?" He watched his daughter try to answer him. She couldn't. "Why hasn't she let you tell them?"

Austin had no idea why Mary had laid the burden solely on her. She would have loved to talk to someone, to get advice. But she only had Mort.

"It's because she wants them to remember her the way she was; strong, vibrant, a force of nature," Mort said earnestly.

"But she told you."

"Austin, I'm her best friend. See, that's what none of you girls ever understood. You all competed for her love, but... Mary didn't need kids to be complete, she needed companionship."

"Why didn't you stay married?" Austin, like her sisters, wished her father had stayed. But Mary had traded him in.

"She said life is too short to spend with one person."

"Dad," Austin pleaded, "I can't do this.

"You can."

"Freud would have a field day with this situation."

"I'm proud of you, Austin."

"Right. I thought parents were supposed to protect their kids."

"You're not a child anymore."

"I never was." Austin stood up to go. Her father was not giving her what she needed. She felt like she was going to explode and she didn't want her father to see her so vulnerable.

Mort jumped up and stopped her, grabbing her hand. "I don't want to fight."

"You're complicit in this too."

"She asked you."

"You're a coward." Austin pulled away from her father. She had had enough.

"She asked you for a reason. There are some people who believe that only God is allowed to take away a life."

Austin stood at the door wanting to leave; yet, unable to. "Do you believe in God?"

"Yes," Mort said. "Do you?"

"Does it matter?" Austin couldn't face her father.

"It matters. Do you believe in God?" he repeated.

"I am not going to have a philosophical argument."

"Philosophical?"

"What?" Austin turned back towards her father.

"You just said philosophical. If you believed in God wouldn't you have said theological?" Mort then asked for the third time, "Do you believe in God?"

"No."

Mort looked at his daughter with a heavy heart. "Then she picked the right person."

July 1982
Dallas, Texas

Dear Daughters,

If there is a god, and I'm not claiming that there is, but if there is a god then why did he make the male species so flawed? You note that I am not capitalizing the letter g in my perpetual indecision about the presence of the great lord almighty despite our weekly attendance at Father Brennan's Mass – and yes I realize that our priest has the same name as the priest in *The Omen*, Austin you were quick to point that out... although I think you're still a bit young to see films like that. I didn't see my first R rated film until I was fifteen. But I digress; I was talking about god's decision to make men so ignorant.

A man is in the White House and is refusing to mention the word AIDS. A health crisis is developing and our leader is staying silent. Two of my dancers are sick and the government is doing nothing to make people aware of this deadly disease. Carter may have sucked as a President, but Reagan blows. Why is he refusing to mention the word? What is he so afraid of? If a woman were in office, she'd be attacking this disease head on. But our country is not ready for that kind of power.

I like men, hell I love men, but they are all... as Miss Tillie used to say... certifiable schmucks. And, yes, an old Black woman using the word schmuck is a sight to behold. I suppose what makes the men I've consorted with in my life worthwhile is that they gave me you three, my beloved daughters. My remarkable women. I don't know what I would have done if I had sons. I don't think I would have capably raised them like I am raising you girls, to be capable. To be extraordinary.

Austin, you never cease to amaze me with your strength and determination. You may be the strongest woman I know and you're still just a little girl. I guess Mort, even though the man drives me crazy, did something quite wonderful by giving me you. You are creative, like me, and I know you're going to make an impact on this world. A lasting and important impact.

Carolina, you are stunning. A natural born leader with a photographic memory. You are stubborn and opinionated and you could be president if you wanted to. Carolina Tillie Baxter. Yes, it definitely has a distinguished presidential ring. And of all the people I've ever met in my life, you probably have the best shot at the oval office. Hell, if an actor who refuses to mention the word AIDS can do it, so can you. You are the most by-the-book person I've ever met. No skeletons in your closet, darling. Shoot for the stars, you'll make it.

Dallas, my beautiful Dallas, you are the sweetest child in the world. You love wearing pink bows. You make me tie them in your pigtails every day. And you put them on your little dolls. And since I'm no longer below the poverty level, I can afford to give you your own doll ... and plenty of them. Prince William was just born in England ... and because you are my little princess maybe I'll just have to make a match for you. I know, that's not very feminist of me, planning an arranged marriage for my baby, but just imagine it, a real life princess! You personify the word good. You are a good girl. A good person and whatever you decide to do in your life, I guarantee that you will be good at it.

Speaking of good and flawed, Sully is a good father but a flawed man. Mostly due to his excessive drinking.

Oftentimes, he has one too many bourbons after work. These Texans take their drink very seriously. When I was in Scotland for the Edinburgh Fringe Festival, I saw some heavy drinking. Everyone there has doughy faces with red noses, from the drink. But they have nothing on my Sully. His home bar takes up half of a football field and he is his own best customer. He tells me that he needs a drink at the end of the day to unwind. Sure, who doesn't need a drink. But three? Four? Come on. I understand that his work is very important. He's in oil ... which is also his favorite subject and he talks about it ad nauseum. To be honest, there's only so much interest I can feign in oil.

A side effect of the excessive liquor is that we don't have sex as much as we used to. Sex with Sully was amazing. I miss it. Sometimes I'd send you kids to Mort's or Roger's for a vacation, just so Sully and I could indulge in a week of decadence. You two would be enjoying new experiences either seeing shows in New York City or hiking off the coast of Washington while Sully and I would be indulging in our own adventures. Oh, the sexual thrills we used to have. He would leave me begging for more. Begging. Now, we rarely have sex. I read somewhere that too much liquor slows down the blood rush from the heart to the penis. Maybe that's it. Or maybe he's bored and I'm not a shiny new thing anymore. Hell, I'm thirty-five. That's old.

John Belushi just died. He was thirty-three ... like Jesus. Three years older than Sylvia Plath and three years younger than Marilyn Monroe. The blonde bombshell died at thirty-six and look at how much she accomplished. She was a sex symbol, a movie star and a bombshell. I'm just a bombshell. A bombshell who wants another baby. I worry that I'm getting too old to have one. Plus the chances of having a baby with Down Syndrome after thirty-five are five times greater than when I had you, Carolina. I've memorized the statistics. But I'll throw caution to the wind. I really want another daughter... I'm just not convinced Sully is the man I want to father the baby.

I want to have sex, but I also want to stay faithful to my husband. Roger and Mort may not have taken the marital vows seriously, but I always did. And I know Sully does too. He's a Republican for god's sake. A real Reaganite. Hey, maybe I do believe in god if I can use expressions like god's sake. Anyway, because I have all of this pent up frustration, sometimes I feel like a ticking time bomb about to explode. Sometimes, I take my anger out on you kids. Oh, I don't hit you, I would never do that, but I do yell... a lot. And I'm sorry. I'll try to control myself. I'll try to be better. But sometimes it's hard.

Remember, no matter what...

I love you Carolina, Austin and Dallas,
Mom

Fifteen

Austin laid down her tiles. Tick. Tick. Tick. She added pop onto corn, using the P on a triple letter space to also spell Pi. Twenty-nine points. As she laid down each tile, it sounded like a precursor to a bomb exploding. Tick. Tick. Tick. She knew that any trigger could detonate her pent up anger and she wanted to release it when she was ready. She needed to diffuse her tension. She looked at Dallas. "I think I figured out why Ilsa gets on the plane."

"She really loves Laszlo?"

"No. In the end, being left behind really sucks."

Dallas rested her hand on Austin's arm. "You can always come stay with me, you know. Me and Peter. If you don't want to be alone."

"Really?"

"Of course, we're family," Dallas offered, her smile belying the fear that Austin would actually take her up on the offer. The last thing Dallas needed was another person to babysit.

"I'm okay here," Austin said, surprised by the comfort she felt from her sister's touch.

"Really? Isn't it just a little, morbid…I mean, staying where you shouldn't."

"Why shouldn't I?"

"I dunno. I mean, without Mom, it's not really a home."

"Right." Any form of comfort was immediately gone and Austin felt herself going in for the kill. "The way our mansion in Dallas wouldn't have been a home without her?" Austin jumped up from the table. She needed to control her rage. Tick. Tick. Tick.

"What are you talking about?"

"When we left Sully, you didn't talk to any of us for a year. You blamed everyone for Mom leaving your dad. But things weren't great, you just whitewashed them, like you always do."

"Austin," Carolina warned, but Austin couldn't stop.

"When it comes to your childhood, Dallas, you've created a complete revisionist history." Austin didn't know what she was doing. Her sister was too easy of a target, it seemed almost unfair to pick on her, but Austin couldn't help herself, she just felt like she was always in attack mode these days.

"My father was a good man," Dallas insisted.

"Sure, they all were."

"Why are you picking on her?" Carolina asked.

"Boy do I love these trips down memory lane," Baltimore muttered. "Especially when I'm not a part of the memory. Jesus, I need a cigarette." She looked at Carolina pleadingly.

"I told you I don't have any." Carolina turned to Austin. "Why are you picking on Dallas, she didn't do anything."

"You'd prefer I pick on you?" Austin sneered.

"At least I can defend myself."

"Hey," Dallas exclaimed, "I can defend myself. Don't talk to me like I'm not here."

Austin looked at Baltimore. "More pot?"

"Yes, please."

Carolina shook her head. "It's illegal, you know."

"Some laws are meant to be broken." Austin smiled cruelly. "And I bet you fifty bucks there are two packs of unopened cigarettes in your overpriced purse."

"Can we please not do this," Dallas begged.

"I said I was out," Carolina insisted.

"Or maybe you're just not good at sharing." Austin grabbed Carolina's purse before her sister could protest. "One hundred dollars. I'll even throw in the brand. American Spirit. I bet you tried to quit but you couldn't, so you figured hey, I'll smoke the 'healthy' version of impending death."

Baltimore grabbed the purse from Austin and rummaged inside. She pulled out a pack of American Spirit cigarettes. "Oh my god—you lied to me."

"I'm trying to concentrate," Dallas said as she arranged her Scrabble tiles over and over again to no avail.

"Give me those." Carolina grabbed the cigarettes back from Baltimore and glared at Austin who finished rolling her joint. "So cliché."

"You want to know what's so cliché?" Austin said after taking a long toke and handing the joint to Baltimore. "Lonely workaholics who fill the vacuous void in their life by digesting smoke instead of meals."

"At least I stay in the game."

"What is that supposed to mean?"

"I work," Carolina said emphatically. "I work hard and I succeed. What are you planning to do, Austin? Live off the royalties from your one book for the rest of your life?"

"Absolutely." Austin felt like a caged tiger. She paced, unable to stay still and ready to attack anything or anyone who came near her.

Carolina lit up a cigarette and laid into Austin. The litigator at her best, refusing to let up. "How come you moved back home? Why haven't you written a book in the last five years? You're still riding on those laurels?"

"As long as I can. That's what makes me an artist."

"Where's the follow up?"

"In my head. Tucked away neatly."

"Bullshit. You need to prioritize. Make time for the important things."

"Right, Carol…ina, because you know so much about that."

Carolina glared at her sister. She knew exactly what she was referring to and she also knew that she was at fault. But she refused to apologize. In order to succeed as a woman in a man's world one had to make sacrifices. And the night of Austin's Seattle book signing was one of those times. Carolina had been determined to make the signing. She missed the big launch in New York City because she was helping Matthew with a deposition, but she had no excuses for this one. She told Old Man Schaefer that she needed to leave by seven to make her sister's book signing and he had no problem with it; yet, the night of the signing there had been a last minute work session which Carolina couldn't get out of. Well, maybe she could have, but she didn't want to. She was trying to make senior partner and she wanted to do everything she could to ensure her future. After the work session, Carolina raced over to Left Bank Books; yet, the signing was over. Everyone had gone home. But at least she had tried. She had made the effort.

Austin remembered the evening differently.

March 1983
Dallas, TX

Dear Daughters,

Let me tell you something about trust, respect, loyalty and love. There is none when it comes to men. I trusted Sully. With all of my heart, I trusted my husband. He was different from Mort. He was different from Roger. He said he would never lie to me and, in turn, I knew I would never lie to him. With that one statement, "I will never lie to you," I knew I was finally safe. I was in a relationship where I was protected, where I didn't have to put up my usual protective shield, where I could let down my ever present guard. Where I could just be me. Finally be me.

I guess *just me* wasn't enough for Sully.

I'd fallen so deeply in love with him and he ripped that love away. My girls, I can't eat, I can't sleep. I know it's fresh and raw and I'm sure time will heal my battered heart. I will not get into the fact of who he fell in love with (the fucking cow Donna Luiso). But that bastard lied to me. The joke is, he used to mock Mort for all of his deception and lies, but he ended up doing the same thing. He fell in love with someone behind my back... why?

Girls, when a man stops having sex with you, there is a good goddamn reason for it. And it isn't 'work.' It isn't because he's too drunk or too tired. It's because he has found a younger, shinier, prettier version of you. When I demanded an explanation, he said, "It just happened."

Bullshit, things don't "just happen."

Donna was Sully's secretary. It really can't get more cliché than that... oh, yes it can, the babysitter, although Mort has the monopoly on that one. It's inevitable, I suppose, that men fall in love with their secretaries. One, because of the proximity. That short skirt is fairly easy to hike up when it's just a desk away. Two, because of the status. A secretary is a paid worker, which immediately gives the boss a higher status. It makes him feel strong, powerful, virile. Three, because Donna Luiso is a gold digging peroxide blonde whore who wears fake colored bright blue contact lenses and had the patience to wait just the right amount of time until Sully was feeling vulnerable enough for her to make her move. See, I never blame the men in these situations. They are idiots who think with their cocks. They are weak. But as women, we are strong and manipulative. We know how to hook a man if we want. Again, sex is one thing... but love. The bastard actually thinks he loves her. That will last two minutes, but when those two minutes are over I will be gone. I'm tired of this shit.

Why are women so cruel to each other? There would be more women in the Senate and House of Representatives if we didn't spend so much time afraid of each other's power. If we didn't spend so much time sleeping with each other's men. Why can't women band together and celebrate each other's force? Why are we so hell bent on destroying each other and undermining our collective strength? We are fucking with the wrong gender. It makes absolutely no sense.

I thought Sully loved me as much as I loved him. I can forgive him for the excessive drinking. I can even forgive him for the whore Donna Luiso as I'm pretty confident that men were born to whip out their dicks the second they see an adoring young thing. What I cannot forgive him for is the lying. Because he promised... he swore he would never lie to me.

He has broken me.

I feel like everything in my life is falling apart ... except for you girls. Why does life move in cycles like this? When did I become so jealous? Why am I not living the life I'm supposed to be living? When did I start letting other people make me so sad? I'm a hypocrite, I know. I occasionally fuck someone else; yet, don't want him to. I guess I don't mind Sully having sex with others, since I don't seem to satisfy him (which is ironic, because I am horny all of the time AND desperate for sex, which is why I now have to go elsewhere because he won't fuck me). I think it's because I've ALWAYS been clear with my paramours that I love Sully and won't leave him, but Sully jumps into a fantasy world, with children ... LITERALLY girls half his age ... Donna Luiso ... it's gross. Maybe it makes him feel younger, maybe he likes being the cliché daddy figure ... but the fact that he pretends to them like I don't exist ... well ... it makes me nauseous. If I left him, he'd be sad. He'd be alone, but maybe he'd prefer that. Who the fuck knows? Like a true repressed Republican, he refuses to ever TALK about anything that is on his mind. He's just repeating patterns. I feel nauseous. It's like Mort all over again, why aren't we enough for each other? Why do I need more? Because he does? Or because I do? What am I going to do?

I need a seismic shift in my life. A good one. I don't want anyone to die, but I want ... I want ... I want to be happy. I want to be loved. Does Sully love me ... enough? I guess that's the real question. I'd rather him cheat on me and me know about it. He needs the feeling of the chase like I need coffee.

Am I an enabler or an idiot because I keep falling for the same mold of man? Instead of building us ... Sully's building himself. And I get the worst of him, the tired, inebriated, whining Sully ... he saves the best for others ... and that's not fair ... that simply makes me seem like a moron for staying.

I'm not making the same mistake I did with Mort. I'm not waiting seven years to make a definitive decision. We're waiting til the school year's over and we're getting the hell out. Yes, Carolina I realize, yet again, you are class president and yet again I will be ruining your life by uprooting you. One day, you'll thank me. Let's be honest, you were not meant to be debutantes...you are three smart, vibrant young ladies who are not meant to be repressed members of the Junior League. You are meant to be more than ladies who lunch. You are all destined for extraordinary adventures. Like Sally Ride. She's the first American woman to make it to space. Imagine that. We're breaking every glass ceiling there is. Sally Ride. Isn't that just a perfect name for an astronaut? Maybe I'll name my next daughter Sally. Anyway, I'll have enough money from the divorce that I, that we, can live anywhere in the world. And I know exactly where I want to go. We'll road trip back east and see what mischief we can get in along the way. I'll even take you to Hershey Park. Our final destination will be the blue house on Money Island. We love that place, it's probably more our home than any of the others...we've spent every summer there since Carolina was a little girl. Fourteen summers.

We don't need men, girls. We just need a roof over our head and a room of our own where we can create. Okay, I stole the last bit from Virginia Woolf, but if you're going to steal, steal from the best and Woolf and Plath and Dorothy Parker are the best for me.

I've written my tenth and final commandment: Whether you fall in love or lust, don't you ever, ever trust. Trust each other girls, count on each other girls, because men will always let you down.

In the future, I will use men for my own enjoyment. I will fuck them, suck them, allow them to take me every which way since Friday. They can wine me, dine me, seduce me, woo me and satisfy me, however, I will never ever count on them. I will never trust them.

And I will never ever marry again.

I love you Carolina, Austin and Dallas,
Mom

Sixteen

Austin had only been to Seattle once before. She was nine and she and Carolina had visited Carolina's dad for two weeks on Orcas Island. The girls had flown into Seattle, where Roger picked them up and drove them to the coast. Austin didn't remember too much about the trip, they did a lot of hiking and swimming, but she didn't understand Carolina's father's strict, military precision. There were rules for everything and, even as a nine-year-old, that wasn't the way Austin rolled. Twenty-five years later, she didn't recognize anything. Her media escort picked her up at Sea-Tac airport and drove her directly to the gig.

Ever since her book had leapfrogged to the top of the *New York Times* Best Seller list, Austin had been on the move. Random House wasn't sure if they were going to take a risk on her; yet, once the big sales numbers started coming in, they went into overdrive to organize Austin's book tour. Both Janis Stein and the in-house publicist, Bernice Addison, worked together to pull off a twenty city tour. Austin was nearing the end of the tour and couldn't think straight. She had been in too many airports to count, eating too many forgettable sandwiches on the run, enduring onerous conversations with nameless book escorts taking her to and from her gigs. All of the hotels blended into one and her hand was numb from signing so many copies of the book.

Despite her exhaustion, Austin was excited about her signing at Left Bank Books. She hadn't seen Carolina in quite some time and was looking forward to reconnecting with her sister. It was all arranged for Carolina to come to the signing and then they would go out to dinner. Austin would expense it and show her older sister that she too was a big success.

Yet, as Austin watched the crowd pouring out of the rain into the store for the event, there was no sign of her sister. It was almost seven and Carolina, with her almost obsessively chronic need to be on time, was absent. Austin pulled out her cell and dialed, just as the store clerk approached her.

"Miss Baxter, we're about ready to—"

Austin waved her off as she listened to the ringing on the other end of the line. Finally, when Carolina's voicemail message played, Austin hung up.

"Let's give it five more minutes," Austin said, eyeing the crowd who had now filled the small reading area to capacity. There were approximately a hundred black metal folding chairs. All occupied, save the one in the front row that had a Reserved sign on it. Carolina's chair.

Austin turned towards the store entrance, in time to see a small figure fighting with the door. The wind had knocked off her hat and her yellow anorak was soaked. The slight woman finally won her war with the door and bounded in, clutching a plastic grocery bag to her chest. She came up to Austin and the store clerk.

"Excuse me, is this the signing for *Pandora's Box*?"

Austin chuckled. The girl, despite the fact that her black hair was plastered to her caramel skin, was stunning. Her dark eyes sparkled and there was a vibrancy in her voice that excited Austin. She felt something stir inside of her that she hadn't felt since she met her college girlfriend.

"It is." Austin smiled as she nodded to the placard behind her. It showed a picture of Austin with the words: "*New York Times* Bestselling author Austin Baxter reads excerpts from 'KEYS TO PANDORA'S BOX'."

The girl looked from Austin to the sign and back to Austin.

"Oh my god, you're—" The girl was speechless.

"I am," Austin teased. "But I'm afraid I'm at a loss, because I don't know who you are."

"Oh, sorry. I mean, I'm Sarah. Sarah Garcia." Sarah awkwardly opened the plastic bag, revealing a well worn copy of Austin's book. "I've read *Pandora's Box* three times. It's absolutely brilliant. I'm a huge fan." Sarah blushed. The chemistry between the women was palpable.

"Thank you Sarah Garcia." Austin led her to the front of the room. "I must have known such a huge fan was coming, I saved you a seat." Austin stopped in front of the reserved chair and tore up the sign.

"How can I ever thank you?" Sarah flirted.

"You can take me out to dinner after the signing," Austin said boldly before turning around and taking her place at the lectern.

"I should call 911 again." Carolina's voice jolted Austin out of her reverie.

"You were supposed to be there," Austin said.

"I had to work."

"So you chose work over me."

"It was important," Carolina insisted.

"So was my reading."

"It was five years ago, can you let it go?"

"You could have at least called."

"You could have at least stayed," Carolina shot back. "I came by when I was finished. We were supposed to have dinner."

"I got a better offer," Austin snapped.

"Will you guys just leave it alone," Dallas screamed and stormed out of the room.

This was a toxic environment and she needed somewhere quiet to breathe.

January 1984
Baltimore, Maryland

Dear Daughters,

I'm getting married again.

And I found a way to get that bastard Sully out of my system. His name is Reggie.

The day your school ended, as promised, we packed up the car and left Sully. He begged us not to leave and was markedly contrite, but when I make up my mind to do something, there is no turning back. You have to have courage to get what you want, especially when the unknown is scarier than the familiar.

Leap and the net will appear.

Gotta see where the wind takes us. We took a long road trip across the States. You kids were so excited to see the sights and we hit them all, from giant balls of twine to Elvis's birthplace. We were snaking our way up the East Coast after hitting every amusement park from Disney World to Six Flags – yes, I am the perfect mother – when we stopped in Baltimore. It was just supposed to be an overnight stay, I mean, what is there to do in Baltimore other than see the Inner Harbor and have some Maryland crabs? It was just going to be a quick in and out between visiting the monuments in D.C. and heading up to Philadelphia to see the Liberty Bell. I didn't even choose a nice hotel and Sully's money has allowed us to stay at five star hotels. We just pulled off the interstate to the first blinking orange sign.

I suppose this is where fate intervened.

So, we were staying at a crappy little Howard Johnson's in some small town off of I-95 called Pikesville and the room was tiny. Despite being a part of a hotel chain, the one story hotel was also mildly creepy, think *Psycho* complete with an Anthony Perkins-like hotel manager. After ten minutes, we were all feeling a bit of cabin fever, especially after being cooped up in the station wagon, so I wanted to take you girls to the pool, but it was too late. The sign said it was closed. Who closes a pool at nine o'clock? Against Carolina's protestations we went anyway. I mean, what's the worst that can happen? We get yelled at by some pimply-faced assistant manager making minimum wage? Or knifed to death by Norman Bates? Okay, I admittedly sometimes let my imagination get the best of me. Anyway, we had the entire pool to ourselves and we swam for half an hour. My little Dallas, it's the first time you let go of me in the water and doggie paddled all by yourself. Imagine, you had your own pool in Texas and you officially learn to swim at a Howard Johnson's pool in Baltimore. Delicious irony. Anyway, after all that swimming, we worked up an appetite. So, we got a bite to eat at the jazz club next door. Carolina, you were very eloquent in listing the reasons why it was an 'inappropriate' place to bring children; however, I believe it's never too early to get an appreciation for Charlie Mingus. He had ALS. What a waste. He was such a gifted musician. Speaking of gifted musicians... let's talk about Reggie White, the delicious crooner who seduced me with the first note out of his mouth that night.

We sat at a red leather booth near the band and you girls all had grilled cheese sandwiches. I had a dirty martini, but I literally could not even take a sip I was so smitten by Reggie. He sat at the baby grand playing jazz like he was born to play. His fingers moved so fluidly. I loved Roger's hands, but Reggie's fingers were... extraordinary. Long, smooth and facile. His entire body was spectacular. Roger was handsome, Mort was distinguished, Sully was rich but

Reggie was ... extraordinary. The minute I saw him I knew I wanted him. And I definitely wanted a baby with his DNA. Have I mentioned how good looking and talented he is? Tall, dark and handsome; my own Luther Vandross.

We're getting married tomorrow.

Okay, okay, I know what I said about never marrying again, but it's a woman's prerogative to change her mind. Plus Reggie's always on the road. He'll be the perfect husband ... there when I need him, gone when I don't. Your little sister will be born soon and when she is, I promise to finally settle us in the island house. Reggie will come visit us. But I need to put my girls first, don't I? After all, you are my priority. Sometimes it may not seem that way, but I love you. I love all of you.

And I promise, once my little Baltimore Sally Baxter pops out, we are on our way.

I love you Carolina, Austin, Dallas
and (in utero) Baltimore,
Mom

Seventeen

Dallas sat on the toilet and looked towards the tub. The last person in the bathroom had pulled the curtain shut, had it been Baltimore or Austin? Dallas couldn't remember, but she was grateful for the confessional curtain separating her from her mother's corpse.

"Hi," she said tentatively, facing the tub, "it's Dallas. I know I haven't seen you in a while. I'm sorry."

Talking to her mother felt oddly comforting. Dallas regularly confessed her sins. She liked clearing her conscience and easing her mind. She and Peter went to church every Sunday and, as far as she knew, she was the only one of her sisters who kept up the faith.

"Forgive me mother, for I have sinned." Dallas started to laugh. Instead of sitting on a chair talking through a screen to a priest, she was sitting on a toilet talking through a gold vinyl shower curtain peppered with orange and red gerber daisies, to her dead mother. Her laughter quickly turned to tears and she grabbed a pink towel off the floor to cover her mouth and muffle her sobs. She didn't want her sisters to hear her. Finally, she was able to compose herself and she turned back towards the curtain.

"Hail Mary, full of grace. Our Lord is with thee. Blessed art thou among women, and blessed is the fruit of thy womb,

Jesus. Holy Mary, Mother of God, pray for us sinners, now and at the hour of our death. Amen."

She touched the curtain, willing herself to open it. She could not.

"Hail Mary Baxter."

September 2002
The Island House, CT

Dear Daughters,

Baltimore has just left the nest and, for the first time in thirty-five years it's just me. Me and my men. Ha. Seriously, sometimes I feel like this house has a revolving door. I should have a notch for every conquest. Fifty-five and I'm still sexual. Still sensual. More so than I've ever been. Sex gets better with age, why is that? Are we more comfortable with our bodies? God knows. I still look great, a dancer's body after all of these years, but I'm enjoying the small paunch in my belly and the softness in my tush. I feel like a woman instead of a little boy. That's the problem with dancers, we are required to have little boy bodies. Tiny bodies with big heads. Like lollypops. No fat, no fun. I love looking and feeling like a real woman. I feel like I have the libido of a seventeen-year-old.

I think my life is just beginning.

Now that my girls are gone, I'm going to put myself first. Okay, I might have put myself first before a little ... a lot. But you know what they say, when a plane goes down, you have to put the oxygen mask on yourself ... before you put it on your kids. And I needed the oxygen mask to give me enough strength and patience to raise my four girls. So I've spent a lot of time chasing men. So I've spent a lot of time letting men chase me. I think it gave you girls a healthy attitude towards men. Two of you are married already and I know Austin and Baltimore will find their soul mates, somewhere. Remember girls, you will have many loves in your life. Our puritanical society says that we are only supposed to have one soul mate. Well, I have had four ... and each resulted in an extraordinary daughter.

When you go through my letters after I'm dead, which will hopefully be in forty or fifty years after I've retired to Palm Springs and done my last pas des deux, you kids will wonder why there was such a huge gap in my correspondence to you. Maybe, because I was raising four incredibly active girls. Also, with the invention of the Internet, who really writes letters anymore? It's all about the e-mail. Still, you can't really save e-mails in a lavender scented underwear drawer. But I've been just as guilty as the rest of the world, trading in tradition for convenience and emailing instead of writing you letters. I've also been quite busy raising my girls. The last eighteen years can be summed up in five words: delicious chaos mixed with heartbreak.

In other words, life.

I'm no longer artistic director of the Womyn Warriors. Dance is a young woman's game and I am no longer young. Plus, after Wander died, my heart was no longer in it. Fucking Reagan. We lost so many. Keith Haring, Anthony Perkins, Arthur Ash and my lovely Wander. Had we known, had Reagan said something... maybe it could have been prevented. My beautiful friend. You stood by me through it all, all the dancers, the husbands, the children. You were the longest male friendship I ever had. And I miss you like crazy. It was not a pleasant way to go. You were so frail, so uncomfortable, so defenseless. It's not fair. Life isn't fair. Hopefully you are up in heaven, dancing with Nureyev. I love you and I miss you, my friend.

At least, considering the circumstances, Wander died relatively quickly. Remember that girl Karen Ann Quinlan... the one the pollster called me about? Her father pulled the plug in 1976 and she died nine years later. NINE YEARS LATER. I can't imagine what she went through. I can't imagine what her family and her friends went through.

Why preserve a life that is irretrievably lost? Speaking of which, our country is at it again, trying to preserve a life that is irretrievably lost. Terri Schiavo is in a vegetative state and her husband wants to give her death with dignity, but her parents are opposed to it. Which brings me again to the question I asked myself a quarter of a century ago: If I were in a similar situation to Karen Ann Quinlan or Terri Schiavo, who would I want as my Power of Attorney? Back then, it had come down to Wander or Dana... neither of which is an option now. So, I'm left with my four girls. But that's neither here nor there. What's important right now are my girls. You are vibrant and filled with life and adventure and I couldn't be more proud. As I state in my seventh commandment: Be kind, be passionate and be forgiving but above all remember, life is for the living. And you are all living your lives to the fullest. Veni, Vidi, Vici.

Like mother, like daughter(s).

Carolina, you haven't been home much. But you're a big time lawyer with a lovely husband and a fabulous career. You've moved on and I applaud you for your courage. It's hard to leave the safety of the nest and the minute you could fly, you did... clear across the country. I wish you'd come back more often, but I know you're happy with Matthew and that is what is important. He is a good man, Carolina... but remember, good men still stray so keep an eye on him. Encourage him. The minute a man thinks you have achieved more than he has or doesn't need you, he starts to roam. You are such a strong woman Carolina, I just hope he appreciates you for who you are and not for what you are to him. Do you understand?

Austin, you are destined to be the most famous of all of us. Random House just bought your book proposal and it's absolutely brilliant. I appreciate you letting me read it and give you my six cents. Now I know that I was right in insisting that you read all of the classics. George Eliot, Virginia Woolf and Maya Angelou. Gotta study the best to be the best. You've proved that books should be gateways to new worlds, not just pulp. Your professional life is set; now, you just have to find someone to settle down with. Aren't there any nice men in New York?

Dallas, you've just moved in with Peter and are embarking on the heroic profession of teaching. I know it's not as showy as Carolina and Austin's careers, but it is a career nonetheless. Teaching, in my humble opinion, is the most valiant profession one can choose, as you are molding young minds. Shaping young futures. Personally, I think you were good enough to become a concert pianist, but you wanted to settle down. And that is a choice too. God knows I was never settled ... until now. And it's nice. It's nice to grow roots somewhere.

And my little Harvard girl, Baltimore ... you can and will do anything your stubborn mind sets out to do. You are so beautiful, so brave, so funny. I am so proud of you and all that you will do in this world. Life is an empty canvas just waiting for you to paint it: black, blue, red, gold, green ... any color you choose will work. That's just who you are.

As for me, I finally feel settled. Funny, I never felt settled until I came to this house. I understand what it means to nest somewhere. I will die in this house. I really love it. And I love Roger for giving it to me. I suppose I love all of my husbands. No, I don't suppose, I do.

I do love all of my husbands.

But not as much as I love my girls.

I love you Carolina, Austin, Dallas and Baltimore,
Mom

Eighteen

Baltimore kept rearranging her letters. She had an excellent word, but if she was going to win, she wanted to do it with a flourish. She scanned the board to see if there were any better options.

"Time's up." Carolina shook the egg timer, ensuring that every last drop of sand had emptied out.

"Turn it again," Baltimore whined.

"You're not twelve. We're not modifying the rules for you anymore, Miss Harvard." Dallas had just returned from the bathroom and hadn't felt any better. In fact, looking at the scorecard, she just felt frustrated. She was in last place. Her most impressive word had been ROBOT with the B on a double letter and the word on a double score for twenty points. How could she compete with Baltimore and Austin, who played each other on Facebook and knew all the two letter words like KA and EF and QI? Who used words like Qi in every day conversation?

"Fine." Baltimore finally put her letters down. "But I bet I could have done something better." She lifted up each letter as she counted up the points. "That's ten, one, one, one, one, one, double s is two, one, one, one is twenty. Triple word score is sixty. Plus fifty for using all of my letters. That's 110 points. Looks like little Baltimore has taken the lead!"

Austin wrinkled her nose. She had a substantial vocabulary; yet, she'd never heard of the word. "You can't just add erastia onto zoo and count it."

"I can and I did."

"What the hell is zooerastia?"

"You don't want to know. But it's a word."

"I challenge you." Austin jumped up to get a dictionary.

"You'll regret it."

"I still challenge you." Austin found the oversized Webster's dictionary on the bottom shelf of the bookcase, sandwiched between an old set of Encyclopedias and Mary's collection of Jane Austin. She blew off the dust, which had collected on its pages and flipped to the end.

"Fine. Challenge me. Just because zooerastia wasn't in your book, doesn't mean it's not a word."

Austin furiously paged through the Z section, scanning for the word.

"I've never heard of it." Dallas had seven vowels and a B. There was no way she would win this game. She wouldn't even come close.

"It's not a fifth grade word."

"Wow." Carolina made a disgusted face as she found the definition on her phone.

"That's disgusting." Austin located the word, annoyed that Baltimore was right.

"What? What is it?" Dallas pleaded.

"It's a word," Austin conceded. "Once you know, you'll never get it out of your mind."

"What?" Dallas said louder, frustrated at being ignored. Again.

Austin dropped the heavy book on the table. "Why is a word like that in your vocabulary?"

Baltimore grinned as she tallied up the scores. "I'm a sociology major. I study different forms of behavior."

"Variant behavior," Carolina offered.

Dallas looked back and forth between her three sisters. If she were invisible, they would still take more notice of her. She stood up and screamed, "Will someone please tell me what the fuck zooerastia means!"

Everyone looked at her and she sat back down. Baltimore started to giggle. "You just used the 'F' word!"

"I don't like being out of the loop and feeling stupid."

Baltimore couldn't stop laughing. "You just said it."

"What?"

"The definition. Fuck. Zooerastia. Fucking animals. Bestiality. Sexual intercourse with an animal. 110 points." Baltimore turned over the timer. "Your turn Dallas."

"I don't feel like playing anymore."

"Told you it would titillate your prurient mind."

"My mind is not prurient and I'm tired of defending myself." Dallas was starting to get angry. Really angry. Breathe, she thought to herself, just breathe. But she couldn't relax. Not here. Not with her sisters pushing her buttons for their own pleasure.

"You're just bitter that you're losing. You can't handle the fact that I'm smarter than you are."

"Just because I didn't go to a precious Ivy League school, doesn't mean that I'm any less smart than you are. And I'm happy. I have a husband. I have a job. What do you have Baltimore?"

"I'm twenty-six. You're not supposed to have anything at twenty-six."

"Really?" Dallas smirked. "At twenty-six, Carolina made the law review. At twenty-six, Austin had already sold her first short story. And at twenty-six, I was already married." She waved her wedding ring finger in front of Baltimore's face.

"Things are different now. My generation is more lost than yours."

"Your generation? You're four years younger than I am."

"In dog years, it's twenty-eight."

"You're not a dog, you're a basket case."

"Maybe I inherited it from Mom."

"Mom wasn't a basket case." Austin looked up from her tiles. It was now or never. She was going to have to come clean.

"Yes she was." Carolina stared at Austin.

"No. She wasn't."

"Oh, no." Carolina was getting angry. "She just happened to drown herself in the bathtub because she was perfectly sane. 'Cause that's what all sane people do. Wake up, eat Cheerios and decide, 'It's a bit cloudy out today, so I think I'll take a bath instead of a shower and, whoa, I'm slipping, I'm slipping. Fuck it: Glub. Glub. Glub.'"

Austin took a deep breath. "No, Carolina. A basket case is someone who finds out she has ALS and does nothing as the disease slowly eats away at her body. Until the only functioning organ left is her brain and it's completely helpless to stop the eroding body around it. Someone who decides to voluntarily remain trapped in her dying shell. That's a basket case."

Despite the raging storm outside, it was dead quiet inside as Carolina, Dallas and Baltimore stared at Austin, who was now little more than a stranger to them.

November 2007
The Island House, CT

Dear Daughters,

I dropped the turkey.

Who in the hell drops a turkey? Mary Elizabeth Baxter, that's who. It wasn't even that heavy. Twenty pounds. Baltimore, you were a big baby. And that turkey was like carrying two baby Baltimore's. And I carried you until you were five. Does this mean your mother's getting old? Say it ain't so. I may have just turned sixty, but I still have the body of a twenty-five-year-old. Okay, maybe a thirty-year-old ... but I look good, damn good. I have spent a lifetime battling the muscle aches and bone pains that are everyday luggage for a dancer, but now that I'm retired, I expect to be pain free. I have paid my dues. I expect my life as a retiree to be pain free (unless it's in the bedroom ... too much information? Still?). You're not little girls anymore, I'm sure you all have active sex lives ... though Carolina ... looking at you and Matthew across the table, I think you need to be doing it more. Please don't fall into the habitual once a week or, gasp, once a month routine. Sex is an integral part of a relationship and I'm guessing it has not been a priority for either of you.

Look at Dallas, my baby gets laid all of the time.

I suppose you're blushing if you're reading this, baby ... but it's obvious the way Peter looks at you. He is still in love with you. He is still insanely attracted to you. Anyone can see it in his eyes. Baltimore, I assume you have a healthy sexual appetite as you seem to have a different partner every time we talk and Austin ... well, let's leave it at the fact that I love Sarah and I think she's good for you. I don't understand what you do, but I approve of her. Where was I? Oh, yes, the dropped turkey. Despite my clumsiness, it was a wonderful Thanksgiving. At least, I thought it was a wonderful Thanksgiving... it was certainly lovely to have all of my girls under the same roof again.

I'm sure when you rewrite history, it won't necessarily go down as one of the better Thanksgivings in history... Baltimore sulked, Carolina was moody, Dallas was embarrassed and Austin worked her hardest to alienate everyone. And I was so klutzy I dropped the turkey. I still can't believe it. I spent most of my life strong enough to lift ninety pound dancers, but I'm too weak to hold a twenty pound turkey? Ridiculous. That should be a good story for the grandchildren. Grandma Dropsy. Thank god for Sarah. Austin, you know I'm not a big fan of the whole lesbian thing, the idea of going down on another woman... don't get me started. What do you actually do? How do you do it? Don't answer that. You can't answer that because you won't read these letters til I'm dead, but someone should write a book. When I'm dead you should write the book, or at least do a set of illustrations so that clueless straight people like me understand the mechanics.

But who am I to judge, it's your life.

I have to admit, for a lesbian, Sarah is a godsend. If you insist on dating a woman, she is definitely the best. And I have pushed you girls to aim for the best. Anyway, the turkey dropped and the four of you, my beloved daughters, just sat there in horror. Well, Carolina sat in horror, Dallas made a face of disgust and Austin and Baltimore laughed. Not terribly helpful. Peter and Matthew managed to stand up. Again, not terribly helpful. It was Sarah who actually did something. She wasn't just a passive observer but an active participant. She was the first to jump to my aid and she counted aloud to eight while she scooped up the turkey, managing to slide it back onto the plate and put it on the table. She then told us about the Sarah Garcia eight second rule: If food is on the ground for less than eight seconds, it is perfectly acceptable to eat. I have a feeling if it took her nineteen seconds to get that bird off the floor, it would have been the Sarah Garcia nineteen second rule. What a girl! You all ate the slightly askew bird, well, everyone except my little vegetarian who was more than happy with the Tofurky sandwich I made. Baltimore, darling, I think it is sacrilege to eat turkey made out of tofu ... but that is just my humble opinion.

Still, my entire family was with me and, in my book, that constitutes a wonderful Thanksgiving. I'm sorry if I was a bit tired, I've had a bug for a little while and I just don't seem to have as much strength as I usually do. I'm sure it will clear up in no time. Just a bit dizzy and tired, that's all. Oh, klutzy ... I suppose I should now add klutzy to the list.

I am thankful for all of you. You are my life.

I love you Carolina (and Matthew)
Austin (and Sarah)
Dallas (and Peter)
and Baltimore,
Mom

P.S. You're never going to believe it but I'm choreographing again. Well, not physically but mentally. When Sully died last month, I had an unexpected reaction. Deep and intense sadness. I knew I loved the man, but I guess I never realized how much until he died. And then the grief wouldn't stop pouring out of me. It was like I turned on a faucet and this rush of emotion flooded out and made me reexamine all of my loves. And I did love Sully, very much. I loved all of my husbands because I'm the kind of person who dives headfirst into a relationship. Anyway, I was doing some soul searching, and like my grief, this poem flooded out of me. I sent it to Maxine, whose daughter is the artistic director of the Womyn Warriors (yes, that makes me feel VERY old) and they are performing it next month. I'd love to get down to the city to see them. Catch lunch with Mort and take in a performance.

All men die.
No matter what they say, no matter
what they promise, they will die.
So, you have two choices:
ONE
You can jump into the relationship with
open arms and an open heart
and know that one day
your arms will be cut off at the limbs
and your heart will be speared like a pig,
ripped out of your body and dripping
on the splintered stake...
TWO
You can enter the relationship with one eye always open.
With the knowledge that they will die
and because you know that, you will be able
to build up enough of a protective shell
to deflect the pain when it comes.

Believe me, I wish I was smart enough
to choose the latter path...
to be able to protect my heart with the push
of a button or a flick of the wrist.

To have an ever ready shield to protect it from pain.
But, I'm one of those people who dives
headfirst into relationships
and even though I know, unequivocally,
that one day the pain will eviscerate my entire body
so that I can't eat,
sleep
or sometimes even
breathe.
I take that chance.
Because I'd rather have a month,
a year
or several years
of pure, unadulterated happiness,
than always have to sleep with one eye open.
I choose the pain of loving fully
rather than facing
the exhaustion and numbness
of holding up
an ever present
protective
shield.

Nineteen

"Mom had ALS?" Carolina was the first to break the silence.

Baltimore seemed dazed. She was still digesting the shock of information. Dallas was similarly wrapped up in her own world as she mumbled "fuck" over and over, but no one was paying attention.

"What exactly is ALS?" Baltimore wanted to know.

"Lou Gehrig's disease," Carolina answered in her lawyer voice as her body instinctively went into organizational mode. "He got it...Lou Gehrig got ALS and died when he was thirty seven."

"How do you know that?" Dallas asked.

"Mom. She was obsessed with celebrity deaths. Remember her obsession about how old people were when they died; Marilyn Monroe, Jimi Hendrix, Jesus."

"Jesus. That's right." Dallas murmured.

"You still haven't told me what it is," Baltimore demanded.

"Amyotrophic lateral sclerosis. It's a progressive neurodegenerative disease. Motor neurons die, so the brain's ability to initiate and control muscle movement is lost. ALS leads to paralysis and eventually death. Essentially, everything in your body degenerates except for your mind. You're trapped in your body."

She paused for a moment, reflecting. "Shit. That's hereditary."

"Children of people afflicted by ALS have a ten percent chance of developing the disease," Austin said, looking at a Chinese food menu. She guessed no one would want to deliver from the mainland, especially in this weather; however, she was strangely hungry. She was craving General Tso's chicken from Dragon East.

Baltimore finally looked up, although her eyes were still glazed. "Wow, Carolina, between Alzheimer's and ALS, you're totally screwed."

Carolina jumped up and ran to the bar. "I need a drink."

"We all need a drink." Dallas joined her, topping off her Bloody Mary again. "Fuck."

Baltimore looked out the window. Even though it was mid-afternoon, the sky was almost black. The clouds were low and the rain pelted against the window with fury. "So, this was a planned death?"

Austin tentatively grazed her hand against Baltimore's shoulder. "That's what I've been trying to tell you."

"Right. The whole *civilized and ladylike fashion of drowning*. So, this means ... "

"That our beloved fucking Mother decided to plan a sisterly reunion with her death," Carolina snapped. "That she selfishly decided to kill herself before talking to any of us about it."

"She talked to me," Austin said, simply.

"Of course she talked to you, you were here." Carolina was furious. She bit every word, clipping her sentences. "There are four of us, Austin. It was our right to know."

"It was her choice."

Carolina's controlled dialogue quickly devolved into a vituperative rant. "That's bullshit. She obviously wasn't in her right mind. If it was her choice, then you should have had the common sense to overrule her choice."

"We're not in a court," Austin said.

"You should have called me." Carolina's voice was hard. "I would have been able to talk her out of it. I could have helped."

"Mom specifically didn't want you to know. She was afraid you would have talked her out of it."

"Of course I would have talked her out of it," Carolina growled. "Suicide is wrong. It's fucking wrong."

"Is that the Bible or your conscience speaking?"

"You could have done something."

"I did." Austin took a deep breath, hoping to ameliorate the three words that followed...

"I killed her."

December 2007
The Island House, CT

Dear Austin,

I need you to come home.

I love you,
Mom

Twenty

"She had ALS," Austin reminded her sisters. "Her body wasn't functioning. She was too weak. I had to do it."

"You are fucking kidding me," Carolina screamed.

"Her mind worked perfectly." Austin kept speaking in a neutral tone. She was not going to let Carolina upset her. "It was exactly what she wanted, she just needed a little help."

"You murdered her." Carolina was red faced.

"I assisted her suicide."

"That's illegal."

"You gonna call the cops on me?" Austin asked patiently.

"I don't know."

Baltimore grabbed Carolina's hand. "Carolina."

Carolina looked at her baby sister. "She committed murder."

"She's your sister."

"And she killed my mother."

"Yes." Austin smiled. "It's all very oedipal."

"I'm so glad you can make a joke about this." Carolina felt a panic attack coming on. She needed to run. She needed to get out of the house. She felt locked up in an asylum and Austin was leading the pack of crazies.

"Carolina, you've only had a minute to digest it. I've had almost two years."

Dallas finally joined the conversation. Her words came out little more than a whisper. "Mom was sick that long? She didn't seem sick last Christmas."

"Did you ever see her get up from her chair?"

"I thought she was tired."

"She still had it together then, but she went downhill, fast. Yesterday, she was having trouble breathing."

The realization suddenly hit Baltimore. "God, Mom was alive yesterday."

"If you call it alive."

Carolina opened the door, she had to get out. To breathe fresh air; yet, the storm pelted her immediately with hard rain and she slammed the door shut. "It still doesn't give you the right to do what you did."

"Had you been here ... Had you seen her ... you would have done the same thing." Austin was starting to get irritated. Her sisters had absolutely zero clue.

"Don't you dare tell me what I would have done." Carolina was now looking into her future. "Right. Well, I'm screwed. I was planning to be a judge one day. Not with these skeletons out of the closet."

Austin looked at her with incredulity. "I'm not planning to go public with this, I was telling you guys as a courtesy."

"Assisted suicide is illegal—"

Baltimore jumped in, "Not in Oregon."

"We're not in Oregon," Carolina exploded.

"I hate our government," Baltimore mumbled.

"What you did is morally wrong. It's reprehensible, it is—"

"How did you do it?" Dallas piped in.

"What?" Austin didn't understand. Why would Dallas want to know? But her prissy sister walked up to her and stood way too close, invading her personal space.

"Show me how you did it, exactly. I want to know."

"No." Austin tried to move, but Dallas grabbed her arms.

"She was our mother too, Austin, I want to know what her last few minutes were like." Dallas pulled Austin's hands up to her own throat. "I want you to show me!"

"I'm not going to show you." Austin shook free and shouted, "You think I enjoyed it? You think I wanted to kill my own mother? I don't wish my last week on anyone ... FUCK. You have no clue what's been going on in this house. None of you do. Carolina, you haven't been home in three years. Dallas, you refuse to deal with the slightest hint of dysfunction; hey, Mom started dying right in front of your eyes and YOU DIDN'T NOTICE. And Baltimore, you're so fucking self-absorbed, you can't see past your own terribly oppressive life fraught with important collegiate decisions."

"What?" Baltimore piped up. "Me? I'm on your side."

"There are no sides, here. There is only reality." Austin sat down, exhausted by her own rant. "Mom was dying and wanted to expedite the process. She gave me no choice but to help her. I have to live with this, okay. The three of you are uninvolved, personae non grata, not culpable. So go be a judge Carolina, you're off the hook."

Carolina looked at her sister and said quietly, "But you're not."

"What are you talking about?" Baltimore asked.

"She killed our mother. That is a punishable offense."

"By who?"

"Any court of law." Carolina turned back to Austin. "It's our obligation to report you."

"You're crazy." Baltimore wondered, at this point, if they were all nuts. She suspected insanity was hereditary as well.

"Am I?" said Carolina. "I think the crazy person is one who can get within inches of the woman who bore her, push her under the water and watch her die. That is the crazy person."

Austin jumped up. "You have no idea what you're talking about."

"Don't I? You killed my mother."

"Our mother." Austin grimaced. "You don't have proprietary rights."

"Neither do you."

January 2008
Island House, CT

Dear Austin,

I mean it. Come home.

I love you,
Mom

Twenty-One

It was almost a Mexican standoff as the girls stood close to each other refusing to move. Austin, at 5'7" had to tilt her head up to glare into the eyes of her taller sister. Eventually, Austin broke the tension with an easy laugh.

"I need a drink." She grabbed Carolina's half empty glass. "You definitely need a drink." She went to the bar and grabbed four fresh glasses, pouring healthy shots of Absolut Citron in each of them. Her back was to her sisters as she feigned a bright attitude, "We should all be drinking. Technically, this is a wake, right? So let's drink."

She turned and deposited the four glasses in each of her sister's hands, ending with Carolina. "Let's drink. And toast." She raised her glass. "To Mom." She looked around at her sisters, waiting for them to drink. "This is what she would have wanted."

Dallas couldn't look at Austin as she took her drink. The second the rain stopped, she was getting off the island. She was getting away from her sisters, from the madhouse and she was never coming back. She and Peter had their share of problems but they were manageable problems, not like this nightmare.

Baltimore looked at her drink. She was now convinced that Austin had lost her mind, hell, if she were forced to kill her own mother it would have probably thrown her off the deep end as well. She sipped her drink, wondering when she should reveal her own secret...since everyone was coming clean.

Carolina continued to glare at Austin as she downed her drink in one gulp. The only thing keeping her relatively sane at the moment was the vodka, which was helping to numb the pain. When Carolina drank, it kept her panic attacks in check. She was furious. Her mother hadn't told her anything. She was the oldest, she should have known. She should have been involved. She slammed down the empty glass on the table and continued to glare at Austin. "What you did was illegal."

"What I did was compassionate." Austin was eerily calm. "Do you have any idea what it feels like to lose control? Of course you don't. You've been in control your entire life. Straight A's from the second you left the womb. We all admit it Carolina, you're the best. The one sister everyone should try to emulate. Hey, your marriage is the only thing you've ever failed at in your entire life."

"Your point?"

"You want to be a judge? Don't judge a person's actions until you've walked a mile in her shoes. How's that for an appropriate cliché? You would have done the same thing."

"That's bullshit, and you know it. Help me out here. Baltimore, Dallas, would you have killed your mother?" She looked at her younger sisters, silently pleading with them. Baltimore turned away and Dallas looked down at her drink. Carolina was baffled by their apathy. "I'm living in an asylum. You people are nuts. Austin committed a felony..." She blinked a few times. Something wasn't right. She felt a strange numbness flowing through her arms. "I don't feel so good."

"You've had a lot to drink," Dallas offered.

"No. It's not that. What's happening to me? My arms—" Carolina was desperately rubbing her arms, trying to stimulate feeling. Soon her hands felt stiff. She stumbled towards the old high back, overstuffed floral chair their mother favored. "I can't feel my fucking le—." She collapsed into the chair like a broken puppet, wanting to speak; yet, no words would come. Her body betraying her.

Baltimore and Dallas rushed over to their sister, whose body was completely rigid. Only her eyes vividly expressed anguish.

"Carolina? Carol?" Baltimore shook her. "What's the matter with her?"

"Carolina!" Dallas screamed.

"Carol!" Baltimore shook her harder.

Austin observed her sisters' anxiety with a detached bemusement and wandered back to the table. "I guess the game's over." She methodically dumped the Scrabble tiles back into the bag, their noise filling the silence.

Baltimore stared at Austin. "Um, what's happening?"

Dallas continued to attend to her eldest sister. "Carolina, can you hear me?"

"She can hear you perfectly." Austin said as the game tiles clanked against each other. "She can see you perfectly. She just can't do anything else ... perfectly."

"What did you do to her?" Dallas finally turned to Austin.

"You can't judge someone unless you walk a mile in their shoes, right?" Austin grinned. "Look, I knew she wouldn't understand. She's too clinical. She had to be shown. It was the only way." Austin pulled out a small envelope from her pocket, with traces of white powder in it. "Don't worry, it's not permanent. Doxycyclinal. Clinically speaking, it causes progressive supra nuclear palsy. In layman's terms, it causes temporary paralysis of all muscular functions. The brain works, the body doesn't. Carol can now walk a mile in Mom's shoes."

Dallas wanted to vomit. "You poisoned her?"

"I'm educating her."

Twenty-Two

Several days before her sisters descended on the island, Austin had her last serious conversation with her mother. She'd been putting it off, but Mary insisted. Sometimes it was easy to ignore her mother just by looking out at the water. Austin could spend hours looking at the water, dreaming away her days and trying to gain inspiration from nature. She loved the water, she had practically grown up on the island, spending every summer there since her birth.

Mary definitely believed that the best part of living on Money Island was the view. The big bay window overlooked the entire body of water and Mary spent most of her days sitting inside on the high back, overstuffed floral chair, remembering her past with great nostalgia and planning her future with great aplomb. Today was a rare balmy fall day and despite the crispness of the air and encroaching weekend storm, Mary had asked Austin to help her outside. She and her daughter rocked back and forth on the porch swing, overlooking a lone sailboat.

"I wish you wouldn't eat junk food," Mary said, not looking at Austin. She wondered if the young couple aboard the small craft were lovers. She could just discern their outlines but couldn't see their faces. She guessed they were happy simply on her premise that everyone deserved to be happy.

"I like junk food." Austin slowly savored each chip. This was her third to last bag and she couldn't be bothered to go to the mainland for more. It was just a quick boat ride over to Old Man Winters' store, but she was too lazy to go. For someone who never cared about what she ate, Austin was starting to feel the sulfites from all the packaged foods she preferred. It was probably time to do a cleanse or at least eat well for a while. It might help her writer's block; healthy body... healthy mind sort of thing. Maybe Monday she'd do a big shop. Even borrow a car and drive up to the new Whole Foods. Fill the refrigerator with fresh fruit and vegetables. Maybe.

"We need to talk about it." Mary's voice interrupted her daughter's ill-fated diet plans.

"No, we don't."

"Austin, I'm going to die. Sooner, not later and I need your help."

Austin did not want to have this conversation. Her mother had been haranguing her for months. Most of the time, she had managed to deflect her mother's pleas. She even went so far as to ingest a paralyzing drug to enable her to feel what her mother was feeling. For fifteen minutes, Austin had understood her mother's disease; yet, the visceral experience was not enough to sway her to do her mother's morbid bidding. "They'll find a cure."

"If they couldn't find a cure for a Hall of Fame baseball player, I don't think they're going to find a cure for a four time divorcée," Mary scoffed.

"Four?" Austin liked Baltimore's dad, Reggie, an occasional visitor to the house. And although he never lived with the family, he always sent them fabulous gifts from around the world, from his various gigs as a traveling musician. Of all of Mary's husbands, he was probably the least husband-like; yet, Austin didn't think her mother ever got around to properly divorcing him. Mary told her that the luxury of still being married meant that she could have affairs, but men knew from the outset that they could not be possessive.

"The papers from Baltimore's father just came through." Mary paused for effect. "I wanted to take care of business before I took care of business."

"You're not funny." Austin hated when her mother made jokes about death.

"I'm not laughing," Mary said earnestly. She tried to move; however, it was too much for her and she relaxed back into the swing.

"Can I get you a pillow, or something?"

"Why, do I look uncomfortable?" Mary joked.

"Are you enjoying yourself?" Austin snapped. "This is not why I came back."

Mary looked at her daughter. Austin had never broached this subject. She rarely talked about her personal life, about her relationship, about why she hadn't delivered the sequel to her bestselling book.

"Why did you come back?" Mary asked plainly, waiting for an answer. When none came, she pressed on. "A famous novelist. Touring the country. You had your pick Austin. Fellowships from California, a grant in England, offers from universities... a nice girlfriend. Why did you come back?"

"You summoned me."

"Fine, don't tell me." Mary could now see the faces of the young couple on the sailboat. She was a slight redhead and he was a burly brunette. They both wore bright blue anoraks and were laughing. The man had his arms wrapped around the girl's small waist protectively. They were no more than twenty-two, twenty-three... younger than Baltimore. And, yes, they did look happy. Mary observed her serious daughter. Austin looked anything but happy. There was a deep pain, a sadness behind her eyes: A sadness of someone who had lived too much in too short of a time. Mary supposed that she was responsible for some, if not all of the more immediate sadness.

"Do you know why you're so special?"

Austin looked at her mother, surprised by the question. "I have no idea."

"Life is strange, Austin. There are so few things in it that you can plan out... because while you're busy planning, some higher power up there is just going to fuck up your plans."

Mary remembered visiting California when she was a young dancer. Her troupe was doing a show across the street from a tiny theatre that featured a poster of elderly women. Mary was fascinated that women that old could still dance and she caught a matinee the following day. Each of the broads, the youngest was 83, had legs that went on for miles, kicks that rivaled hers and the energy of twenty year olds. They looked gorgeous in their corsets and boas and she knew, right then, that her destiny was set. She focused on her daughter. "There's this theatre in Palm Springs that only hires dancers in their eighties. I saw a show there when I was on tour and I've spent the last four decades planning my retirement, as an octogenarian burlesque dancer in Palm Springs."

Austin started to laugh. While she spent most of her life watching her mother dance or choreograph, she considered her long retired.

"What? You don't think I could make it? With these gams? I was born for it." She managed a chuckle before her voice took on a more serious tone, "Now I can barely move my legs. See, someone up there is fucking with me. So, you know what I'm gonna do? I'm gonna take control. I'm not gonna wait until a breathing tube is shoved down my throat and some strange nurse is wiping up my shit. I want out. I've had a good life. No, I've had a great life. And I have my four girls to show for it."

"I hate to burst your bubble, Mom, but we're not that impressive."

"Are you kidding? A big shot lawyer, a teacher, a writer and a…. what is Baltimore these days?"

"Psychology? Anthropology? Something 'ology.' "

"She'll figure it out. You switched majors three times."

"You switched husbands four."

"Life is too short to spend with one person." Mary knew she had to change tactics. Her daughter was not as amenable to her request as she had hoped. She needed to manipulate her into doing it, but first, she had to peel away the protective layers. She had to get Austin to a place where she would have no choice but to help her. "How is your father?"

"I thought you still spoke to him." Austin bit the inside of her cheek. She knew where her mother was going and she tried to prevent herself from getting annoyed.

"I do." Mary smiled. She knew exactly which buttons to push. "I was wondering if you did."

"You're not going to do this," Austin mumbled.

"What?" Mary asked innocently.

"This. This. This," Austin said, getting frustrated. "Pick an argument to get me riled up so I feel bad and placate you by doing what you want."

"I would do that?"

"You're manipulative, Mother."

"How can I be manipulative?" Mary asked sweetly. "I can't even get up."

"You're doing it right now," Austin said with anguish in her voice.

"What?"

"Making me feel guilty. I'm not buying into it."

"I'm not asking you to. I'm just asking you to help me die."

Mary watched Austin jump up and walk to the front of the porch. She raised her voice a little so that her daughter could hear her, even though she was pretending not to. "What? You're the only one who can do it. Carolina will come up with some legality why it's ethically wrong to prematurely end my life. Dallas can't handle blood and Baltimore's too young, it would scar her."

Austin raced back over to her mother. She was furious. "You're worried about scarring Baltimore and not completely fucking me up?"

"You're different," she said gently, "you're my Austin." Mary nodded to her daughter to sit back down. Austin sat at her mother's feet and, with effort, Mary placed her hand on her daughter's head.

"Four daughters. Four cities. Well, technically Carolina's a state, two states; but she was my first and I hadn't made the city decision yet. Poor girl. I think she always felt left out in a way. That's why she pretends to be Carol. Carol, hmmpft. What a stupid name. But you ... you're my Austin. My radical. You wrote progressive plays that almost got you kicked out of Princeton. Your father wrote articles for the Times which teetered between slander and Pulitzer. You're the only one of my girls who has the cojones to do this."

"Cojones?" Austin didn't know her mother spoke Spanish.

"I slept with a Mexican gardener last year. Picked up a few things."

"How many men have you slept with Mother?" Austin challenged.

"How many have you?" Mary challenged right back, staring into her daughter's eyes until she found the answer she was looking for. "Never?" Mary looked at Austin with surprise. "Not even one? How can you be gay, you're so much like me!"

Austin glared at her mother. While she was a strong advocate for equal rights, it was pretty much limited to equal rights for women: Mary had always bordered on the edge of homophobia.

"I just wonder if there's something I could have done," Mary questioned aloud. "You know, it's not legal in the eyes of god."

"Says the woman who is asking me to kill her," Austin sputtered. "Look at the Commandments, Mother. I don't think *Thou Shalt not be Gay* is one of them, but I'm fairly sure *Thou Shalt not Kill* is somewhere in the top ten."

Mary ignored Austin. She had her exactly where she needed her. Now, she needed to layer on the ammunition. "You were named after the best city in the world. A democratic, liberal artistic community thrust dead center in a repressed, Republican mess. You're a paradox... and you have no choice. I'm not strong enough to do it. If I do it, I'll do it badly. And it's rather awkward to almost kill yourself. Best if it's done right the first time. One never lives down that kind of embarrassment."

Mary struggled for a moment to catch her breath.

"Mom?" Sometimes Austin hated being the only one around when her mother got like this. The depression she could handle, the frailty she could not.

"I can't feel my legs anymore. It was okay when I was just stiff, but my body's crumbling. It's going to happen anyway, a prisoner trapped in her own body. I'm just sorry I can't say goodbye. But it's for the best. Carolina wouldn't understand. None of them would.

"My first mistake with Carolina was not really naming her after a city. She's not even really one state. Carolina, but is she North or South? I could have easily gone with Charlotte, but I couldn't get that song out of my mind. *Carolina In My Mind.* I inspired James Taylor you know. Slept with him. Twice. Bastard. Never gave me credit. Carolina's driven, but she's not happy. Gotta be happy, Austin. Now Dallas, she's happy. Didn't plan to have two of my girls in Texas. Ironic. Wanted to make it up to Taos, but the water broke a week early. Still, there are worse places to give birth. My Dallas. She's a good girl. She plays it safe, but that's what Dallas is; a planned community of safe players."

"Mom, maybe it's time for bed." It was still early enough for Austin to try to get some writing done. Or at least stare at the blank screen of the computer. She was getting good at that.

"Your old mother's on a roll. Besides, there's only Baltimore left, unless I have any more girls out there I don't know about. Baltimore's my free spirit. She's too young to quite figure out what she wants, but she's special. All my girls are special, they were born in the best cities in the world."

"Technically, Paris is the best city in the world."

"Not such a fan of the French." Mary turned her attention back to the couple on the sailboat. They were a stone's throw away, just pulling up to the dock. The brown-haired boy was probably one of the Braverman grandkids. Edna and Saul Braverman lived on the far side of the island and had too many kids and grandkids to count. Baltimore had briefly dated their youngest son. Mary turned back to her daughter.

"So, I was thinking Friday."

Twenty-Three

"This Friday?" Austin asked. Mary had been asking for this favor for over a year. She'd ask it casually in passing and Austin would ignore her. She'd ask her aggressively over dinner and Austin would deflect her. Austin assumed after the whole "If I try your pill and don't agree" the subject was moot; yet, Mary was pressing on with her unreasonable request. And this time, she was making a direct plea for a result only a few days away. Austin repeated the question, "This Friday?"

"This Friday," Mary confirmed.

"This Friday doesn't work for me."

"There's nothing wrong with this Friday, Austin. You have no plans. It's also convenient. You can call your sisters Friday afternoon and they can come in for the weekend. That way Carolina won't miss work and Baltimore won't miss class. But no funeral, I want you to scatter my ashes. You have to promise me that."

"I'm not promising you anything."

"I was in labor with you for seventeen hours." Mary smiled.

"You're using guilt to get me to kill you?"

"Why, you almost killed me then, why not again?"

"Stop making jokes!" Austin screamed. She fought back tears she rarely shed. How dare her mother. How dare she manipulate her like this. It wasn't fair.

"Look, I've already come to terms with this, and I need you to understand. I'm taking control. It's not going to get better from here. I can try to fool myself or use my last few months to 'find' myself, but I don't have to... I'm not lost." Mary looked back at the water. It was one of the few things she was going to miss. Her water and her girls. But she didn't, she couldn't let her girls see her like this. She wanted them to remember her as a strong, vibrant woman. Austin could handle it. She was a writer, she could and would use the pain in her writing the way Mary had used her pain in her dance.

It was the burden of an artist to use pain as a creative catalyst.

Mary's attention turned back to her daughter. "I've enjoyed the journey... and now, I'm ready for it to end. Help me, Austin." This was it, Mary thought, now or never. She had one more motivation up her sleeve. After that, she would have to figure out something else. Probably call Mort. But he wasn't the right person to do this. Austin was the right person. "Okay. Get me a spider from the garden."

"Why?"

"Just get me a spider. There are plenty hanging around the Swiss chard. Go on, I'll still be here when you get back, I'm not going anywhere."

Austin jumped off of the porch, glad to be rid of her mother; albeit, only temporarily. The weather was stunning, unseasonably warm for this time of year and it felt good to walk barefoot through the grass. She grabbed an empty can of SpaghettiO's from the recycling pile and wandered over to Mary's haphazard garden. The garden had always been one of her mother's pride and joys. She had hoed a small patch of dirt in the corner of the backyard when they first moved into the house. Each year, the garden expanded a little as she added more vegetables. Dinners were often pastas and salads filled with the fresh cabbage, cauliflower, onions, broccoli and spinach Mary grew. She had a green thumb and even when her mobility started to falter, she kept her garden up by barking orders to Austin, who did not possess her mother's gift with greenery.

Walking through the rows of leaf lettuce and radishes, Austin felt bad that she had let her mother down. She hadn't planted the seeds in time and most of the garden had failed miserably. And the few plants that did manage to bloom didn't taste as good as they had in earlier years. The lettuce was wilted and the carrots were stunted. Still, Mary complimented her and assured her that the following year the garden would regain it's strength. Often times, gardens had off years. Austin only wished that her mother was just having an off year as well.

No matter what Austin decided to do, it was fairly clear that Mary would not be around to see her garden the following year.

Austin spied a decent sized Yellow Garden Spider sunning himself against a stalk of cauliflower and shooed him into the can. She didn't have a lid and quickly ripped off a piece of lettuce as a makeshift cover. She carried the spider back to her mother, who was resting on the porch with her eyes shut. Austin's heart suddenly beat faster as she rushed over to her mother. "Mom?"

Mary spoke without opening her eyes, "Are you afraid of spiders?"

"What do you want, Mother?" Austin was irritated. Of course she wasn't dead. Though that would have solved everything. When it was her time to go, Austin thought she'd like to die like this; peacefully swinging on a beautiful day overlooking the water. Not violently. Not prematurely. Not by the hand of her daughter.

Mary opened her eyes and managed a small smile. "I want you to do exactly what I say. No deviations, no permutations. Promise?"

"Whatever."

"You have to promise me, Austin. Don't make a dying woman beg."

"Fine. I promise," Austin said reluctantly.

"Pull two legs off of the spider."

"Ew."

"Just do it."

Austin rolled her eyes. Mary was always illustrating points by having her and her sisters do ridiculous things. Once Mary had smelled smoke on Baltimore when she was thirteen. That night, Mary sat at the table with Baltimore and Dallas and put a pack of cigarettes in front of each of them. She would not let them get up from the table until they had smoked an entire pack. At the time, Carolina was in San Francisco and Austin was living in New York but the story was legendary. Dallas gave up after half a cigarette and never touched them again. But Baltimore and Mary sat at the table across from each other matching each other death stick for death stick. Finally, with only two cigarettes left in the pack, Baltimore's eyes rolled back in her head and she vomited all over the table. That broke her of the habit, which she had only picked back up a year ago. Mary had done a similar move on Austin when she was sixteen and came home drunk one night. Her mother told her that it was fine if she drank, but she should drink with her. She should learn to hold her liquor if she was going to be a drinker. Austin matched her mother shot for shot of whisky; yet, Austin could only handle three shots before she threw up.

Mary Baxter's sixth commandment in life: "If painful lessons are inflicted, then your teens won't be addicted."

Her mother's rhyming laws were both legendary and ridiculous. Still, they seemed to work. Austin dumped the spider on the porch, quickly holding it in place with one of her fingers. Grimacing, she pinched one leg off and then another. The spider sat, frozen.

"What's it doing?" Mary asked from her seat.

"Nothing. It's not moving." Austin watched the spider that just lay there motionless.

"That's because you've taken away its mobility," Mary said harshly. "Now, that spider is completely alive and, if spiders can hear or think, she's listening to this. And she's trapped. She'll die because she has no one to feed her, unless of course you want to take that task upon yourself."

Austin didn't answer her. She just stared at the hobbled spider, willing it to move.

"If she could talk, she would beg you to end her life." Mary continued, "What kind of existence is this for a spider? Her friends and family are in the garden. They were happy there. They could go wherever they wanted. Eat whatever they pleased. Now, she's trapped. She can't move. She's going to die. The question is, how long will she have to live in pain before she's put out of her misery?"

Mary used every ounce of strength to touch her daughter's shoulder. "What are you going to do Austin? She's waiting."

Without warning, Austin smashed the spider with her fist, the small body oozing underneath her skin. She started to bawl, uncontrollably. Shaking as the realization of what had happened and what would happen coalesced.

Through her daughter's sobs, Mary said quietly, "I'm ready to go, darling. Please, let me go."

Twenty-Four

Austin looked at the slight watch on her wrist. Her mother insisted earlier that she take it, but the delicate leather band already felt like a heavy weight. 4:15. Her sister had been sitting immobile since three thirty.

"It's been forty-five minutes," Dallas screamed. She had been pacing back and forth for the last three quarters of an hour and it was making Austin dizzy.

"I know," Austin said.

"How long is this supposed to last?"

"I don't know."

"How long?" Baltimore chimed in, also furious, although she had directed her frustration in a stationary manner as she sat devotedly next to Carolina without moving.

"I said, I don't know," Austin defended herself. What she did know was that it was too long, way too long to be under.

"Take a guess, Dr. Kevorkian," Baltimore snapped.

Austin looked at her sisters. When she took the drug, she had been under for a very short time, just long enough to understand what it meant to feel paralyzed. She had also been warned exactly what was going to happen whereas Austin had tricked Carolina into taking the doxycycline. Austin had doped her drink. Last week, when Austin tried the drug, she and Mary sat tranquilly next to each other until the drug wore off. Her mother had even sung to keep her calm. Now, it was complete chaos. It was happening all wrong.

"Fifteen minutes," she finally confessed.

"Austin!" Dallas was almost apoplectic.

"What? I didn't plan it this way."

"Which way did you plan it?" Dallas barked. "Poison one of us to understand Mom's condition and hope that we don't die too?"

"She promised it would work," Austin said helplessly. She took her mother's word. It had worked for her, so of course it would work for her sisters. But it didn't. It had all gone terribly wrong.

"Who promised?" Dallas asked.

"Who promised?" Baltimore echoed.

"It doesn't matter."

"It absolutely matters." Baltimore jumped up and got in Austin's face. "Who promised?" Baltimore's brain went into overdrive. The only 'she's' in Austin's hermit-like life were her editor, her ex-girlfriend and her mother. Who would recommend doing something as idiotic as this? Who would want to show by example? Of course it was their mother. Leave it to Mary to manipulate Austin into taking the pill to understand her condition. Complete insanity. "It was Mom's idea, right? She put you up to this. Look at me, Austin. Did you drink the oxy-whatever-it's-called? Answer me."

"Yes."

"Oh Austin." Dallas's voice lost its edge. It was a mixture of pity and disgust.

Baltimore grabbed Austin's wrist, digging her nails into her sister's skin. "How long were you under?"

"Ouch. Fifteen, maybe twenty minutes."

"Then why has she been under almost an hour?"

"I don't know." Austin pulled away from Baltimore and crouched in front of Carolina. This was not the way she had planned it. She and Mary had discussed it. Her mother convinced her if her sisters didn't approve or understand what she had done, she should show them. One example would be enough, but she had enough of the drug for all three. They had apportioned the three doses into little bags. Austin had only needed to show Carolina, but the lesson should have been over by now. This was taking too long. Much too long.

"She's had a lot to drink. Maybe that somehow increased the potency or slowed down the poison. I don't know."

"Well, what are we supposed to do?" Dallas asked.

"We should let her sleep it off."

"She's not sleeping."

"Jesus, Dallas. It's an expression. It has to go through her system."

"Well how fucking long is that going to take?"

"Is fuck your new favorite word?"

"Fuck off." Dallas jumped up and ran over to the phone. "We should call someone."

"No, we shouldn't."

"A doctor. We should call a doctor."

"So she can find Mom in the tub and Carolina on the chair?" Austin looked at her sister like she was a complete moron. Maybe she was: Dallas certainly wasn't handling the situation with any clarity. "We're not calling anyone."

"I don't care. This is too dangerous." Dallas started to dial the phone; however, Austin yanked it away from her, pushing Dallas to the ground and victoriously cradling the phone.

"Ha. I'm stronger than you are, Dallas."

"You're psychotic," Dallas cried. First Baltimore had pushed her and now Austin. And now Carolina wasn't there to save her. Dallas hated herself. She hated her weakness and her status in her ridiculous family. She was the bottom of the hierarchy. With Peter, she was an equal. At school, she was a god. Here she was a nobody.

Invisible.

"Give me a break." Baltimore helped Dallas up. "If someone wanted to call someone, I'd pull out my cell. We're not gonna call anyone."

"Thank you," Austin said. "Someone else who's thinking logically."

"Oh please," Baltimore snarled. "You're not scaring anyone Austin, you're just pathetic."

She walked over to the liquor cabinet and surveyed the bottles. Finally, she grabbed a half full bottle of Grey Goose and started to climb the stairs, calling back to her sisters.

"I'm going to sit with Mom."

March 2009
Island House, CT

Dear Daughters,

When you read this I'll be dead.

It might be in a month, it might be in a year or three or five. I've done a lot of reading on this disease. Too much reading. It's depressing as hell. The average lifespan once someone is diagnosed with ALS is three years; however, there are people who have beat the average. One guy, who has been lifting weights, has lived with the disease for ten years. Another man has committed himself to homeopathic treatments and is successfully living with it after eight years. I don't know where in that average spectrum I'll fall ... the only thing I know is that as soon as I see signs of the disease starting to win, I'm going to forfeit.

I've been lucky and the disease is moving incredibly slowly for me. I've fallen a few times and I've had a major case of the dropsies, remember that turkey? But other than stiffness, I'm doing okay. I knew something was wrong when my muscles felt so fatigued. A dancer has a dancer's body her entire life, no matter how old she gets. Yet, my body was feeling far too run down for someone as young as I am, so I finally went to a doctor in New Haven. I was given every kind of test and scan known to womankind and was diagnosed with Lou Gehrig's disease.

Fuck.

The doctors wanted to give me meds to slow the disease. They wanted to sign me up for clinical trials. They wanted to monitor my regression. They wanted to retard my death: I wanted to embrace my life. So I went to see *Quantum of Solace*. Hell, at least I got closure on the whole *Casino Royale* thing. I mean, why in the world would you create a two-parter James Bond? Stick with the formula; it works. I am glad that I lived long enough to see Daniel Craig. He's my favorite Bond yet. He combines Sean Connery's physicality, Roger Moore's dapper humor, Timothy Dalton's brooding, Pierce Bronson's sultriness and even Lazenby's charm. But enough about Bond, more about me. So, I got the delightful diagnosis, went to see the latest Bond film and then popped into a bar and flirted my ass off.

I still have it, girls.

And I came to a definitive decision. I don't want to spend my last years or months or days in and out of hospitals. I want to spend them remembering. I want to spend them living. Some people may see that as quitting. As losing. As giving up. I sometimes think it's braver to walk away than to fight, especially if you want to keep your dignity. I don't like this disease, I don't like it at all. The mind works and the body doesn't. Who wants to be a vegetable, completely dependent on other people? I have always been a strong independent woman and I don't want to have to start relying on other people now.

So, I called Austin. I needed to tell someone and she was the most logical choice. If I told the islanders like Edna Braverman, they would become too cloying; bringing me coffee cake every day, wanting to sit with me, wanting to talk. Who wants to sit and talk when their nerve cells are dying? I am far too private of a person and, frankly, I wouldn't be able to handle the looks of pity. I can handle the disease better than I could handle those plaintive looks. Those looks are a mixture of "you poor thing" and "thank god it's not happening to me." Sometimes it's hard to decipher between the two. The nice thing about Austin is that she's not big on pity. I like that.

Some people might call that emotionally stunted, I call it practical.

Initially, I just wanted her to check in on me once in a while. She was busy writing and seemed happy living with Sarah ... but when she found out, she packed up her life and moved in with me. It's not what I thought I wanted, but I can't say I'm disappointed. It's been nice to have her here. It's been helpful. But she never leaves. My disease has been an excuse for her to become a hermit. I'm not sure what you are hiding from darling, but when I'm dead you must promise me that you will start living again.

Carolina, Dallas and Baltimore, please don't be mad at me that I kept this from you. If I had my druthers I would have kept it from all four of you, but I needed some help and Austin was the most logical choice. Now, don't get all snippy. I can hear you girls fighting. "I'm the oldest, I should have known." Right, Carolina? Well you, my darling, are a hotshot lawyer. How would you have handled this? Probably put me on every macrobiotic diet out there, hired physical therapists and sent me into the city three times a week for some clinical trial. No thank you.

Dallas, love, you are so busy with Peter and your students, I didn't want to burden you with another problem. You are so good at your job and so needed in your community that dealing with a sick mother would have split your focus and not allowed you to do your very best. It wouldn't have been fair to you.

Baltimore ... my guess is you screamed the loudest about not being involved in my illness. Darling, trust me, the longer someone can go before really, truly losing their innocence, the better. You are still a child. Yes, I know you're an adult in your twenties, but it is also a time of adventure, of discovery, of self-exploration. Dealing with a sick parent would have put a huge weight on that journey. You're probably angry now, but I know I did the right thing.

Trust your mother.

The only people who know about this are Austin, Mort and Reggie. Roger's mind is pretty much gone, ironic, huh ... ALS and Alzheimer's: opposites on the disease spectrum. Sorry, Carolina, you really hit the jackpot of the genetic pool. And Sully's dead, may he rest in peace, the rich bastard. Reggie wanted to come back, but I told him the best way he can help me is to live his life and tell me stories so I can live vicariously through him. He has kept up his part of the bargain and his stories are priceless. He has been dutifully calling me biweekly with detailed accounts of his musical adventures ... more like his musical shenanigans; he is a wicked, wicked man ... in the most delicious of ways. Every time he calls, I get to travel to Morocco and Berlin and Prague without leaving my home. He embraces life with a courage very few people have. I hope you girls get to spend more time with him as you get older, and he promised that he will step up as a parent when I'm gone. Not just to Baltimore, but to all four of you. And of course Mort knows. Throughout it all, Mort has been my best friend. We talk every night on the phone, gossiping about our day. Not that I have much to gossip about, but it's nice to hear his voice and it's nice to relive our memories. It's funny, when we talk about the good old days ... they actually are good old days. I suppose age gives you the luxury of revisionism. And Mort and I are on the same page: We decided together that it would be Austin who helped me die. Not an easy decision for parents. But the right one.

Austin, my artist, my writer. To write, one has to dig into pain. To embrace it rather than gloss over it. I mean, have you read *Pandora's Box*? You'd think the heroine had the worst childhood in the world. I notice you killed her mother in the first chapter. Just like Bambi's mother. Maybe you were trying to tell me something. Anyway, when it came to mothering, I did my best. In retrospect, maybe I finally understand that my mother did too. It's not easy raising girls. But I did it and as far as I can tell, you four are well on your way to reaching your potential. Where I failed, you will succeed.

Jesus has nothing on my four babies.

And I suppose in addition to my girls, I am leaving behind a legacy. The Womyn Warriors have survived for several decades and the lives they have touched have been immeasurable. Looking back, my best work definitely came from my pain. Your four fathers, as much as I loved them, gave me rich material for my work. The pain they caused me fueled my creativity. I suppose, in a sick and twisted way, involving Austin in my struggle is my selfish way of helping her do her best work. Darling, you've been trapped under Sylvia Plath's bell jar since writing your first book... maybe this 'experience' will break the glass and unlock your power. The point is, I don't want the other three of you to blame her for participating in this. It was my choice. I was always in control.

I have been in control my entire life. Until now. And I am okay letting go. Honestly other than my beautiful daughters, what I will miss the most is the sex.

No one ever thinks about senior citizens having sex, but we do. And we like it. We like it a lot. It's... slower than it was when we were younger. But the hormones are still active. Even after my men dried up, I didn't. I guess that's why God created masturbation. I can't even move my fingers that well anymore... You can't imagine what it's like to be trapped in your own body. Maybe, if I were a couch potato my whole life, I would have been used to this sitting thing, but I was a dancer. I had... the most beautiful legs. I'd sometimes dance sixteen hours a day. My feet were bloody until I was twenty…And I used to complain…Imagine that. I used to complain that my feet hurt.

It's funny the things you complain about which really don't seem that serious in retrospect. Once, I was on a cruise with Sully. Dallas, your father loved the water. Wonderful cruise. Too much food. Crappy ports, but, overall, pretty wonderful. Quite luxurious. So, the day comes when we return to the States and for some reason the crew hadn't anticipated that everyone would want to leave the ship at once, so the lines to get off went around the ship, twice. You've never seen people so angry. It was like the entire previous fifteen days were negated by the two hours of inconvenience these people had to experience. I even felt myself getting antsy, and I'm not that antsy of a person. With four daughters, how can you be?

The guy behind me…tall, balding, with extremely kind eyes said, very quietly, "We could be waiting in a line for bread and water."

Wow. Now, there's a perspective.

I'm not angry anymore. I was. Boy, was I. When I started to feel the stiffness, I cursed my body for getting older. When I started to have trouble breathing I cursed the scientists for not finding a cure. When my body shut down around me, I cursed God for…just for. He's an easy target, you know. But He's also comforting. Someone who listens, unconditionally.

I've had an amazing life. I saw the world. I had four successful daughters. And I don't want to die in a hospice with tubes down my throat. I don't want to wait in line for bread and water.

I'm ready.

I love you Carolina, Austin, Dallas and Baltimore,
Mom

Twenty-Five

Baltimore sat on the edge of the tub and stared down at her mother's body, which was partially submerged in the water. She was a beautiful woman, even naked and dead in the antique claw-foot tub. Drinking from the vodka bottle, Baltimore remembered taking a bath with her mother when she was a little girl. They used to sing a song, just the two of them. A made up ditty that was theirs.

With her hair that hangs down to her belly
And her ears which point up to the sky
She's got a smile that makes you feel so happy
And a face as sweet as cherry pie.

She made her mother promise not to sing it to her older sisters. From the clothes to the dolls to the boyfriends, Baltimore wanted something that was just hers rather than a hand me down from one of her older sisters.

It was a routine, just theirs: When Baltimore was a little girl, Mary would brush her long often tangled hair in the bathtub. And sing. They would sit in the bathtub together, naked, Mary's long legs taking up the length of the entire tub while Baltimore sat in front of her playing with her Barbies. She remembered once, when she was no more than three, a man walking into the bathroom and peeing while they were singing.

"*With her hair that hangs down to her belly*," Baltimore sang as she watched the man curiously, "*and her ears that point up to the sky*." Baltimore smiled at the man, trying to get his attention before she turned around to her mother. "Is that my new daddy, Mommy?"

"No darling, he's just a friend. C'mon, keep singing." Mary continued the song, "*She's got a smile that makes you feel so happy. And a face as sweet as cherry pie*."

Those were some of Baltimore's happiest memories. Not the random dudes streaming through the bathroom, but the solidarity between her and her mother. They always had a special relationship. All of her sisters took a part of their fathers with them: Carolina was clinical, exact and a perfectionist like her father Roger who was in the military. Austin was intense like Mort, both writers who spent more of their lives critically observing rather than passionately living and Dallas was indeed Sully's daughter: a clean cut, rule follower who always swam with the crowd.

While Baltimore didn't inherit her father's musical prowess, she shared his passion for life. She also shared his inability to commit. Both Mort and Sully were more father figures to Baltimore who only saw her dad on rare occasions as he was often touring the world. The most time she spent with him was a night in Paris when she and one of her college roommates were backpacking through France. She read in the paper that the Reggie White Band was playing *Caveau de la Huchette* – an underground club on the Left Bank. Excited, she grabbed one of the last seats in the crowded club and watched in awe as her father played the piano like Thelonious Monk. Baltimore knew she was biased, but her father was that good. He sang in both French and English and the crowd ate him up. Afterwards, she approached him, pushing through his throng of admirers. He was thrilled to see her and he dragged her out to a late night dinner where he kept ordering bottles of wine and entertaining her with funny stories about his latest tour. At three am, they finally called it a night and she gave her father a ferocious hug, unwilling to let go.

Random sightings of Reggie were par for Baltimore's life. She never knew when she would see him or for how long. He always visited Mary when he was in the States and Baltimore made sure to keep her life flexible enough that when her father was in town, she could see him. But most of their relationship was electronic. She kept up with him through his Facebook fan page more than visits or phone conversations.

Mary had been enough parent for her and had raised Baltimore with the confidence to do anything she dreamed. So, then, why hadn't she given her the courtesy of saying goodbye?

Baltimore knelt down next to her mother, took her lifeless hand and started to bawl.

October 2010
Island House, CT

Dear Daughters,

This is the last letter I will write to all of you. I wrote individual letters earlier this year, when my hands had not yet betrayed me. This is the last group letter to my beautiful daughters. I'm using this new program where I speak into the computer and it prints out what my voice says. Very clever, but this is it. I am not going to prolong the life of a body that is ready to go. It is time. I am done. I am ready. Fall is fully here and I will be gone before the first frost.

Don't mourn for me because I had a wonderful life. I had four wonderful daughters and you each made me very proud. I know I wasn't the best mother and I apologize for anything I ever did to hurt you. You have all reached for the brass ring and grabbed it with courage, grace and light. You have made me incredibly proud. You are my biggest accomplishments.

You are my joy.

I love you,
Mom

Twenty-Six

Left alone with Austin, Dallas thought she was going to go crazy.

She couldn't sit still and kept looking at Carolina, touching her to make sure that she was still alive. What kind of version of alive was this? A perverse thought in the back of Dallas's mind told her that she should be grateful Austin hadn't decided to poison her: She had her girls to teach, her teams to coach, her piano to play, her husband to love. She felt her heart beating way too quickly. She didn't belong here. She didn't fit into this family reunion. This was not the family she signed up for. She had her family. Peter was her family.

Dallas sat down on the couch in the lotus position, closed her eyes and took a deep breath, trying to soothe herself with a mantra. "I have created my own life. I've established my own routine. I have my own boundaries." She repeated the mantra three times until she believed what she was saying. Yet, when she opened her eyes and saw Austin biting back a laugh, she exploded. Dallas was so fucking tired of everyone making fun of her. "Go ahead, laugh. Jesus. Why did I even come back? I tried to get away from this madhouse. I don't even know you people anymore."

"You never knew us," Austin said.

"Why?" Dallas snapped. "Because I didn't make sense in our family of over achievers. I could never color outside of the lines or connect the dots into my own pattern. I followed the rules. I was a follower. I fit the mold. Sue me."

"Oh, so now that Mom's dead, you've decided to have a pity party for yourself?" Austin was so tired of her sisters whining and complaining all the time. Mary had given them all the tools to succeed in life. She had done her job. "You have a good life Dallas. Mom raised you well so don't start biting the hand that fed you."

"You are just filled with lovely little metaphors aren't you?"

"Look, if you really think you're ready to open your eyes to the reality of life, be my guest." Austin lowered her voice, "But you can't handle ugly."

Dallas bristled, "I can handle as much ugliness as you can." Her sister had no fucking clue what she had gone through. None of her sisters had. None of them had been in the position of loving a man so much and betraying that love through a lie that would sever their bond if it were ever discovered.

"No. You can't," Austin said. "You created this perfect little world far away from your severely dysfunctional family. You live in your surreal utopia with your perfectly manicured lawns and your perfectly pristine buildings. Your perfect little suburban Garden of Eden where nothing evil ever happens."

"Is that what you think?" Dallas was genuinely shocked. "I teach at a private school so I'm inured to the problems of society? I can't feel anything? That's priceless. You've elected to isolate yourself in your house with your mother... what do you know about what I deal with on a daily basis?"

"Your mother?" Austin smiled, catching Dallas's slip.

"What?"

"You just called her '*your mother*.' Isn't she *your mother* too?"

"It's just an expression," Dallas snarled.

"More like a Freudian slip."

"You're impossible to talk to," Dallas sputtered. "You ... you just keep twisting things around."

"I'm just saying that maybe you'd feel more culpable if you had used the expression *our mother*. She stopped being all of your mothers a long time ago."

Dallas looked at her sister. She wondered which one of them was it who was really unable to handle the truth. "You're right."

"I am?" Austin was confused. The Baxter sisters rarely conceded an argument, especially to each other. Even if they were wrong. It meant admitting defeat and they had all been raised with a competitive nature that precluded defeat. She looked at her younger sister taking the bait. "How?"

"When mothers are so fucking self-absorbed they put themselves before their children ... then they stop being your mother." Dallas smiled smugly, observing Austin's stunned reaction. Her sister never acknowledged that Mary was not a good mother. Neither did Baltimore, and Carolina wasn't around long enough to realize it. She hadn't seen Mary's negligence. Only Dallas saw, really saw, how selfish their mother was. A mother's job is to put her children first and Mary never, ever put her children first. And Dallas was tired of whitewashing the truth.

"Austin, I still remember when Mom married Baltimore's father. I was just a kid, but I remember. Do you? Do you remember? She ignored me. She ignored all of us. It was "Reggie" this and "Reggie" that. Reggie became her life and we were pushed into the background. She was not the perfect mother, Austin. No one can be. Heck, she didn't even come close. Every week she'd fall deeply in love and ignore us while she pottered about with her latest husband or lover or boy-toy. Nothing like being abandoned in your own home, over and over again."

Austin didn't know where this was coming from. Sure, when Mary fell in love, sometimes Austin felt like a second-class citizen. But abandoned? Sure, her mother had spent long stretches away from her girls ... especially when she was in between husbands, but she had to live too, didn't she? Besides, Austin had acclimated: She had kept herself busy as a child in order not to let her mother's absence affect her. One of the reasons she had become such a good lacrosse player was all of those hours she had spent working on strengthening her non-dominant hand, making obstacle courses to increase her agility and practicing her shots in the net. Biting back a wave of sadness, she admitted to herself that she had become used to being alone. Her sisters were around, but her mother was absent. Why was her mother gone so much? It didn't matter now, but Austin felt like Dallas had suddenly ripped the curtain away and shattered the illusion. Still, her mother always came back to her. Eventually, she always dumped her men and came back to her daughters. That is what mattered. Mary came back.

Austin glared at her sister. Now Dallas was changing things around, composing a different draft of her life ... how could she talk about abandonment, how could she judge? She had no idea what Mom was going through, she hadn't been around. She had disappeared. They all had. They had moved on with their lives in Philadelphia and Seattle and Boston.

They had escaped.

Dallas interrupted Austin's revelations. "When I got married, Peter became my family. I know I'm a priority to him."

"But you're still part of this family." Austin refused to let the argument drop. "You chose to forget about that responsibility. You abandoned Mom. You all did."

"I had an abortion," Dallas blurted out, knowing that would shut Austin up. She finally won a round, and it was with the smartest sister of them all. After enjoying a moment of stunned silence, she smiled triumphantly. "Still think I can't handle the ugliness of life in my perfectly pristine world? Still think I would be the last one Mom would ask to kill her? I've already killed someone, I have a track record," she shouted.

"Dallas—"

"—Still think I couldn't have handled it, Austin? Hell, I could have given you tips. Jesus, you're so busy preaching to all of us that we shouldn't judge a book by its cover, but that's all you ever do to me. You think because things look perfect on the outside, they're equally perfect on the inside? Wake up, Austin. Everything is not what it appears to be."

Austin didn't know what to say. She certainly hadn't seen this coming. "I ... I thought you guys really wanted kids?"

"We did. He does ... But I don't." Dallas's voice was now little more than a whisper, "I always thought I'd have them, lots of them and how different it would be for them than it was for me. How I'd take them to field hockey practice and piano lessons and pay attention to them. I guess I had painted this life for myself and it was going right on track ... but when it happened, I panicked."

Austin didn't know what to say. She had never seen Dallas this vulnerable. She hadn't remembered ever having a serious conversation with her sister. Their relationship had been superficial, always dancing on the surface and never daring to cut through the top layer. Austin was seeing, really seeing her younger sister for the first time. Carolina and

Baltimore were such big personalities, often sucking the air out of the room with their physical energy that Dallas was often overlooked.

And Austin was one of the biggest culprits.

Dallas kept talking, unaware that her sister was looking at her instead of through her. "I suddenly realized, I don't want kids. I don't want to be a Mom. I don't want to be like Mom. She ruined me. I just want to take care of me. Me and Peter."

"Wait," Austin said, unsure if she was hearing correctly, "you're blaming this on Mom?"

"I don't think people should have kids just to have them. If they're going to have them, they damn well better put in the time to love them and care for them and spend time with them. So, yes, I am blaming Mom. I refuse to fuck up a daughter the way she fucked me up."

Austin nodded. Mary had fucked them up. She had fucked all of them up.

Dallas looked into her sister's eyes. "And at the end of the day, I want to jump into my sweats, pour myself a big glass of red wine and watch bad reality TV. I want to be selfish."

"What did Peter say?"

"I didn't tell Peter." Dallas started to cry. "I couldn't. It would break him. It would break us. I told him I was going for my yearly pap smear and I did it, right in the office. I made him dinner that night. I taught the next day. Life goes on, right?"

January 2010
Island House, CT

Dearest Dallas,

When I sat down to write individual letters to my girls, I chose to write to you first. Why? Because I realize you've never really been put first. At least, I haven't put you first and I'm sorry. Too little too late, but I am sincere in my apology. Carolina is a natural leader and an obvious first and Baltimore is bossy enough to push herself into the first position. Plus, she's the baby and enjoys a special attention that way. Austin, a fellow middle daughter, has always stood out and she and I have always had a special bond ... perhaps because she is Mort's daughter. But you, my precious daughter, have always seemed to get the short end of the stick. I could spend this last letter to you apologizing, but instead, I'd rather spend it talking about how much I love you. How the little moments in your life have added up to one of the fullest and most wonderful lives a mother could hope for. How proud you have made me all of these years.

You have made me so proud, Dallas.

I remember your first piano concert. Not the silly recitals, but the first concert when you insisted on wearing the pink velour dress and matching bow. I wanted to paint your nails pink too, but you didn't want the audience distracted when they watched. You were so focused, so calm. I was a nervous wreck as that audience poured in to the auditorium, but you were filled with grace. An angel on stage. And then you played and I couldn't believe that I had created someone so talented. So beautiful. So filled with music and joy. You were the only performer who, after you took your bow, pointed to your teacher. Even then you were humble and gracious.

Your wedding day was one of the most gratifying moments in my life. Carolina got married in a civil ceremony, Baltimore will probably be married on a beach and Austin is gay, so fill in the blank there. You were the only daughter I was able to give away. I still tear up thinking about how beautiful that day was. How beautiful you were in your traditional gown and church ceremony. It was straight out of a bridesmaid's magazine. Your sisters in pink taffeta standing up for you and Sully and I walking you down the aisle; our little girl between us, a combination of the best of what we both had to offer the world.

You are magical my darling. I successfully fucked up four children, but you will inspire hundreds, maybe thousands depending on how long you teach. Every student in your social studies class, every kid who comes to learn how to play the piano, every field hockey player you coach, you are profoundly affecting their lives. You are making them better.

I'm so very proud of you for many reasons. Please don't tell your sisters, you are my favorite. You have always been my favorite daughter.

I love you Dallas,
Mom

Twenty-Seven

Dallas continued to sob.

Austin wanted to comfort her, to hold her, to tell her that it would be okay. But she just stood there, uncomfortably, across the room, unsure of how to make the first step. Austin's awkward silence and Dallas's sobs were interrupted by a loud voice from the bathroom upstairs.

"Why doesn't Mom smell?"

Baltimore staggered down to the living room. She wasn't drunk, but the alcohol had definitely focused her senses and she realized that the facts were not adding up. There was a big hole in Austin's story. And the one thing Baltimore hated more than anything else was being lied to.

"Why doesn't Mom smell? She should smell. Dead bodies smell."

"Let it go, Baltimore," Austin said, her attention still focused on Dallas.

"Who died and left you boss?" Baltimore jeered. "Oh, I guess Mom did."

Baltimore walked to the shelf containing the Russian dolls. She violently opened one, yanking out the dolls inside one by one and setting them down.

"You know the problem with these fucking dolls? The smallest one has absolutely no purpose. See, you've got this big one. The one that holds all the other ones." She opened and closed the doll, making a loud clacking noise. "She's the mother. She contains all these other dolls inside of her. Protecting them. She's like a kangaroo, and all of these other dolls are like baby kangaroos safely tucked away in her pouch. So, you've got the mother." She put the big doll down and looked over at the immobilized Carolina. "Then the big one who everyone reveres." She glared at Austin. "The talented one who everyone worships." She sneered at the sobbing Dallas. "The perfect one who everyone admires." She held up the tiniest doll with great disdain. "And then you get to the end and there's this shitty little piece of wood. The baby. She doesn't hold anything inside of her. Hell, you can barely see her. I call her ... Baltimore."

Baltimore gently placed the tiny doll at the end of the row, whirled around to Austin and slapped her.

"You didn't let me say goodbye."

March 2010
Island House, CT

Dearest Baltimore,

I see myself in you. Your spirit, your determination, your stubbornness, your zest for life. Your sisters have gone on to do great things with their lives, but I have a feeling you will journey farther and venture further. Not in the showy way of setting legal precedent like Carolina or the glamorous way of writing a best seller like Austin. Not even in the simple way of Dallas molding young lives. Something ... different. Something ... special. Maybe you'll stop global warming. Maybe you'll adopt an orphan from Indonesia. Maybe you'll start a revolution in a third world country. Maybe you'll do all three. I wouldn't put anything past you my darling, you have more spirit in your little finger than most people have in their entire bodies.

I remember when you bicycled from San Francisco to Los Angeles a few summers ago. "Why?" I asked you. "Because I can and I want to for those people who can't," you responded. You then trained for a year and raised almost ten thousand dollars to fight AIDS. Why? Because you could. That is just the kind of person you are. When you crashed on the second day and needed twenty-two stitches in your forehead, you told them, "Stitch it up well enough so that I can ride tomorrow." And you did. You didn't even consider stopping or taking time to heal. Nothing ever stops you, Baltimore. Not even a gash in the face. When someone tells you no, it makes you that much more determined to say yes.

Keep saying yes. It will lead you to remarkable places. We live in a world of naysayers where it is so much easier to say no than to say yes. Keep saying yes and let the wind take you on the journey that is meant for you. Of all my daughters, I believe you have enough courage to let go and let the river flow without pushing it. You are in for an extraordinary journey as your life is truly just beginning.

I love you my beautiful baby daughter. Please consider this my goodbye. I couldn't bear to face you. More than any of my girls, you represent life. Unabashed, free, passionate, courageous life. And when death faces life there is a mindfuck that occurs where death is suddenly given false hope. She sees light and energy and is given a false courage, which makes her believe that she can face the pain and the suffering. Death catches a glimmer of hope where she believes she can journey on because she has caught the contagious energy of Life.

And I couldn't be tempted.

Also, it's hard enough to do what I'm doing without seeing what I once represented. And when I look into your eyes, Baltimore, I see myself.

I'm so very proud of you for many reasons. Please don't tell your sisters, you are my favorite. You have always been my favorite daughter.

Goodbye, my sweet daughter. Be strong. Be brave. Be bold.

I love you,
Mom

Twenty-Eight

Baltimore went over to the shelf of Matryoshka dolls and started to throw them like a crazed woman. Her sisters watched in awe as she opened every set, savagely throwing mothers and babies around the room. Decapitated heads in various shapes broken off from their bodies and landing on the floor.

A macabre doll graveyard created from a grownup's temper tantrum.

"Hey, guess who dropped out of Harvard last semester?" Baltimore was laughing hysterically as she continued to fling the dolls. "Surprise! No point keeping that a secret anymore." She ignored her sisters' surprised looks. "I signed up for the Peace Corps three weeks ago. I'm going to Cambodia. I'm going to help lepers."

Exhausted, Baltimore finally flopped into the couch next to Dallas. "I thought I'd have time to tell her, to say goodbye. She would have been proud of me. I used to envy you, Austin. I wanted to be you."

From the high back, overstuffed floral chair, Carolina spoke in a hoarse whisper, "You dropped out of school?"

Dallas stopped crying. Baltimore stopped speaking. Austin stopped breathing. They all turned to Carolina and started speaking at once.

"Carolina."

"Thank god."

"Are you okay?"

Carolina cleared her throat and spoke again, more clearly, directing her question to Baltimore, "You dropped out of Harvard?"

Baltimore nodded meekly.

"That would have killed Mom," Carolina said, as she slowly rolled her neck and began to stretch out her stiff muscles.

"Luckily, that's been taken care of already," Baltimore said. "Thanks Austin."

"Get her a washcloth. Go," Dallas ordered her younger sister.

"Get her a washcloth. Go," Baltimore imitated her, frustrated that she was still the one ordered to do things. "Get her a washcloth. Get her a washcloth," she growled as she bounded up the stairs.

Carolina continued to stretch her body gingerly. First she moved her fingers, then her wrists, then her elbows. She remembered an old acting exercise she had taken as a high school elective where the drama teacher had the students warm up their bodies limb by limb. She was stretching cautiously, examining each limb and praying that everything would work again. That no part of her body would have lasting paralytic effects.

"I think I finally understand what you meant by relaxed," Carolina said to Dallas as she struggled to pull something from underneath her.

"How do you feel?" Dallas knelt beside her, feeling a deep sense of relief that she hadn't lost two of her family members in the same day.

Carolina found the offending object beneath her and looked at it. "Spending an hour with your ass glued to a Ken doll is not my idea of a fun afternoon, but I'm fine. A little stiff, but I'm fine." She tossed the Ken doll on the table and continued to stretch before turning to Austin and exploding, "What the fuck were you thinking?"

"I wasn't."

"You've committed two felonies in the last twenty-four hours."

"I know."

"I could have you arrested."

"Then you could be my lawyer," Austin said earnestly.

Carolina glared at her as she continued to stretch. "You took that stuff too?"

"Mom ... made me," Austin confessed.

"I've never felt anything like it. It was unbelievable. I heard ... I saw everything. I felt ... hot, cold, itchy ... that's what was happening to Mom?"

"Only hers wasn't temporary."

"Poor Mom." Carolina finally realized what Mary was going through. And how she ultimately wanted to preserve her legacy. And the lengths she had to go to make sure that it was done right.

"I know." Austin bit the inside of her cheek, trying to prevent herself from crying.

They looked at each other, hard.

Everything Carolina had ever believed, all of her ethics and mores and principles were suddenly upside down. As a lawyer, she thought clinically. There was no black or white, there was only the law. Legal opinion had become her Bible. Yet, as a daughter, everything she had ever championed flew out the door.

"I would have killed her too."

April 2010
Island House, CT

Dearest Carolina,

I can only imagine how furious you are. And it's okay. It's okay to be angry. It's okay to let go of your rage. Sometimes I worry that you keep everything so bottled up you're going to explode. You are human. It is fine to feel. It's okay to hurt. You're allowed to hurl things and scream. You can cry.

You are so smart, Carolina. Such a leader. How did I create such a magnificent daughter? You are such a force to be reckoned with. Matthew wasn't strong enough for you and I pray you don't judge yourself on his idiocy. He was, as my Scottish lover Frazier once said, a feckin eegit. You are a powerful, strong, talented and amazing woman and there is a man out there who will recognize that power and not feel threatened by it. Right now, the hurt with Matthew is too strong. But mourn it. Recognize it. Accept it and move on. Remember, whenever God closes a door, somewhere he opens a window. Yes, I realize I'm quoting The Sound of Music, but like I've always said, quote from the best.

Maria may have left the abbey, but she ended up with sexy Captain Von Trapp.

Don't hate me because I didn't include you in this decision. I almost did. You would have been far more efficient in handling my disease than Austin, but I didn't need efficiency, I needed detachment. Someone who I could still help. And you don't need my help. You've been independent since you were a very little girl.

I'm so very proud of you for many reasons. Please don't tell your sisters, you are my favorite. You have always been my favorite daughter.

You are now the matriarch of the family, Carolina. And I know that I am leaving my family in good hands.

I love you,
Mom

Twenty-Nine

"Carolina!" Dallas cried. She couldn't believe what she was hearing. After all of her posturing, her lawyering, and her preaching, Carolina had changed her mind.

"I would have killed her too. Absolutely," Carolina said, finally understanding what had gone on in the house. The deterioration with which Austin had been forced to cope. "You want to try the drug? Austin, do you have any more of this stuff?"

"Yes." Austin smiled.

"No!" Dallas said.

The sisters sat in silence for a moment while Carolina continued to stretch. The stillness in the room was interrupted as Baltimore bounded down the stairs. "Why doesn't Mom smell?" She tossed the wet washcloth to Dallas, who put it on Carolina's forehead.

"Answer me." Baltimore walked over to Austin, who had settled on the couch after Carolina came out of her coma. "Why doesn't she smell, Austin?"

"I don't know."

"I'm not a biology major, but I happen to know a little something about dead bodies."

"Why?" Carolina chuckled. "Because you watch *Law and Order*?"

"*CSI.*" Baltimore sneered at her eldest sister and turned her attention back to Austin. "Look, her body's been decomposing for over fourteen hours. What time did you kill her?"

"I don't remember," Austin said flatly.

"Yes you do," Baltimore insisted. "Like the doctors on TV who are always telling each other to call the exact time of death. When we were kids and we played doctor and killed our Barbie dolls, we always announced their time of death. So, my guess is when you killed OUR MOTHER you would have taken a second to mentally jot down the time."

Austin's silence infuriated Baltimore. "It doesn't make sense. It's impossible. If she died yesterday and we didn't get here until this morning, she should smell. She should smell a lot. SO, WHY DOESN'T SHE SMELL?"

Austin grabbed one of the battered Matryoshka dolls from the couch and squeezed it, focusing her attention on the doll. Baltimore and Carolina both looked at her, then at each other before simultaneously realizing.

"No," Carolina said.

"You didn't," Baltimore accused.

Dallas looked at both of them. "What? What am I missing?"

Austin shook her head, unable to speak.

"That's just sick." Baltimore stood up. She needed to get away from her sister. From the stranger who had betrayed her.

"What am I missing?" Dallas whined. She had no idea what they were talking about. Who cares that their mother's body didn't smell. That's the last thing they needed, to be cooped up in a house with a fetid corpse.

"She couldn't," Carolina said.

"She couldn't what? If someone doesn't tell me what's going on, I'm gonna kill *myself*!" Dallas screamed, before the realization finally dawned on her. Dead bodies only smelled when they had been dead for a good amount of time. And if their mother had died the night before, her corpse would have been noxious by now. Which meant that the body was fresh. It was newly dead. The potential answer was so horrifying she could barely get out the question. "Wait, Mom was still alive when you called us? Austin…is that true?"

Austin closed her eyes, trying to block out the noise; yet, the memories of the morning thundered into her head.

Thirty

Austin helped Mary prepare to die.

She twisted the worn brass taps, as steaming water thundered into the antique bath. It was six o'clock. The schedule was set. Help Mom die at six, call her sisters at six fifteen and greet them the following day at noon. Mary had organized the schedule down to the seven red-eye options Carolina would have.

Austin watched as bubble bath and salts mixed under the taps. Lavender. Mom's favorite. She loved the odor. She claimed it reminded her of her childhood.

Austin gently lifted her mother and placed her in the tub. She watched as Mary relaxed in the warm water, resting her body against the curve of the porcelain. Austin watched her mother slide down the side of the tub, the bubbles surrounding her head like a watery halo. There was thunder grumbling just outside the window, almost mimicking the sound of the rushing water, creating an ominous soundtrack to the task at hand.

"I'm ready," Mary said, looking angelic.

Austin crouched next to the tub. She placed both of her hands on her mother's shoulders, preparing to push her under the water; yet, she couldn't. She tried, but she couldn't. She just froze in place. Austin looked at the tiny watch that rested atop the pink towel, crumpled on the floor. It was five after six. She was already behind schedule, she was supposed to call Carolina by six fifteen.

Austin looked at her mother. "I can't."

"Yes. You can," Mary said resolutely. "We've been through this."

Austin tried again; yet, she couldn't.

"Your sister isn't going to be able to get a flight out," Mary warned.

"I know." Austin broke down. She had prepared for this moment. She was willing to do it; yet, when it came time for the actual doing of the deed, she was paralyzed. Fitting, she thought, considering the circumstances.

As Austin bawled, Mary watched her daughter. She knew she had to be dead by morning, but there was still time. She owed that to her daughter.

"Turn off the water."

"What?"

"Turn off the water, it's full enough. You don't want it to overflow. Turn it off."

Almost in a daze, Austin complied.

"Do you have your cell?"

Austin felt the sleek phone in her pocket. Janis insisted she carry one around as her editor was one of those people who preferred to communicate via text rather than actually speak to people.

"Yes. Why?"

"Call Carolina."

"What? I thought you didn't want her to know." Austin shouted, "What are you talking about?"

"Sweetheart. There are limited flights to Hartford tonight. Carolina's going to need at least an hour to pack and organize before getting to Sea-Tac. You need to call her now."

"But..."

"Just do it." Mary gave her daughter a look. She loved the warm feeling of the hot water. Soon it would get colder, that would be uncomfortable; however, it was a small price to pay considering what she was asking.

"It's ringing," Austin said shakily.

"Hold my hand," Mary instructed.

"Carolina? Hi...Mom's in the tub." Austin looked at her mother. She saw the pain in her eyes. The exhaustion of trying to keep her little body going. "No, I'm still here, sorry. Yeah, she's...um, dead." Austin never took her eyes off of her mother. "Stop yelling. I don't know. What? I found her this way." Austin started to cry. "I guess she drowned...What? Um, she looks...happy?" Austin felt a laugh bubble up inside of her. It confused her, but she let it out. "Sorry, no, I'm not laughing. I have something stuck in my throat. She looks serene, I guess would be the best word. Like she intended to do it. So, maybe you could fly out here. Yeah, I'm gonna call them next." Austin hung up, letting the phone slip out of her hand.

"Now Dallas."

"Can I just wait a minute, please." Austin sobbed as she held her mother's hand, listening to the grumbling thunder, which warned of the impending storm.

Thirty-One

"So, Mom was alive when you called us?" Baltimore couldn't believe her sister's gall. "So, when did she die?"

"Wait, you called us while she was still alive?" Dallas still couldn't digest everything: Mary's audacious request. Austin's weakness. Austin's strength.

"It was a lot easier than I thought," Austin admitted. "She held my hand." She looked at Carolina. "I told you Mom was dead while she was holding my hand."

"Us too?" Baltimore demanded.

"It just got easier and easier. It's like, because I told you she was dead, I knew that I could do it. I had... a deadline."

"Poor Austin," Carolina said.

"Poor Austin?" Baltimore shouted. "That's bullshit. Mom was alive when you called us. So, when did she die?"

Austin took a deep breath. There was a finality in what she was about to say. "Time of death: Eleven-thirty."

"Last night?"

"This morning."

"We got here at eleven-thirty." Baltimore was shocked.

"Oh, Austin," Dallas said sympathetically.

"That's why Mom doesn't smell," Austin explained.

"I don't envy you anymore," Baltimore said.

Thirty-Two

Mary didn't envy what her daughter had to do. It was almost eleven thirty. Austin had called Carolina just after six and Dallas at ten. She had left several messages for Baltimore, who finally returned her call this morning at eight. Now, it was just a matter of time.

"I'm ready," Mary said, breaking the silence of the last several hours. She couldn't even feel the water any more. She refused to let Austin drain the tub, or put in more hot water. She didn't want to give her daughter any more excuses. It was time.

"It's time."

"No," Austin said.

"Carolina will be here in a few minutes. Probably Baltimore too, if she was able to get a ride. Dallas will be late, Dallas is always late ... but you only have a few minutes before they get here. It's time," Mary repeated, locking eyes with her daughter.

Mary's look gave Austin strength.

Austin leaned over the tub and put her hands on her mother's thin shoulders, pushing her frail body under. Suddenly, Mary's body went into fighting instinct as she tried to resist, violent thrashing against the water; yet, her opened eyes continued to beg Austin to finish her task.

Austin moved her hands to her mother's head, completely submerging it. She looked away, no longer able to bear her mother's eyes boring into her. As the body convulsed and twitched under the water, Austin stared at the pink bath towel crumpled on the floor, remembering seeing her mother in it the night before.

She wasn't sure when the jerking stopped. She wasn't sure when the silence started or when the room felt so deathly still. She just remembered the sound of the water taxi breaking her from her shocked stupor, standing up and walking out the door.

Austin looked out the window at the approaching water taxi. She could make out the small figures of her sisters, huddling against the wind. She supposed she should eat something.

As she went downstairs to microwave herself some Macaroni and Cheese, she did not turn around. Her own face etched with pain, was the polar opposite of the serene smile of the corpse lying in the bathtub.

Austin had finally been able to give her mother the gift of death.

September 2010
Island House, CT

Dearest Austin,

I'm not sure what to say to you that hasn't already been said. Having you here these past few years has been invaluable. Your help, your companionship ... I don't know what I would have done without you. And asking you to keep my secret was a tremendous burden. And I am grateful that you were able to do it. You're more like your father than you know, I only hope that you will try to spend more time with him. Try to give him more of a break. He's flawed ... all men are flawed, but your father is particularly flawed. He is also particularly wonderful and I couldn't have survived this disease without him.

You need to get on with your life, honey. You and Sarah were good together. Now, don't get mad at me, but I called her. And I found out that the reason you split up was me. Well, inadvertently, me. You kept my secret from her as well ... she thought you were leaving her because you weren't ready for commitment, but it was really so you could be my nursemaid. Honey, she loves you. And I know you love her. I may not understand your choice to love another woman but I understand you. And I've seen how lonely and how miserable you are. You were your best when you were with her. Go back to her. She wants you to go back. I want you to go back. And you want you to go back.

She's expecting your call.

Parents are not supposed to have favorites. It's considered bad parenting. But one thing I can never claim is being a great parent. I have four fantastic girls but you, my darling, you are the best of the best. I'm so very proud of you for many reasons. Please don't tell your sisters, you are my favorite.

You have always been my favorite daughter.

How else could I entrust you to do what needs to be done?

Why else would I think that you could do the unthinkable?

You did the right thing, Austin, because by killing me, you have saved my life.

I love you so much,
Mom

Thirty-Three

No one spoke.

The revelation was too terrible; yet, each sister knew, in her own way, that Austin's act had been necessary. That, if put in the same position, they would have done the same thing.

Dallas looked out the window. It was almost magic hour and the rain was finally letting up. The sun was desperately trying to peek out from behind the clouds. The once angry waters were almost placid.

"It stopped raining. The police will come and then ... What happens?" Dallas wondered aloud.

"We notify the people who loved her. We have a service. We go back to our lives," Carolina said.

"It just feels so ... unresolved." Dallas still had an uneasy feeling in her stomach. She was someone who craved closure.

"Life doesn't resolve itself," Carolina said.

"That's seeing the glass half empty."

"Dallas, you're the only one who sees the glass half full."

"My glass is broken," Austin said.

"I don't even have a glass," Baltimore piped in.

Dallas turned from the window. "Hey, I love my life. Who can say that, really say it and mean it?"

"Not me," Austin said.

"Nope," Baltimore echoed.

"Definitely not," Carolina agreed.

Baltimore looked at Dallas, observing the slight lines under her blue eyes, seeing the errant hairs frizzing out at the hairline of her bob. She realized how much work it must take to be perfect. What a burden it was. "You're just happy because you're in the perfect relationship," she said wistfully.

"No she's not," Austin said.

"Austin," Carolina warned.

"What?" Austin was tired of the lies and pretexts. "I mean, Peter's great and everything but she didn't tell him about the abortion."

"Austin!" Carolina repeated.

"You had an abortion?" Baltimore was stunned. After a few seconds of contemplation, she really saw her sister through a new lens. "Wow. You're not perfect."

"At least she only lied to Peter." Carolina started in on Austin. "Lying to someone else is forgivable, but lying to yourself—"

"—I'm really not in the mood—" Austin protested.

"—For someone who almost killed two people in the last four hours, I think you can put yourself in the mood. What's keeping you here? What are you hiding from? If you're a writer, aren't you supposed to get out there and observe life? Seems to me, you've spent the last year observing death."

"—Do you know what happens to a spider when you pull off its legs?"

"If you're not going to answer the question—"

"—I can't write," Austin said as her sisters all looked at her. "I write one book which manages to land on the *New York Times* Best Seller list and all of a sudden, I'm a fucking celebrity? People expect things from me. I can't figure out my own life and other people, strangers, expect things from me. Jesus, I have no idea how I wrote that book. I just did it."

"It was a really good book," Dallas offered.

"Thank you." Austin bit back tears. "But one isn't enough. Once you write one you have to write a second and a third."

"Did Harper E. Lee ever write anything other than *To Kill A Mockingbird*?" Carolina asked.

"Yes. But it doesn't matter. Harper E. Lee hasn't spent her advance and doesn't have a publishing house threatening to sue her." Austin sighed. "Do you know how many self-help books I own? I just can't write the second book. And I've tried everything; Yoga, meditation ... even Kabbalah—but I didn't get the whole red string thing. I mean, if you're gonna find yourself, shouldn't you do it privately ... not announce to the whole world 'look at me ... I have a red string ... I'm Madonna.'"

Austin was starting to lose it, the events of the last few hours ... of the last few years finally breaking through her psyche: the stoic veneer shattering. "I'm not Madonna ... Madonna was the perfect mother, right? Not "Like a Virgin" Madonna, the "is a virgin" Madonna—the virgin mother. The Virgin Mary. Ha. Our Mary was no virgin. She slept with the fucking gardener. So, the original Mary has Jesus, who becomes God, right? So then our Mary has me who she chooses to play god, on whom she generously bestows the power of life or death."

Austin laughed. "But I have to give her credit. She asked for help. She wasn't afraid to show her weakness. I'm terrified. What happens when people realize I am far less than they expected. I write a book and people think they know me. They don't know me. I don't know me. Mom never knew me. She raised the bar so high, so impossibly out of reach. I could never live up to her expectations."

"It's the burden of being her favorite," Carolina said. She no longer hated her sister, her feelings for her were more like a combination of awe and pity.

"What?" Austin disagreed. There was no way that she was the favorite. Baltimore was the beautiful baby. Carolina was the great success. Dallas was married and happy. Her sisters were all far more successful than she was.

They made their mother proud.

"You were her favorite," Carolina repeated. "Don't worry, we all know it. Show of hands in favor?" Carolina and Dallas both raised their hands. Reluctantly, Baltimore raised hers as well.

"You were the most like her, Austin. I was too focused, Baltimore did her own thing and Dallas was too ... good."

"I live with the burden," Dallas said, perhaps finding her sense of humor for the first time in her life.

"You're not that good." Baltimore laughed.

"I used to be so jealous of what you guys had," Carolina said, without a trace of bitterness in her voice. "It's like you were a conduit for her. She never got to explore her creative side, so she lived vicariously through you. You were like ... this vessel that Mom could manipulate to her will."

"Okay, that's just creepy."

"You need to get out of the house, Austin," Carolina continued. "Whatever happened with Sarah, work it out, make it up, go back to her. She was really good for you. Go carve out a life for yourself."

Austin looked at her sister. She was right. She needed to start living again. Start writing again. And Sarah would take her back; the only reason they had split was because Austin wanted to protect her from the sadness of watching Mary die. It was time for her to move on with her life.

Mary's death had allowed her to live.

"Thanks ... Carol."

"Carolina."

They smiled at each other for a minute before Austin ventured, "So ... we're good?"

"Yeah. We're good." Carolina looked around the room that had been her refuge for her entire life. A nest which her father had built and her mother had maintained. She was now the matriarch of the family. "I'm going to miss her."

"Yeah." Austin bit the inside of her cheek, willing herself to be strong.

"Me too," said Baltimore.

After a minute, they all looked at Dallas who remained silent.

"What?" Dallas rolled her eyes. "I'm not a monster. Just because she fucked up my self-esteem, sense of self and identity doesn't mean I won't miss her. She's my mother," Dallas admitted.

"Parents are supposed to fuck up their kids," Carolina announced. "It's part of the evolutionary cycle."

"What do you do when there are no parents left?" Austin wondered. She vowed to spend more time with Mort. To forgive past mistakes, to see if they could build their fractured relationship.

"You work with what you've got." Carolina looked gently at Austin, compassion finally blooming in her face. "When the police come ... I'll say, I was here too ... I was here too when she died. When Mom drowned. I was here."

"So was I," Dallas said immediately.

"Me too." Baltimore hugged her sister. "You're not alone."

"I know," Austin said, acknowledging her sisters' generous gift.

In the distance, the sound of the water taxi whirred on the water. Baltimore ran to the window and nodded back to her sisters. They walked out of the door and waited.

Together.

39874203R00182

Made in the USA
Middletown, DE
27 January 2017